The Weird Detective Adventures of
Wade Hammond
Volume 2

By Paul Chadwick

Off-Trail Publications
Elkhorn, California

Acknowledgements
With thanks again to Bill Blackbeard, Larry Estep, and Paul Tozer for help in compiling this volume.

"Satan's Shrine," Copyright © 1932, Magazine Publishers, Inc.
"The Corpses' Carnival," Copyright © 1932, Magazine Publishers, Inc.
"Teeth of Terror," Copyright © 1933, Magazine Publishers, Inc.
"Fangs of the Cobra," Copyright © 1933, Magazine Publishers, Inc.
"Murder Bait," Copyright © 1935, Magazine Publishers, Inc.
"Scented Murder," Copyright © 1935, Magazine Publishers, Inc.
"The Murder Maker," Copyright © 1935, Magazine Publishers, Inc.
"The Grinning Ghoul," Copyright © 1935, Magazine Publishers, Inc.
"The Terror Train," Copyright © 1935, Magazine Publishers, Inc.
"Murder on the Air," Copyright © 1936, Magazine Publishers, Inc.

Cover artwork Copyright © 1934, Standard Magazines, Inc. for *Thrilling Detective*, January 1935

THE WEIRD DETECTIVE ADVENTURES OF WADE HAMMOND: VOLUME 2
Copyright © 2007, Off-Trail Publications
ISBN-10: 0-9786836-4-1
ISBN-13: 978-0-9786836-4-1

All Rights Reserved. No part of this book may be reproduced or transmitted in any form by any means, electronic or mechanical, including photocopying, recording or by an information storage and retrieval system, without written permission of the publisher, except where permitted by law.

OFF-TRAIL PUBLICATIONS
2036 Elkhorn Road
Castroville, CA 95012
offtrail@redshift.com

Printed in the United States of America
First printing: April 2007

CONTENTS

Introduction 5

SATAN'S SHRINE 7
    Detective-Dragnet, March 1932

THE CORPSES' CARNIVAL 23
    Detective-Dragnet, December 1932

TEETH OF TERROR 37
    Ten Detective Aces, May-June 1933

FANGS OF THE COBRA 49
    Ten Detective Aces, October 1933

MURDER BAIT 61
    Ten Detective Aces, June 1935

SCENTED MURDER 75
    Ten Detective Aces, September 1935

THE MURDER MAKER 95
    Ten Detective Aces, October 1935

THE GRINNING GHOUL 107
    Ten Detective Aces, November 1935

THE TERROR TRAIN 127
    Ten Detective Aces, December 1935

MURDER ON THE AIR 145
    Ten Detective Aces, February 1936

Appendix: The Wade Hammond Stories 169

Introduction

We last visited the career of Paul Chadwick in the first volume of this series. To briefly recap: In the late-'20s and early-'30s, he sold a variety of fiction, mostly to Street & Smith pulps; in the early to mid-'30s, he shifted over to Ace with the Wade Hammond series, and later the Secret Agent X and Captain Hazzard novels; he's mostly absent from the fiction scene from 1941-47, then resurfaces, writing detective and western stories into 1952 when he disappears once again.

And there it stood until a letter turned up—addressed Hampton, Connecticut; dated April 29, 1969—from Chadwick to famed editor and publisher Leo Margulies. Chadwick had sold a few stories to Margulies back when Margulies ran the Thrilling chain, thus prompting this opening: "You probably remember me from the 'old days.'" Chadwick had heard from neighbor and fellow veteran of the pulps, Walter Snow, that Margulies was starting a new western magazine, and was submitting a 2700-word short titled "No Limitations." The new magazine, presumably, was *Zane Grey's Western Magazine*, which had been a Dell digest from November '46 to January '54, and which Margulies' Renown Publications revived with the issue of October 1969.

Chadwick closed, "I have been in the newspaper field for the past 10 years; though at one time my name was quite well known in the Western magazines and I would like to get back into them. Best of luck in your new venture and count on me if your market develops."

That ten years accounts for the 1959-69 period, still leaving his activities in the mid-'50s a mystery. The fact that Chadwick worked in print journalism certainly reflects on the Wade Hammond stories. As Chadwick occasionally points out, Hammond is a newspaperman by day, although we never see him working. He's a reporter like Dr. Watson is a physician. "[Hammond] was a globetrotter, soldier-of-fortune and newspaper correspondent by profession, not a detective." ("The Murder Maker") Hammond's professional experience emerges from time to time: "Hammond, sprawled in a big armchair, dropped his cigarette into an ashtray, untangled his legs and got up. He crossed the room in four quick strides. Ten years of newspaper and police work had taught him to answer phone calls promptly." ("Doctor Zero") And when he examines a typewritten note in "The Corpses' Carnival": "Wade answered quickly. 'See those lines under the words? Any newspaper man knows they mean italicize.'" Okay. So that doesn't make Hammond a Woodward. Or even a Bernstein. Maybe not even a Jimmy Olsen. But it does show, on Chadwick's part, some consideration of the newspaper business, suggesting that he may have been a bit of a Wade Hammond himself, that is, a moonlighting newspaperman, and that Wade may have been his imaginary alter ego. If true, then Chadwick's absence during WWII may owe to some Hammondesque globetrotting correspondent work following the Allies. His early published work appears in the mid-'20s making a birth date around 1905 most plausible, and also making him too young for WWI and too old for any meaningful soldiering in WWII.

And that's as many aces as we'll pile onto this house of cards. . . .

John Locke

Detective-Dragnet, March 1932

Out of the black maw of the river came a struggling man. His strange, sobbing cries rent the night. For his wrist was gashed by the claws of a beast!

Satan's Shrine

WADE HAMMOND'S muscles were growing cramped as he crouched by the bale of jute. His eyeballs were smarting as he stared off into the fog, watching the spot where the wharf and the warehouse wall formed a right angle against the dark sky. There was good reason to be alert tonight. Death roved the waterfronts.

A tugboat sounded its whistle close at hand. It gave a coughing bellow like some wounded sea monster risen from the depths. Wade's fingers tightened over the butt of the .38 Colt automatic in the deep pocket of his overcoat. The straight line of his lips grew harsher. He was close to being nervous tonight—as close as he ever came.

A half-dozen detectives from the homicide squad were watching the docks to right and left of him. But his mind was ill at ease. One of their number had already been slain; another seemed under the shadow of death. No one could predict what gruesome thing might happen before the night was over. His own name might be on some assassin's list in the black pages of the criminal world. Some unnamable thing might be creeping out of the darkness toward him at this very moment; just as it had crept upon Cleve Neilson and Detective-Sergeant Burnett, leaving the mark of fear on their cold, dead faces.

Strange cases always fascinated Wade Hammond. Yet in this case there was little save horror, and a sense of being up against something hideously inhuman and uncanny. But he had volunteered his services to Inspector Thompson, and he intended to go through with it.

Tiny spots of green and red showed out on the river. A siren wailed, and a long finger of blue-white light sprang across the water, playing over the docks and pilings.

The police boat!

Near here on successive nights past, the bodies of Neilson and Burnett had been found floating face down. First the wealthy young clubman, then the sergeant of detectives who had been assigned to investigate his murder. And now "Big Jim" Gordon, following Burnett's footsteps, had failed to report at headquarters.

That was why the police siren was moaning out there, why grim-eyed men with guns were watching the docks tonight. Would the horror repeat itself again; would Gordon be found like the others? Was it already too late to help him?

Wade Hammond had taken part in more than one manhunt but tonight he was hunting an intangible foe. No man of the regular force knew what to look for or what to expect. The bodies might have been dumped from a boat, or been thrown from the end of a dock. Autopsies had indicated the presence of some mysterious poison in the blood. The theory was that Neilson and Burnett had been dead before the water of the river entered their lungs.

But the police wanted results, not theories. They wanted to find the murderer and trace the man who had disappeared.

The police boat's siren sounded again. The beam of the searchlight continued on up the river. The mist closed sullenly in.

With it there came to Wade's ears a sound that sent prickles racing up his spine and made him glide forward to the edge of the dock. He stood there, staring down into the dark water, every nerve taut.

Then it came again—a blowing, sobbing gurgle as of something or someone struggling in the water. Wade whipped his flashlight out. He turned its beam downward; then he almost cried out.

A white, staring, tortured face looked up at him from the river's surface for one terrible instant. The eyes seemed to be pleading. The mouth opened, and again came that inarticulate gurgle; the throat-rattling gurgle of a desperately wounded or dying man. But the face itself was what sent Wade into instant action. It was the face of Detective Big Jim Gordon.

WADE tore his overcoat off; then the coat of his suit. He removed his shoes, hardly taking time to untie them. He rested his flashlight on the edge of the dock so that it still shone on the water. He blew one shrill blast on the police whistle that had been given to him by the inspector. Then he made a clean dive into the icy water.

The sound of the whistle would bring detectives on the run. Wade hoped to reach Gordon before his feeble strokes ceased.

He saw Gordon's big head go under, then come up again. He saw the man's great arms lash the surface in a frenzied effort to keep afloat, as though, with death close at hand, his powerful body had summoned superhuman strength to fight.

But, whatever was wrong with Gordon, it seemed to be something that no human will could overcome. When Wade reached him, the big detective's eyes were closed. He was floating, feebly paddling with arms that seemed to be growing paralyzed.

Water drooled from his mouth as he turned his head. Glazed eyes met Wade's.

Wade slipped his strong arm under the massive shoulders of the detective, who had been the champion wrestler and strong man of the force.

Recognition showed in Gordon's tortured eyes for an instant. He expelled the water from his mouth in a stertorous gasp. His tongue rattled as Wade kept him afloat. He moved his lips. The voice that issued from between them seemed to come from a long way off—from a man snatching one last moment of life from the grave itself.

"Watch—the—curio—dealer—he's—" Another ghastly rattle cut off Gordon's words. He gave a wrenching sob that shook his whole body.

"Wait, old man," said Wade softly. "Keep quiet now. Wait till I get you ashore. You can tell me the rest then."

But, as he towed the detective closer to the piling, he understood why Gordon had made such heroic efforts to speak. The man's great body had gone suddenly limp. The light had passed from his eyes. Big Jim Gordon would never go out on a murder case again.

Wade's blast on the whistle had taken effect. Torches flashed on the wharf above. He could hear excited voices. Then a rope snaked down.

Wade slipped it gently around Gordon's body. He waited till they had drawn Gordon up before taking advantage of the rope himself. When he reached the planking of the dock, they were working over Gordon, moving his arms and chest to expel the water from his lungs and start the breath again.

Dripping and shivering, Wade stared into the gray eyes of Sergeant Foley, in charge of the dock patrol. Foley's ruddy face showed hard, worried lines.

"Where did Big Jim come from?" he asked.

"I don't know," said Wade. "I heard him cough and choke just after the patrol boat passed. He was almost dead when I reached him. I'm afraid it's too late to help him now."

Foley nodded morosely, his fingers still feeling for Gordon's pulse. "I've sent for the ambulance," he said. "But you're right—it's probably too late. Did he say anything before he went out—while he was in the water?"

Wade repeated the five words of the incomplete sentence that had come from Gordon's dying lips.

"It doesn't seem to make much sense," said Foley bluntly. "Maybe he was out of his head. Any idea what he meant?"

"No," said Wade, "but I'd like to work on that lead if you and the inspector will—"

Wade suddenly ceased speaking. One of the police detectives had given a sharp exclamation.

"Look there—on his hand—what's that?"

Wade stared down, his eyes widening. The plainclothes man was holding Gordon's hand palm upward, turning his flash upon it. Crimson mingled with the water on the skin. It oozed from five small gashes.

Wade and Foley bent closer. The detective-sergeant's breath quickened perceptibly. Wade's lean face was as set and expressionless as a mask.

"My God—they look like the marks of claws!" Foley's voice was hoarse.

Wade spoke quietly, tensely. "That's what they are. See the way they're spaced and how they pull in one direction?"

ALL of them standing around the dead man had the same uncanny feeling of mystery and horror. The night seemed to shut them in, setting them apart from other men, giving them a glimpse into a world of fantastic terrors. Those wounds on Gordon's dead hand seemed out of place along the riverfront of this great city—yet they were unmistakably the marks of claws.

Wade looked up and saw that even these regulars were shaken. Their faces seemed to have paled. Fear showed in the depths of their eyes.

Foley spoke harshly, breaking the silence. "We'll go over every foot of this dock and the ones next to it. Then we'll search the street front. Someone must have dumped Gordon into the river. He couldn't have been attacked by an animal here. In spite of those marks we don't know what killed him. There don't seem to be any other wounds on him."

Wade slipped his overcoat back on. He was hardly conscious of the wet clothes beneath.

A clanging bell at the end of the dock announced that the big police ambulance had arrived. Wade saw figures hurrying forward through the mist. One was dressed in white like a ghost.

They were carrying a bulky, box-like affair between them. A pulmotor. He watched while they attached the life-saving mechanism to the still form of Big Jim. But even that failed, as the first-aid had, to rouse any spark in Gordon's body. The young interne in white made an examination with his stethoscope, then snapped the instrument shut.

"We can't do anything for him, chief," he said. "If he was alive when you first got to him there must be something wrong besides exhaustion or drowning."

Foley nodded. "They probably got him like the others," he said. "Poison of some sort, I guess. Take him up to the station house. The inspector and Doc Weston will want to have a look at him." Then he turned to Wade. "What about those wet clothes of yours, Hammond? You'd better go along with the boys in the car, hadn't you?"

Wade considered. Wet clothes had never kept him from a manhunt yet. They couldn't stop him now if there was any possibility of Foley's men getting the murderer tonight. But he doubted that they would—and he wanted to be there when the medical examiner looked Gordon over.

"O.K., chief," he said shortly.

He helped them carry the pulmotor and Gordon's body back to the waiting ambulance. On the way to the station house he was silent, revolving in his mind the strange thing that had happened.

They laid the detective's body out under the bright lights in the squad room of the station house. Inspector Thompson and Weston, the acting assistant medical examiner, came in ten minutes.

Wade told his story briefly while the doctor examined the body. He rolled Gordon's eyelids back, squinted at his throat and nostrils, and prodded his skin here and there with a blunt instrument. Inspector Thompson watched owlishly. The doctor finally straightened up.

"No good," he said. "Only a careful autopsy will show the exact cause of death. There are some indications of poisoning—dilated pupils with symptoms of cyanosis on the skin. But the latter might have been caused by prolonged submergence in cold water."

"What about those marks on his hand?" Wade's voice held a strained note that he couldn't quite control. They were no longer out in the dark and mist now; but Gordon's dying words still rang in his ears, and those weird scratches had impressed him deeply.

"Eh?" Weston bent down and examined the hand with the five wounds on it. Thompson was staring intently, too. It was the first they'd heard of them.

The doctor's voice rose excitedly. "That's odd. Those are claw marks, if I know anything. Some large animal has scratched him."

Wade nodded. "We thought the same thing," he said. "What do you make of them? They rather upset the poison theory, don't they?"

Weston began going over every inch of Gordon's body. He did not answer until he had made certain there were no other wounds.

"I don't know what to think. We'll get busy on an autopsy right away. I'll have my report ready by morning. This is a hellishly queer case."

While the doctor was telephoning arrangements to have Gordon's body taken to a place where the autopsy could be performed, Inspector Thompson turned to Wade.

"What do *you* think, Hammond? You were the one who found Big Jim. Have you any theories as to what he meant by those last words?"

"Not much," said Wade. "But with your permission I'm going to look for that curio dealer he spoke of. If there's a shop like that down near the docks we'll locate it. But we mustn't blunder. I wish you'd let me handle this alone at first, inspector. We've got to find something to work on."

"Go ahead," said Thompson. "I'll back you up."

Sergeant Foley called as they reached his desk outside. He reported that his men had found nothing suspicious around the docks or on the front street. Wade took the receiver when Thompson had finished speaking.

"You didn't see any curio shop did you, chief?" he asked.

"Not on the front street," said Foley. "There's a couple of junk shops back from the river; but they're locked up tonight, and they're too far from the water for anyone to have carried Gordon without some of us seeing him."

"Thanks," said Wade. "I'll look them over myself in the morning."

He wasn't satisfied. He pinned faith somehow in Gordon's last words. He reasoned that a man with only a few moments to live would say the most important thing first. And Gordon had said: "Watch the curio dealer."

WADE'S early morning shower was interrupted by the sharp jangling of the telephone. It was Thompson calling from headquarters.

"We've just got Weston's report," said the inspector. "The autopsy showed traces of cyanide in Gordon's blood. It didn't come through the stomach. He must have inhaled it. Thanks to your efforts there was very little salt water in his lungs. Weston, and Dermott, the toxicologist, have proved that fumes of hydrocyanic acid killed Gordon. This is a strange business, Hammond. It gets queerer as we go along. I can't figure how poison and the claw marks of an animal go together."

"Neither can I," said Wade, "but I'm going to see if I can find out."

"How?"

"Find the curio dealer who is mixed up in this—the one Gordon spoke of."

He paced the front room of his big apartment as he dressed. Around the walls were the trophies and souvenirs that marked Wade Hammond as an adventurer, world traveler and soldier-of-fortune. There were guns, knives, and the skins and stuffed heads of big game. Also mementos of his exploits as a freelance criminal investigator. Two huge bookcases contained as complete a library of criminology as could be found in the city.

Wade lit a cigarette, made sure that the clip in his automatic was filled, and then set out.

When he reached the waterfront street in his roadster he could hardly visualize it as the scene of last night's terrible experience. The mist had cleared now. Big trucks ground along over the cobblestones. Taxis were whizzing away from the half-dozen nearby ferry slips. Scores of pushcart peddlers were passing with their two-wheeled vehicles piled high.

He parked his car in a side street and began to hunt for the two "junk shops" that Foley had mentioned. They were both, as the detective-sergeant had said, away from the docks. Neither was open when Wade first passed by.

One had only nautical goods in the window. It was more like an old-fashioned ship chandlery than a curio ship. The other interested Wade more. The name Leo Bruner showed in faded gilt lettering above the door.

He saw stacks of old books, antique brass lamps, an odd assortment of inkwells, coins, and dusty pieces of furniture. Some of the things unquestionably went into the class of curios.

His eyes snapped with excitement. He had no theory as to how such a shop might have any connection with the deaths of Neilson, Burnett and Gordon. He had only the inarticulate words of a dying man to guide him. But, remembering them, he proceeded with extreme caution.

He breakfasted in a nearby cafeteria, then sauntered past the curio shop again, taking pains to stay on the opposite side of the street.

A small, plainly dressed man with a brown, wizened face was dusting the books in the window. He glanced up as Wade looked across. Wade got a momentary impression of dark, beady eyes, and a high forehead rising above shell-rimmed spectacles.

When Wade reached the end of the block he paused to consider. It might be unwise to enter the curio shop now and arouse the dealer's suspicions, assuming that the man had anything to do with the mysterious chain of murders.

Wade stood at the edge of the curb, smoking and surveying the rundown stores across the way. He was out of the curio dealer's range of vision; but his eyes kept swiveling down the street at an oblique angle toward the front of the shop. What sort of a clientele did Leo Bruner have? Why had he set up business in such an out-of-the-way place?

For nearly an hour no one entered or left the curio shop. Then suddenly Wade leaned forward. A smart sport roadster came to a stop at the corner of the block. A woman got out of it.

She was young and smartly dressed, with black fox furs around her shapely shoulders. Her face interested Wade. It was startlingly pale with finely chiseled features. The only spot of color was that made by her rouged lips.

Wade had seen that face somewhere before. He remembered now, and his pulses tingled. It was Mrs. Cleve Neilson, member of the rich social set, and wife of the murdered clubman. Her picture had appeared in all the tabloids.

It was plain, too, that she was ill at ease. She crossed the street and went down on the other side. Then re-crossed and walked with quick steps to the front of the curio shop. She stood for some moments facing the window as an interested shopper might do. But Wade saw her eyes slanting right and left along the street. Then she opened the door and her trim figure disappeared inside the shop.

Wade was close on the track of something big. The sentence that had come from Detective Gordon's dying lips was bearing fruit. It was more than mere coincidence that the wife of the murdered Neilson was visiting the curio shop.

Wade made one of his quick decisions. He left the curb, crossed the street and entered the shop himself.

Mrs. Neilson was standing near a drapery in the far corner of the store. She turned startled eyes toward Wade. Her slim gloved fingers clutched her beaded handbag nervously. He saw now that her face had a transparent, unhealthy paleness. There were lines under her eyes and around her mouth that even the most flawless makeup could not conceal from a close-up observer. Yet she was still beautiful, as a sickly, poisonous flower might be.

He was careful to let no trace of interest cross his face, resting his eyes on her for a moment only, shifting them quickly to a shelf of books in worn leather covers. But he was aware that the woman was fidgeting, that her gaze was constantly turning in his direction.

Then he heard footsteps approaching from behind the drapery. From the corner of his eye he saw the curio dealer appear again.

The man gave a visible start when he saw Wade. There was a quick interplay of glances between him and the woman. Bruner held something in his hand, a small lacquer box. The woman reached for it, but he shook his head and drew his hand back. Her slim fingers were quicker. They closed over the box, taking it from him forcibly. The man showed his teeth in a smile that held little mirth. He spoke in a voice that had the high, cutting edge of thin steel.

"You will like it, madame. A lacquer box with silver inlay. Not expensive either, and it will make a delightful little gift. Shall I wrap it for you?"

The woman shook her head. "No, I'll put it in my handbag." She spoke so softly that Wade could barely make out what she said. She gave the man some bills, then turned quickly and left the shop.

THE curio dealer came forward, looking at Wade sharply.

"Can I help you?" he said.

"I'm just browsing through these books," said Wade. "You have some interesting volumes here." He spoke casually. He could see the man studying him.

"I get new ones in from time to time. I have a little bit of everything in my store."

"So I see."

The man moved nearer. He adjusted his spectacles and reached upward for a book on a shelf above head level. In doing so his left hand brushed the right side of Wade's overcoat.

Wade stepped away, but not soon enough. The curio dealer's fingers touched for an instant the hard outline of Wade's automatic.

It was cleverly done, Wade had to admit. He could have kicked himself for carrying the gun there. Bruner's maneuver had not been accidental, he felt sure. The curio dealer knew now that he was armed—and knowing that, could guess at other things.

But the man's narrow, wizened face gave no indication that he had made a startling discovery. His manner continued to be that of the suave shopkeeper anxious to please a customer. He placed book after book in Wade's hands, expounding on the merit of each.

Playing his part of the game, Wade bought an old volume on Renaissance architecture. But there was a bleak glint in the depths of his eyes as he left the shop.

Mrs. Neilson's roadster was gone, as he expected. His mind reverted to the lacquer box she had bought. Did it bear any relation to the strange series of events that had kept the police busy for the past three days? How could such a thing have even a remote connection with the hideous claw marks on the hand of the dead detective?

Yet Wade, prompted by one of those inner hunches which had led to his solving more than one sensational crime, felt that it had. He did not leave the vicinity of the curio shop at once. He wanted to find out more about the wizened, dark-eyed Leo Bruner. Behind that high, narrow forehead was, he believed, the diabolical brain which had planned the three ghastly murders. But as yet he was not sure what was the best method of attack.

He saw a number of well-dressed people enter Bruner's shop during the next two hours. They came in cars or taxis. They had the same furtive look that he had detected in the pale face of Mrs. Cleve Neilson. But he didn't get too close. He took pains that Bruner should not see him spying.

Just before noon he decided to go and have a talk with Mrs. Neilson. Bruner should be coming out to lunch soon anyway. The woman was undoubtedly one of the keys to the mystery.

He walked back to his parked roadster, climbed in and headed it uptown toward the swanky residential districts. He stopped only long enough to get Mrs. Neilson's number from a phone book.

A uniformed doorman gave him the number of the suite. A fast elevator whisked him up to the fourteenth floor of the huge apartment building that towered above the west side of the park.

But the maid who met him at the door shook her head.

"Madam left shortly after breakfast," she said. "She has not returned or telephoned arrangements for lunch."

Wade nodded. "Does she often do that sort of thing?"

"Yes, quite often. Madam always comes and goes as she pleases."

"Have you any idea where I might find her?"

"I do not know. Madam never tells us where she goes. Sometimes she stays out till very late at night. She is perhaps visiting friends."

Wade frowned. He did not believe that Mrs. Neilson was visiting friends. His mind switched back to that lacquer box and the curious way in which she had snatched it from Bruner's hand. It was significant, as were her mysterious comings and goings. He took a step forward.

"Listen," he said. "There's reason to be worried about your mistress. I've got to locate her if I can. I'm going in to take a look at her room."

He displayed his special investigator's card. The maid's eyes widened with fear. She stood aside, and Wade entered the apartment.

He went directly to Mrs. Neilson's boudoir. For a moment he paused, looking around the luxurious chamber with its handsome furnishings. Then he went straight to a small secretary in the corner. It was locked.

"You haven't the key, I suppose?" he said, turning to the maid who had followed him in. She shook her head.

WITHOUT hesitation Wade took a small metal cylinder from his pocket. It was a tool kit of remarkable lightness and compactness. He seldom went anywhere without it.

The handle was hollow and contained an assortment of odd-shaped tools. He took out a jimmy no larger than a tack puller, but made of the hardest chromium steel. This he screwed into the metal handle. In two minutes he had the secretary open.

The maid watched while he ran through the papers inside. There was only a bare chance he would find what he was looking for. Wade knew that. He wasn't even sure himself exactly what it would be.

But halfway through a sheaf of envelopes he paused. There was one craftily worded advertising pamphlet from a well-known society bootlegger. It was addressed to Miss Alice Nailand, 14 Jefferson Mews. Wade put this in his coat pocket and closed the secretary with a snap. He thanked the maid for her cooperation.

Ten minutes later he was driving his roadster downtown.

He stopped at the public library for half an hour and made an intent, but seemingly irrelevant study of some old maps of the city. Then he drove on down to police headquarters and ran briskly up the steps.

He found Thompson sitting behind his cluttered desk, placidly shooing a persistent fly from the dome of his bald head.

"Hello, Hammond. Been wondering when you'd turn up. What's new?"

Wade tapped a cigarette on his left thumb nail. He looked at the inspector intently.

"There are big things in the wind, chief. I've seen and talked to the curio dealer that Gordon spoke of. Now I'm hunting for Mrs. Neilson. Unless I'm soft in the head, that woman was the indirect cause of her husband's death."

Thompson's face had the look of a curious owl.

"Just what do you mean, Hammond?"

"I can't tell you yet. But do me a favor, inspector. Come along. We'll talk to her together. See if I'm right."

"Where is she?" Thompson was putting on his hat and coat as he asked the question.

Wade's reply was enigmatic. "I'm not even sure that I know," he said. "I may be taking you on a wild-goose chase."

Wade felt more sure of himself as they turned into the narrow street known as Jefferson Mews. It was just behind the square on the edge of the city's Bohemian quarter—a quarter, too, where under the gaudy cloak of bohemianism, men and women went to indulge their secret vices.

No. 14 was one of the small but expensive studio buildings with a private entrance. It was just the sort of retreat a woman of means might select as a place for the clandestine gratification of a vicious appetite.

"Look!" said Wade excitedly. He was pointing to a smart roadster parked halfway down the block. "There's Mrs. Neilson's car now. I guess we're on the right track."

The inspector nodded. But he was puzzled when they turned into the entranceway of No. 14.

"The name here isn't Neilson," he said. "It's Alice Nailand."

Wade smiled. "She should have chosen an alias not quite so similar to her own name. It would have been more misleading."

He pressed the bell with his thumb. Then lighted a cigarette and waited. But nothing happened. A minute passed and he pressed it again. There was no answer this time either.

"I'm afraid, inspector, we shall have to find the janitor—or else pick the lock." Wade's voice was grim.

"Do you think that's advisable? Remember who Mrs. Neilson is! She could raise a row if we broke in on her like that."

"I am remembering, inspector. Her husband was quite a big shot, also."

Wade went outside. But he saw that these buildings were not like apartments. It would be hopeless to try to find a janitor. Only the renting agent would have a key. It would take too long to locate him.

He took the tool kit out of his pocket again. He selected an instrument that was his own private invention. It was a gadget as small and delicate as a watch. He called it his "phantom finger." Unlike an ordinary skeleton key which would open old-fashioned locks, this instrument could adjust itself to the most complicated tumblers and was adaptable to any shaped keyhole. Once the adjustable teeth had accommodated themselves to the design of the lock, Wade could set them in place by turning a small knurled screwhead.

Thompson blinked as the door opened.

"It's lucky, Hammond, that you've never been tempted to follow the profession of a burglar."

Wade pocketed his phantom finger and strode forward. They found themselves in an elaborately tiled hallway. The door at the end, leading into the big studio, was not locked. Wade knocked, but received no answer. He turned the knob and they entered.

The light from the big north window had been partially shut off by shades. Wade snapped on the electric switch, then drew in his breath sharply.

The figure of a woman was sprawled on a low divan. One arm hung over the side, trailing on the floor. Her dress was disarranged. Her white face was turned toward the high ceiling. She did not move or speak.

"My God!" said Thompson harshly. "It's Mrs. Neilson—dead!"

Wade nodded. There was no need to verify the inspector's observation. He had only to look at those still, marble white features to know that it was true. His gaze darted about the studio. His mind was piecing things together.

Thompson walked over to the body. He stared down at the still face, then rolled the eyelids back from unseeing eyes.

"I'm no doctor, Hammond, but look—the pupils are contracted. This is another poison case—I wonder if she took it herself?"

"Not poison," said Wade quietly. "The pupils are contracted, you say. It's drugs this time. She *did* take them herself; but I don't think they were the cause of her death. Look—what's that on the floor?"

He pointed to an oblong object. Then picked it up. It was a soapstone bookend wrapped in a piece of pillow casing.

"That's what did it," said Wade. "This is murder, inspector—the same devilish chain we've been following. In an emergency, the killer made use of a crude weapon; but even then he was careful to leave no fingerprints."

Wade felt the dead woman's head for a few moments, running his hand down over her slim neck.

"The blow was a neat one, too," he said. "It broke the atlas and axis vertebrae just below the base of the skull and killed her instantly."

He left the body and began feverishly searching around the room.

"What are you looking for?" asked Thompson.

"A lacquer box," said Wade shortly. "It ought to be here somewhere unless—"

He broke off to examine a streak of whitish powder on the thick-napped rug. Then he began the search for the box again; but it was nowhere to be found.

"If this is linked up with the other murders," said Thompson, "where do your animal's claw marks fit in? And when are these killings going to stop? There have been four now, Hammond. I admit the thing's getting my goat. The press is raising hell with us. The squad is getting a bad name."

"We're up against an unusual type of criminal," said Wade quietly. "I can't explain yet exactly how those claw marks came to be on Gordon's hand, though I'm beginning to formulate a theory of my own. But I can tell you when the killings are going to stop—today. The murderer has overreached himself this time. If he doesn't get me first we'll put an end to his slayings once and for all. Come on!"

In his excitement Wade overlooked a matter of police routine.

"Where are you going?" said Thompson. "We can't leave the body here unguarded before the medical examiner arrives."

"All right," said Wade. "You stay here. I'll go to the nearest phone and get in touch with Doc Weston and Sergeant Foley. When they come I think you'll find it more interesting to go with me. You've never met the curio dealer, have you, inspector?"

Wade located a drugstore on the corner with a phone booth in it. He put in his calls in a snappy, authoritative voice.

Twenty minutes later the men from headquarters had arrived, and Thompson and he were on their way to the curio shop of Leo Bruner. A squad of police detectives followed them in another car.

AS WADE had half-expected, the shop was closed when they reached it.

"Bruner may or may not be in," said Wade. "But it's time we searched his place anyway. This is his headquarters. I think we're going to find some things that will surprise us."

He turned to the detectives then.

"Who'll volunteer to go in with me?" he said. "You remember what happened to Neilson, Burnett and Gordon! There's some hellish mystery here. Bruner is a man with a twisted, devil's brain. He won't hesitate to kill again if he gets the chance. The inspector's life is too valuable to risk."

But Thompson grabbed Wade's arm at this.

"To hell with that stuff," he said. "This is my party as well as yours, Hammond. What's good enough for my men is good enough for me."

The old crime-hunter's face had lost its usually placid look.

Wade grinned in admiration. He had anticipated some such reply.

"O.K.," he said. "Here goes—we won't bother to pick the lock this time."

With the blunt nose of his automatic he smashed the glass in the door and stepped through into the shop. Thompson followed, his own gun drawn.

"Come after us if you hear a whistle," called Wade over his shoulder, "or if we don't show up in fifteen minutes."

The interior of the shop was deserted. There was no sound anywhere. Wade made straight for the draperies near which Mrs. Neilson had stood earlier in the day when she received the lacquer box.

He pulled the draperies aside. There was a long passage behind them, and at the end of it a door. Black draperies hung along the walls of the passage. A dim red light burned overhead. It looked like the mouth of hell. And, mused Wade grimly, it probably was.

He started along a weird, funereal passage. With every step his sense of imminent danger increased. Thompson was close behind him; both had flashlights ready in their left hands in case the light overhead should go out.

But it didn't. They reached the door at the end of the passage. Wade opened it cautiously. It moved silently back on well-oiled hinges. The passage continued straight ahead for perhaps fifteen feet, then turned in a sharp elbow to the right.

Wade stopped dead short.

"Look!" he hissed. Thompson came closer, staring over his shoulder.

In the corner of the passage a grotesque idol of glittering rose quartz faced them. It was mounted on an ebony pedestal and was seemingly of Oriental design. Wade had seen such things on a small scale in the importers' shops, and during his travels through the Far East.

The idol was in the form of a satanic dragon, half lizard, half lion. The eyes were open and glaring, bright points of light reflected in the polished stone pupils. The nostrils flared widely. Fangs showed in a hideous snarl. Huge lion's feet were raised on either side of the head. The five claws on each foot were unsheathed, hand-carved by expert craftsmen from the glittering crystalline stone.

"It's just some kind of a Chink god," said Thompson. "Let's see what's around the end of the passage."

But Wade still stood rooted to the spot. His eyes were fixed on the idol's claws. His face was as inscrutable as a mask. He seemed to be weighing, considering, struck speechless by some astounding thought.

All at once the deathly silence of the chamber was disturbed by a faint hissing. It was barely more than a whisper, like the sound made by a steam radiator on a winter day. Thompson started to move forward; but Wade caught his arm with steely fingers.

"My God!" he said. "Quick—let's get out of here—smell that?"

The air had suddenly become filled with the faint, but unmistakable, odor of bitter almonds. Already Wade could feel a sense of dizziness creeping upon him and a mounting pressure against his eardrums.

He literally hurled Thompson back toward the door through which they had come. The inspector gave a hoarse cry.

"Look—it's closing!"

WADE bounded forward. He reached the door just a fraction of a second before a lock on the outside clicked shut. He flung it open and dragged Thompson after him into the passage. Fresh air assailed their nostrils.

There was a movement of the draperies nearby. Wade caught a glimpse of a brown, wizened face. Then the blue nose of a gun poked viciously out like the head of a snake. Wade leaped aside as the gun jetted flame. He pressed the trigger of his own automatic.

The report was followed by a muffled cry from behind the draperies. A figure lurched into view. It was Leo Bruner, a shattered wrist dripping blood where Wade's bullet had struck.

With a hiss from between clenched teeth, Bruner sprang toward the door leading into the idol's chamber. He seemed too crazed to know what he was doing; driven only by an animal frenzy to seek a way of escape.

He flung the door open. Again came the odor of bitter almonds, stronger than before. Then the door closed behind Bruner. He disappeared into the room where the grinning idol presided.

And then a ghastly, choking cry sounded for an instant from behind the closed panel. It was followed by a silence even more terrible.

Wade jumped toward the draperies through which Bruner had fired. There was a small hidden alcove here. From the wall inside, two small brass valves protruded. Wade's hand flashed out. He turned them both as far as they would go, yet felt instinctively that he was too late.

"We couldn't save him now, even if we wanted to," he said.

"You mean there's poison gas inside?"

"Yes, I guessed it as soon as I saw the idol's claws. That devil is useful as well as ornamental. Bruner had his hydrocyanic gas piped from a storage tank somewhere and arranged to come out the idol's nostrils. Gordon must have been close to the stone image when he got that dose of his. He fell forward, and the palm of his hand struck one of the devil's feet. That explains the claw marks."

"But how about the bodies getting into the water?"

"We still have to verify that," said Wade. "But I think we'll find that it's simple enough. The old Stuyvesant canal runs under this building. I looked up some city maps on my way to your office and found that the canal crossed right about here. It was covered over in 1872 you remember. Bruner found an entrance to the old covered canal in his cellar. That made it easy for him to dispose of the bodies. Gordon, with his athlete's body, was able to live and swim long enough to reach the river even after the dose of poison gas."

"And the first murder—when he killed Neilson? Why did he do that?"

"It's not hard to figure, either. Neilson discovered that his wife was a drug addict. He couldn't make her stop, so he found out who was selling the stuff to her. He came here to warn Bruner privately, not wanting the scandal to get into the papers, of course. Bruner killed him, and afterwards killed Burnett and Gordon to cover up the first murder. They must both have trailed Mrs. Neilson here."

Thompson whistled.

"This second valve," said Wade, "is a ventilating device to clear the air after the gas has been shut off."

Five minutes later they entered. Bruner's body was almost in front of the rose quartz idol. The man's arms were flung outward, his head was down and his knees drawn up, very much like a person praying before a shrine.

They all stared at the horrible sight until Wade broke the heavy silence.

"Satan's shrine," he said grimly. "Bruner got what was coming to him all right. He won't poison any more hardworking dicks now."

Detective-Dragnet, December 1932

Divers salvaging that sunken treasure ship mysteriously died on the harbor's bottom. Others refused to go down, for they held that dead men's gold was better left with the dead. Wade Hammond, private investigator, took the baffling case, and found—

The Corpses' Carnival

WITH two cops at his side Wade Hammond stared down at the huddled figure in the street. Five minutes had elapsed since the gray murder car had made its sensational getaway.

Men and women who had sought cover like scared rabbits when the shooting began were stepping out of vestibules and areaways now and edging in to form a curious crowd.

Wade Hammond spoke softly. "They machine-gunned him," he said, "hit him in a dozen places. They weren't taking any chances."

As he uttered the words his gaunt, bronzed face set harshly. Under the thin mustache line his lips were bleakly grim.

One of the cops looked at Wade and talked from the side of his mouth:

"Who is he and what did he have that they wanted?"

He pointed at the articles scattered about on the sidewalk beside the body. A fat billfold was there, a bunch of letters, two theater tickets and a bundle of newspaper clippings.

"A guy from that car went through his pockets," the cop continued. "I saw him jump back in with something in his hand when I came around the corner. It looked like paper."

Wade nodded. He was still staring down at the pitifully sprawled figure with its thatch of red hair showing against a pool of darker crimson on the pavement.

"You might not know it," he said. "But that's Danny O'Rork of the *Evening Globe*. Those bullets changed his looks—a lot."

The cop spoke again. "Maybe he was mixed up with the mobsters and tried to doublecross 'em like that newspaper guy out in Chi."

Wade shook his head. "Not Danny O'Rork," he said. "I've heard about him. He was a square-shooter, had a clean slate, and all the rest of it. You say one of the killers grabbed a paper from him. O'Rork must have stumbled on a story that would hurt somebody. That's the way I dope it."

"Yeah," said the cop.

Wade bent down and fingered the billfold, while the blue-coats stood by and watched, content to let him do the searching. They knew who he was, knew that, as a special investigator, he had figured in several big murder cases with the sanction of the police commissioner himself. Their faces showed respect.

Wade opened the billfold and took something out of it. His lips were pursed together.

"It's O'Rork all rights—look!" He held up an Associated Press card with the Irishman's name written on it.

The cops nodded glumly.

Wade gathered up the scattered articles from O'Rork's pockets. A letter gave the dead man's address. It was just around the corner. Then suddenly he reached out and picked up O'Rork's keys.

"I'm going around to his place and take a look," he said. "Maybe I can find out what it was those killers grabbed from his pocket. You come with me, Flannery, it's on your beat. Harrison can stay here till the ambulance comes."

In three minutes they entered the house where Dan O'Rork had lived and worked.

The landlady showed them to the dead man's room. It was a drab chamber except for a few theater posters and a college pennant on the wall. The photograph of a girl looked down from the bureau.

"It must be his kid sister or a sweetie," said the cop. "It's going to be tough on her."

Wade nodded. He hovered over the desk, looking down at the sheets of paper, the cigarette butts and the dusty typewriter. He was hunting for a carbon of the paper the killers had taken. But it didn't surprise him when he failed to find it. Few reporters bothered with them.

Then his hand dived into the wire wastepaper basket and came out clutching a crumpled sheet. He opened it, smoothed it out. O'Rork had apparently jerked the page from his machine, dissatisfied with it, then begun again. There was only one line at the top, an incomplete line which didn't seem to make much sense; but it held Wade's interest.

```
...under the name of Clara Scott. Mystery now surrounds
her and...
```

The paper was freshly crumpled; the last thing in the basket. The cop spoke slowly, his eyes still intent on the page over Wade's shoulder.

"Maybe that's the name of the kid in the photo," he said.

"It isn't the name of any girl," Wade answered quickly. "See those lines under the words? Any newspaper man knows they mean italicize."

The cop looked nonplussed.

"It's not a girl—it's a ship," continued Wade. "Wasn't there a steamer by that name rammed in the harbor a few weeks ago—the one they're trying to raise?"

"Say—you're right." The cop's voice was excited. "She was carrying gold in her. They had a story in the paper about it."

Wade grunted. He turned back toward the wastepaper basket. There was nothing else in it except an empty match paper. He started to turn away, thought better of it, and once more his hand dived in.

He regarded the match paper intently, eyes gleaming. It bore an inscription. "Sam's Place, 30 Front Street."

That was down by the water. Just the kind of joint a newspaper reporter would go to get a drink and pick up news about a sunken vessel.

Wade said nothing to the cop; but he slipped the match paper into his pocket. He didn't want to take a chance on any police bungling—not with the men who had knocked off Danny O'Rork. There seemed to him something queer about the murder, something that did not appear on the surface. He'd go down to Sam's Place and take a look around—all by himself.

BUT before Wade did this he called up the *Globe* and gave his story of O'Rork's killing to the city editor. It was only fair that the paper for which O'Rork worked should have the story first. He would have wanted it that way.

When Wade had finished the grim details of the shooting, he asked a question himself.

"What's the latest dope on that steamer, the *Clara Scott*—the one with the gold on it that was rammed in the harbor?"

"She's still there. They haven't got to her yet. The Eastern Salvage Company is doing the work; but a couple of bad accidents slowed them up. Two of their divers were killed. Why do you want to know?"

"O'Rork was working on the story when they got him."

"I think you're wrong, Hammond. It was something else. He'd been poking around the warehouse section over across the harbor. Said he was on the trail of something that would make the hottest copy we'd ever had."

"I thought so," said Wade, and hung up.

He jumped into a taxi and drove to the offices of the Eastern Salvage Company. A desk clerk took him in to see the two partners, Brown and Wheeler, who were in charge of the company's affairs. Brown was a short sandy-haired man with a pink face. Wheeler was taller, stoop-shouldered and slow in his speech. He looked worried.

"I hear there's been some trouble in getting to the *Clara Scott*," said Wade. "Two men lost their lives, I understand."

Wheeler and Brown looked at each other.

"Yes, but we've no statements to make to the press other than those already given. Both deaths were purely accidental—though there's been a lot of talk."

"You don't say." Wade's face was inscrutable. "What sort of talk?"

"We don't care to say." Brown, the senior partner, spoke icily. "It's all absurd."

Wade leaned forward his eyes snapping.

"Listen, Brown—O'Rork, a reporter for the *Globe* was working on the *Clara Scott* story. He was shot a few minutes ago—machine-gunned in the street. There was nothing absurd about that."

"But what has it to do with us?" said Brown. "It sounds like a gangster affair to me."

"Maybe it was and maybe it wasn't. Anyway, I'd like to go out and look your salvage boat over."

"If you want to snoop around you'd better think up a better excuse. We can get along without all this publicity." Brown's voice was nasty.

Wade took out his special investigator's card again and thrust it under Brown's face. The effect was instantaneous.

"That makes it different." Brown spoke grudgingly. Wheeler said nothing. His pink face was expressionless. "You can use one of the company boats," added Brown. "You'll find it at the dock. I'll give you a pass."

A SPUTTERING motorboat took Wade out to the spot where the *Clara Scott* had sunk. Only a buoy marked the place now. It was off the deepest part of the channel, about a hundred yards from shore.

The salvage boat, *City of Portsmouth*, was a broad-beamed, bargelike craft with derrick booms and cumbersome machinery.

Wade looked at it curiously. The captain, Forbeson by name, treated him respectfully when he saw the company's pass. Wade saw that no work was going on.

"I hear there's been a couple of accidents," he said.

The captain nodded. "Yeah, we lost two divers. A twisted lifeline got one. Bailey was his name. Doughton, the other, must have had a heart attack. They sometimes get 'em on account of the pressure. But the other boys got superstitious; they wouldn't go down. If they don't get over their scare we'll have to get new ones."

Wade pressed the captain for details without success. The man had evidently been instructed not to talk too much. Wade wondered if this was a wild-goose chase. What possible connection could all this have with the death of Danny O'Rork?

Then he thought of the match paper he had found in O'Rork's room. He left Captain Forbeson and took the motorboat back to the shore. He'd have to move cautiously, feel his way along. What did Forbeson mean when he said that the divers "got superstitious"?

In the back room of Sam's Place, with beer and whiskey slopped on the narrow counter, Wade found out. Ed Bramberg, the bleary-eyed bartender, whispered the tale to him.

"It's a bad business," he said. "Even the dead don't rest easy when there's gold around." He paused and polished a whiskey glass industriously, turning his eyes away from Wade's.

Wade lit a cigarette and blew a puff of smoke toward the ceiling.

"You mean there's something going on down below on the *Clara Scott?*"

Bramberg turned quickly. "Yes—she's laid there nearly a month now—in eighty feet of water. There's dead men on her—but they ain't resting easy, I tell you. They said Willie Doughton got a heart attack. But it wasn't that. He was in here the day before he died. He'd been down to the *Clara Scott* and he'd seen things—lights and something moving around. The next day, when they pulled him up, he was dead."

A croaking voice at Wade's elbow sounded. Wade turned to face an unshaven barroom loafer. The man spoke hoarsely.

"It's dead men's gold," he said, "and they better leave it be."

The bartender nodded. "You're right, Heinie. That's why the other boys won't go down—not after what happened to Doughton and Bailey. They'll have to get divers in from outside. And even they won't work—after they find out."

Wade was piecing the thing together now. It was another strange and ghastly tale of the sea. A ship full of gold, and dead men on her come to life.

He ordered a mug of beer for "Heinie" and found that the man's last name was Gatzon. He was a thin-faced dock rat with a coppery stubble of beard on his face; not a prepossessing character; but one who interested Wade. He seemed eager to talk about the *Clara Scott.*

"Captain Forbeson knows what he's up against," Heinie said. "He won't get men to go down for him. It'll be months before they raise that gold. Nobody'll go down while those dead men are dancing around on board."

He chuckled harshly and tipped up his mug of beer.

"Put that in your paper—you're a newspaper reporter, ain't you?" he added.

Wade nodded. "Once in a while I do a little of that sort of work."

He left shortly and went back to his apartment. For a time he paced the room with its familiar objects around the walls—the stuffed heads of big game, beads, curios and weapons—all souvenirs of his travels and adventures in various parts of the world.

Then he went to the window and looked out. In his mind's-eye he could still see the sprawled figure of Danny O'Rork, shot down without a chance. A hunch was working inside Wade's brain; a hunch that O'Rork's death and the deaths of those two divers were in some way connected.

He went to see his friend Inspector Thompson down at police headquarters. The old bald-headed man-hunter greeted Wade cheerfully and listened while he talked.

"This shooting of O'Rork isn't what it seems, chief," said Wade. "In my opinion, somebody wanted it to look like a gangster killing. But gangsters don't stop to take papers from dead men's pockets. With your permission I'm going to investigate this thing. It got under my skin the way they butchered O'Rork. Besides that, I think there's something big in the wind."

"Go as far as you like," said Thompson, his face owlish. "But don't get yourself shot. The department needs you even if you don't figure on the payroll."

There was a wealth of praise in that terse sentence. Wade Hammond had figured in some tough murder cases—and figured well.

"O.K., chief," he said, and the two men's glances met in a smile of understanding.

IT WAS dark that night, and Wade Hammond was glad of it, for he had strange work to do. He had hired a dory, and now, with the oarlocks muffled in strips of cloth and an odd-looking black box in the boat, he rowed out toward the place where the *Clara Scott* had gone down.

All afternoon he had been studying up on salvage apparatus. Then he had paid a visit to an old friend of his who worked in the amplification department of a radio concern. Together they rigged up a mechanism such as Wade doubted had ever been employed before. He planned to use applied science in his investigation of the mystery of the sunken ship.

The salvage boat, *City of Portsmouth*, had gone back to her dock. Only the marker buoy floated in the chill water over the spot where the *Clara Scott* lay.

Wade tied the painter of his dory to the buoy, then opened the top of the black box. Wire was coiled inside on a reel. There was a small microphone of peculiar shape. It was waterproofed and weighted with lead. There were also two earphones, a rheostat and three control dials.

Wade touched a switch which lighted a bulb and brought a faint humming sound from the box. Then he lowered the weighted microphone over the side of the dory and slowly unreeled the wire.

Eighty feet of it went down before the wire began to grow slack. Wade slipped the earphones over his head.

Minute after minute he listened, slowly turning the dials on the inner face of the black box. He heard nothing. Then he reeled in ten feet of wire, untied the painter of his boat and drifted till the weighted microphone struck something and caught. He bent forward eagerly now, listened again, and suddenly his face tensed.

There was a sound in the earphones, an uncanny noise of movement. Something was stirring in the black depths below him. Faint vibration came over the wire; then sounds of thumping, and the hollow, ghostly clank of metal as though the dead were holding high carnival down on those rusty iron decks.

A light sweat broke out on Wade's face, though he had been mentally prepared for something of the sort. His fingers trembled a little as they hovered over the dials.

Was the sound he heard merely the grating and thudding of loose metal on the sunken ship in the tidal currents, or was it something more strange and sinister? The words of Bramberg, the barkeeper, came back to him.

"Even the dead don't rest easy when there's gold around."

The next day he went to Sam's Place again and saw Bramberg and Heinie Gatzon. The little dock rat, who seemed to make the place a permanent hangout, greeted him like an old friend. Wade drew the man into a corner.

"Listen," he said. "There are funny things going on down there on the *Clara Scott*. You're right and Ed is right. But I'm going down to find out what they are. Will you help me?"

Heinie Gatzon shivered and drew back.

"Not me," he said. "Let the dead men have the gold. It belongs to 'em."

Wade lifted a twenty-dollar bill out of his pocket and pushed it across the table. Gatzon's fingers closed on it greedily.

"That's yours, and another like it," Wade said, "if you'll give me a hand. I'm going down to take a look at the *Clara Scott* myself."

"You are?" The words came from Gatzon's lips in a gasp of amazement.

"Yes—I'm going to hire a diving suit. I want you to keep the pump going for me. We'll slip out after dark in a motorboat."

"Ever been down before, mister?"

"Once, a good while ago," said Wade. There were few things he hadn't done in his active life. "It's only eighty feet. That isn't bad. Divers went down to three hundred when they were after the F-4.* I know the place to get a suit."

"You ain't told anybody about this?" asked Heinie.

"No, not a soul. Keep it under your hat."

Gatzon shrugged. "I shouldn't do it—but I'll help you," he said. "I can use the dough."

Wade visited a marine supply house and made arrangements for the rental of some diving apparatus. He had a long and confidential talk with the head of the firm. The suit he finally selected, composed of rubber and aluminum alloy, was fairly light but of complex design. It was especially adapted for work from a small boat at depths of not more than one hundred feet. This gave Wade a safety margin of twenty feet.

From the same concern he hired a motorboat with the air pump installed. But he didn't specify where or for what particular purpose he was going to use either the boat or the diving suit.

"A police investigation," was all that went down on the company's records.

---

* The USS F-4 sank off of Pearl Harbor on March 25, 1915 with the loss of 21 crew members. Recovery of the submarine is considered an important event in the history of diving and salvage.

THAT evening, as dusk crept along the waterfront, Wade stopped at Sam's Place and collected Heinie Gatzon. Together they went down to the dock where Wade's diving suit and motorboat had been delivered.

The handling of gas engines was an old story to Wade, and the mysteries of the diving suit had been explained to him by a company expert.

He spent an hour telling Gatzon exactly what to do.

"My life's in your hands, Gatzon," he said. "For every ten feet I go down there's an added water pressure of four and a half pounds. That means I can't descend any faster than the pump can supply air."

"O.K., mister. You kin trust me. I never went back on a pal yet—and any guy that slips me twenty bucks is a pal."

Night had fallen, somber and mysterious, as Wade started the motor and headed out across the harbor. Thin clouds hid the stars. The surface of the water was black except for the occasional red and green running lights of a vessel, or the transient, many-windowed radiance of a ferryboat plowing clumsily along. Wade switched off his own signal lights and took a chance on being run down.

"There might be somebody watching, Heinie," he said. "I want this thing kept between us." His voice as he spoke was low and tense, and his eyes had a glitter to them that presaged action and danger.

He knew what a risk he was running in visiting this boat to which sinister rumors clung. A man inexperienced in diving took a chance just going down. But a great part of Wade Hammond's life had been spent in taking chances. And when he was probing a crime he never let the threat of personal danger stop him. Rather it spurred him on, sharpened the functioning of his already keen brain and made his nerves and muscles coordinate.

But Heinie seemed uneasy as they neared the spot. He puffed on a cigarette hidden in his cupped hand. He jumped when Wade's flashlight stabbed the darkness as he hunted for the buoy.

"Cripes, I wouldn't want to be in your shoes, mister. The dead can see in the dark, but you can't. It'll be dark as hell's sewer down there."

Wade tapped the helmet of his diving suit in which was set a circular lens with a reflector and bulb behind it.

"This takes care of that, Heinie. All I have to do is press a button inside the suit. Then I'll have light enough in any direction I turn my head."

Gatzon laughed shortly. "Doughton and Bailey were old hands at the game. But the dead men got 'em."

Wade didn't answer. His flash had caught the marker buoy. He shut off the boat's engine and they glided up. Then he made the painter fast. The next moment he was getting into his cumbersome suit without wasting any time.

"Start the pump going, Heinie," he ordered.

He waited till he heard the electric motor operating the air pump purr softly as Heinie moved the switch. Then he dropped the helmet over his head and snapped the outside clamps. A tank on his shoulders, which appeared to be an expansion chamber, gave him the look of an enormous humpback.

He waved to Heinie, swung a leg over the boat's side and felt for the ladder. Slowly he lowered himself into the coldly lapping water, and could feel the chill of it as it crept up his body. He glanced across the harbor at the city's skyline with its myriad lights.

For all anyone could say it might be the last time he would ever look at it. His plans might go wrong, or his hunch prove incorrect. It was queer what sort of places a lively imagination and an adventurous spirit got a man into.

Then he let go his grip on the ladder and dropped into the water. He counted off the seconds as he slid slowly down with the air hose and hoisting line unwinding.

Gatzon was doing his part, so far, seeing that the speed of his descent was not too great. But Wade's face behind the goggle glass of the helmet was grim. He began to feel a pounding in his ears and a sense of constriction around his nostrils as the depth increased.

DOWN, down, down, with the chill of the water growing more intense. But he accustomed himself to the throbbing in his head and the coldness that seemed to seep into his very marrow. It wasn't unbearable yet, and wouldn't be. The depth wasn't great enough.

But his scalp prickled as he sensed that he was nearing the sunken ship. Any moment now his feet might touch a part of the huge hulk. His speed of descent was slowing. Heinie was following instructions.

For a moment Wade switched on his helmet light and looked down.

Rising toward him, as though in a giant aquarium, came the ghostly hulk of the steamer. The masts seemed like emaciated, naked arms reaching for him.

He spoke then into the small telephone disc set close to his mouth inside the helmet.

"Slow up a little more. I'm right over her now."

Heinie Gatzon's voice sounded in the communicating phones.

"O.K., boss."

He slipped past a tangle of antenna wires now that dropped from the ghostly masts. The steamer was keeled over on its side. His feet touched the side rail and slipped off. In a second he was sliding down the iron-plated hull until he came to a jarring stop on the harbor's bottom.

He switched off the light and stood in utter darkness as though waiting for something. And then it came. Gatzon's voice suddenly sounded in his ears again. It was a different voice now, harsh and murderous, the voice of a killer.

"You're going to get yours now, Hammond. You asked for it—sticking your nose into other people's business. So long! I'll be seein' you—in hell." A grating laugh sounded.

Then the voice and the laughter ceased and Wade suddenly gasped for air. There was a pain in his lungs as though a thousand needles were being jabbed into them.

He reached up. The air hose and pulley wire at the top of his helmet were snaking down—cut. There was a roaring in his ears. Heinie Gatzon had played him false, had severed his connection with the world above with the deliberate intention of murdering him.

But Wade wasn't surprised. He had anticipated it. He touched a valve at the top of his helmet, blocking the mouth of the air hose, preventing the water that would soon fill it from rushing down and drowning him. At the same instant he opened another valve, and oxygen once more came into his lungs. A meter began ticking inside his helmet.

The tank on his shoulders was doing its work now, saving him from Heinie's treachery. His diving suit was a combination of the air pump and self-sustaining type; a super-safety suit of the latest design. He had kept this from Gatzon, believing that the man hadn't enough technical knowledge to guess it, and expecting that he was in league with those who had killed the two divers and Danny O'Rork. And he had trapped Gatzon into revealing his hand.

But the mystery of the *Clara Scott* was still unexplored, and Wade had air for only forty-five minutes. At the end of that time he would open a third valve, fill his suit with expanded oxygen, and float to the surface.

And now he had work to do. What was the secret of those sounds he had heard and of the divers' deaths? Were dead men engaged in ghostly doings on the sunken boat, or were living fiends at work for their own ends? If so, how did they get there, in eighty feet of water and without surface connection? It seemed too fantastic to be believed.

Wade walked along the side of the huge hull. He felt like a ghost himself in some ghost world. Progress was slow. The ship seemed miles in length.

Then his groping hands touched a waterlogged rope that curled over the side. He pulled it, found that it was tied somewhere above, probably a neglected lifeline which had helped to save some of the poor wretches trapped on the steamer after the crash.

He drew himself up hand over hand, letting a little more air into his suit to make himself lighter. Soon he was standing on the steamer's canted deck.

Then he stopped, his muscles rigid. Up forward he saw a dim radiance in the water. Light, ghostly and iridescent, made a miniature aurora above an open hatch. And as he saw it, perspiration stood out on Wade's body inside his diving suit in spite of the water's chill. Those other divers, Doughton and Bailey, had not been wrong then.

HE DROPPED to his hands and knees and crept forward as silently as the clumsy suit would permit. More than ever he seemed to be living in some fantastic dream. Dead men dancing! It was as though he were among the dead himself; as though he were on his way to join some ghastly revel on the sea's bottom.

He came to the open hatch and stared down. Shadows wavered eerily through the water. A fish flashed its silvery side by him. A huge crab scuttled off.

But the thing that held him spellbound was the light suspended in the ship's hold. Here was no work of ghosts, but of human hands. Wade leaned farther over, trying to pierce the shadowy depths.

Then he stiffened. A faint scraping sound reached him inside the helmet. Suddenly, obeying an impulse that was stronger than reason, he whirled and threw himself to one side almost slipping through the hatchway. Something crashed against him, slipped off his arm.

He turned as a huge figure, dimly seen in the illuminated water, seemed to leap upon him. He realized then that he had been followed, probably seen when he flashed his light that first time as he was descending. Some living thing in the depths had crept upon him with murderous intent.

He backed away from the hatch into the eddying shadows. For an instant he saw the form of another diver—a diver like himself with no air hose or lifeline attached to his helmet. Then the man was upon him, and they were grappling.

Wade clutched at an arm as he saw a hand with a knife upraised. He switched on his helmet light and found himself staring at the glass lens of another diving helmet with a man's eyes behind it, eyes distorted like those of some gigantic crustacean.

The knife probed for him; but he fought it away. And then began the most terrific fight of his life. He had fought on battlefields, city streets and in tropical jungles; but never eighty feet under water with the awful threat of drowning hanging over him as each second ticked away.

This fight bore a resemblance to a slow-motion movie film. Their struggles were awkwardly grotesque; but with death in every movement. One slash of that knife at Wade's suit and the sea water would rush in. He would be drowned like a rat.

They stumbled and groped on the iron deck. They fell, sprawled and rose up again. Wade at last caught the other diver's arm, twisted it savagely and made him drop the knife. But the man broke away, leaped upon him, bore him down, and the next instant they were fighting again.

Wade was gasping for breath, absorbing the oxygen faster than it came from the storage tank. He threw his antagonist off, rose, then his foot slipped. The light in the water around him grew brighter.

For an awful instant he saw what it was. His enemy had locked with him again. They were on the edge of the open hatch. It was too late to move back. They lost their balance and fell. The metal on their suits pulled them down as they turned over and over in a quick descent.

Wade made a desperate attempt to lighten his suit with more air. Lights and shadows revolved before his helmet lens. Then there was a thud, a sensation of the world tumbling in about him; and Wade lost consciousness.

When he stirred again the radiance of the light suspended in the water was still in his eyes. A great fear seemed to be clutching at his brain. He tried to think, tried to clear his blurred faculties.

The meter! The meter in his helmet—telling him when the air supply would be gone!

It was hardly moving now. His tank was practically exhausted. There was not enough left to fill his suit and get him to the top. He was trapped in the hold of the ship, trapped with death soon to come.

HE ROSE stumblingly to his feet. For an instant he looked up at the black square of the hatchway. Then he looked down and his eyes widened in horror at the sight of the crumpled, sprawled form in the water beside him. It was the other diver. The man's helmet had struck an iron bolt. The eye lens had been broken and he had drowned.

Wade turned away with a feeling of nausea. Then he saw the black opening in the ship's side where plates had been ripped away. This was not the hole made when the vessel had been rammed. The opening was too even. He ran through it with a sudden realization of what it meant. He found himself in the mouth of a black tunnel.

Some of the mystery clinging to the *Clara Scott* was solved!

Sections of huge piping, large enough in diameter for a man to stand upright, were bolted together end to end. They led off across the floor of the harbor. This was how unseen men reached the sunken boat.

But there was water in the pipe still, and Wade's head was pounding again as though a trip-hammer were beating against it. The air inside his helmet was growing almost unbreathable. He ran on like a man in a nightmare, half wishing he had used the last of his air in an attempt to rise to the surface.

On and on he stumbled, staring through his eye lens along the black tunnel of the pipe, while the reflected radiance of his own helmet light seemed to dance and zigzag through his reeling brain.

He came up sharply against a blank wall of metal. He stared dizzily and uncomprehendingly for a moment. Then he understood and his heart leaped.

There was a door in front of him, a door leading to an air lock in the pipe. He groped for the handle, opened it, and walked into the shut-off section. Water was here, too. But he shut the door behind him tightly. Subway builders used such air locks. There must be a valve.

He looked for it, found it, and his hand reached for the brass handle as a drowning man reaches for a straw. He turned the valve and heard the hiss and roar of air under tremendous pressure. Suddenly the water in the chamber began to recede. It was being forced out through an automatic vent.

He almost sank into unconsciousness again. With fumbling fingers he groped at his helmet, opened it, and lay gasping in the cold air that now filled his lungs. He got to his feet, wriggled out of his suit, and found the next metal door.

Under his diving suit, close against his side, a flat automatic was strapped. He gripped it now and walked on through the pipe after opening a second bulkhead. He was breathing air, eighty feet below the harbor's surface.

He understood it all now. The amazing ingenuity of the thing was so staggering to the imagination that he wouldn't have believed it himself if he hadn't been there to see it. Yet in a way it was as simple as it was ingenious—and there was no limit to what men would do for gold.

These men, whoever they were, had laid a pipe from the shore to the sunken ship. They had been salvaging the gold that way. No wonder they didn't want divers coming down from the surface. No wonder they had taken murderous steps to see that they weren't interfered with. Gatzon was in league with them. He was a spy, a squealer who was posted to see that outsiders did not become too suspicious, and to do away with them if they did.

Danny O'Rork had probably fallen in with Gatzon, too. Then he had formed a theory, the right one, and had gone prowling around among those warehouses at the edge of the harbor. This fitted into the puzzle, too.

Wade's eyes gleamed. They thought he was dead now. That gave him an advantage.

The pipe began to slant upward and his steps grew more steady. The pressure in his lungs was slowly relaxing.

He came to another door at last and opened it cautiously. There were pipes in it controlling the air supply. A light burned down at the end of a long corridor, and he heard the movement of machinery. He must be in the basement of one of the warehouses. It was here that the thieves had carried out the land end of their ambitious scheme.

He edged along the corridor, gun in hand, past a room where a man in overalls sat watching dials. At the end of the corridor, where it was quieter, he came to another room with a light in it. And here he stopped short.

There were two men in the room. He heard the sound of voices—and one of them was familiar. Wade had heard it somewhere before. Outside in the distance the engine of a motor truck was rumbling. One of the men in the room was speaking more clearly.

"Cliff won't have to worry now that the guy's dead. He'll be up with another load of the stuff soon. Shall I go back to Sam's Place and watch for more of 'em who think they're wise?"

Wade knew who was speaking then—Heinie Gatzon. He stepped into the room, his face harsh, his gun-hand steady. His voice came like the crack of a whip.

"Get up—back against the wall. Any move and I'll nail you both."

The other man turned then, and Wade's eyes widened. So, here was the final explanation of the mystery.

"Wheeler," he said grimly. "You doublecrossed your partner, eh, and the stockholders of your company? Thought you'd do a little salvaging on your own! You knew all the tricks of the trade and tried a new one. But you went beyond your knowledge when you tried murder. That's my line, Wheeler—I study it. I can forgive you this salvaging stunt—it was pretty clever. But I can't forgive you the murder of Danny O'Rork—or those two divers who were killed 'accidentally'! Neither will the murder jury that convicts you. This is going to make some story, and I only wish Danny O'Rork was here to get the credit for it."

Ten Detective Aces, May-June 1933

Wade Hammond was the first to see the man stagger across the green of the Somerset links. And that man was more dead than alive. In his zigzag wake was an invisible trail of horror that started Wade Hammond on the most ghastly case of his career.

Teeth of Terror

WADE HAMMOND had taken his stance for an approach to the fourth green of the Somerset links when he saw the figure running toward him.

His steel-shafted mashie was lifting for the down stroke. His suntanned face with its pencil-thin mustache line was set in concentration.

But he straightened up quickly letting the white ball lie where it was. There was something abruptly arresting about that figure coming across the fairway.

The man's arms were waving grotesquely. He was stumbling, reeling, and a faint inarticulate sound was coming from his lips.

Then Wade saw who it was. Young Keith Rutledge, one of the guests at the Somerset Hotel, and a member of the brokerage firm of Rutledge, Lennox, Coe & Jacobson.

As a special investigator of crime, Wade carried a card in his pocket bearing the signature of the police commissioner himself. He was always being drawn into strange homicide cases. But he wasn't looking for murder under the bright morning sun on this green, seaside golf course.

He didn't connect Rutledge's peculiar actions with crime as the man drew nearer. Yet he saw that something was radically wrong.

Other golfers had noticed Rutledge's odd behavior, too. A half-dozen players on neighboring greens were edging forward, squinting behind their hands, calling excitedly to each other.

Wade could hear Rutledge's strange cry plainly now. It sounded like the horrible babbling of an idiot. It had a ghastly quality that snapped Wade out of his pleasantly relaxed state of mind.

He dropped his mashie beside the bag holding the rest of his clubs. He'd been making the round alone, playing against par and trying to beat his own record, and he was the first to reach Rutledge.

The young broker's face had a strangely livid tint. The pupils of his eyes were dilated as though belladonna had been dropped into them. He was holding his right hand awkwardly in front of him. The fingers, Wade noticed, were as stiff as though they had been frozen.

Then Wade saw that Rutledge's teeth were clamped shut and that he was trying to talk through them. A froth showed at the corners of his lips and Wade's first thought was of hydrophobia.

But Rutledge still seemed in command of his faculties. He pointed to his wrist, made spiral motions in the air, and gestured back toward the way he had come.

Then, as though the effort had been too much for him, he staggered in a circle like a dancer executing a pirouette. Before Wade could catch him he sprawled horribly on the green grass of the fairway.

Wade moved close and stooped over.

"What is it, Rutledge? For God's sake, what's the matter?"

The broker was silent now. The sounds that had come spluttering through his clenched teeth had stopped. His body was stretched out rigidly on the grass, in the throes of some sort of paralysis. Only his eyes rolled, showing that he still lived.

Wade realized with a shudder of horror that he was looking down at a man who was like a living corpse.

Other players were coming up now on the run. There was a babble of excited voices. Lennox, Jacobson and Coe were among them. Each had been shooting a practice round alone—secretly trying to iron out his pet weakness in preparation for the Sunday afternoon match. All were young men of about the same age, partners in the firm of which Keith's father was head.

Coe was plump and red-headed, a man who seemed well-satisfied with himself. Lennox was tall, thin and dark. Jacobson thick-set and blond. They reminded Wade of a vaudeville team getting ready to do an act.

THE swanky Somerset Hotel was a favorite hangout for stock-market men. It had been called a brokers' paradise; with golf, handball, a salt-water swimming pool, a bar for those who knew the ropes, and an assortment of unattached and attractive women included in the guest list. Young Rutledge and his partners were habitues of the place.

"What's the matter?" asked Coe. "What happened to Keith?"

Wade looked up quickly.

"It beats me!" he said. "You saw the way he was running. He was trying to say something; but he couldn't get it out. That froth on his lips looks almost like rabies."

At mention of the dread word, the golfers drew together and stared around furtively. A woman on the edge of the small crowd gave a cry of fear.

"It can't be rabies, though," Wade added. "He's paralyzed, stiff as a board, but he's still alive. Get a doctor somebody."

A caddy detached himself from the group and sped toward the hotel.

As he did so Wade's eyes focused themselves on Rutledge's wrist. Two reddish marks showed there.

He rose suddenly.

"Some of you stay with him," he snapped. "I'm going back to see where he was. He must have been making the round alone."

Coe spoke up again.

"That's right! He was practicing on the fairway between the seventh and eighth greens—trying to get rid of that hoodoo of his. He always sliced his drive there and went into the rough. I passed through him this morning and heard him swearing. He'd driven three practice balls into his favorite clump of bayberry bushes already."

Wade had heard the story of Rutledge's hoodoo. Bets had been won and lost on it in the hotel. The young broker, it seemed, never failed to drive into that one clump.

He started off across the fairway and was joined by Jacobson and Lennox. They, too, had seen the marks on young Rutledge's wrist. Jacobson spoke of them.

"There must have been some kind of wild animal in those bushes," he said. "It bit Keith when he was hunting for his lost balls."

Wade nodded. He had figured the same thing out himself. But he knew there were no wild animals on the links, nothing except a few ground squirrels. A hunch that was almost like the working of a subtle sixth sense was telling him that there was something queer about this. Men with hydrophobia didn't stiffen out like corpses.

They went over the hill and passed down into the hollow where the fairway between the seventh and eighth greens lay. It was one of the most secluded spots on the course, giving a player a sense of isolation.

"There's his bag," said Jacobson. "And there's the last club he used. He must have tried to get out of the rough with a mashie-niblick."

A plaid bag filled with golf clubs lay on the grass. The mashie was some little distance away from it. But Wade was more interested in something else—the clump of bayberry bushes that formed a poisonous-looking light green against the darker background of the fairway turf.

They approached it cautiously. Each man seemed to be thinking of the same thing.

"Spread out," said Wade. "We'll take it from different angles."

They laid their bags down and each selected a heavy club. Then they began beating systematically through the bushes. But no living thing stirred. The clump was only about thirty feet in diameter. If anything had been there they would have seen it. But all they found were two more of Keith Rutledge's lost balls.

"It's no go," said Jacobson. "There's no animal here, but I suppose it might have run away."

Wade said nothing. He was staring at the clump of bushes.

"Coe was apparently the last one to see him," he said. "But other players might have passed through while he was practicing here. It's a lonely spot."

Jacobson gave a start at the subtle implication of Wade's words.

"You don't think a human being had anything to do with this?"

"I don't know," said Wade. "If Rutledge dies I'll think there's something strange about it. He was trying to say something. He had a terrified look on his face."

"And suppose he did—what could it mean?"

"It might mean murder!" said Wade softly.

WHEN they got back to the spot where they had left Keith Rutledge, the group of people, grown larger now, were standing with frightened faces.

A doctor from the hotel had a stethoscope clamped to the prostrate man's chest. His face, too, was serious. He straightened up as Wade edged into the crowd.

"I can't do anything for him," the doctor said. "The man's dead."

A shudder passed over the crowd. Rutledge's strange death seemed doubly gruesome by contrast with the bright sunlight and the open fairway. Wade spoke grimly.

"What's your diagnosis, doctor? Could it be rabies?"

The doctor shook his head.

"Not a chance. A stroke followed by cerebral hemorrhage or embolism is the nearest I can come."

"What about those bites on his wrist?"

The doctor started. Evidently he hadn't noticed them and no one in the crowd had told him. He looked at them now and shook his head again.

"They're hardly more than scratches, Mr. Hammond. I don't think they have anything to do with his death."

"He had that arm held out in front of him," said Wade. "It seemed to be stiff and paralyzed before any of the rest of him. I got the impression that he was frightened and trying to tell me something."

The doctor looked skeptical.

"What's your theory, Mr. Hammond? I know you've done police work. The clerk at the hotel told me that."

"Poison," said Wade shortly. "I don't know much about medicine, doc, but I'm certain that man didn't die a natural death."

His words made a sensation in the crowd. Coe looked at him and his reddish face turned pale.

"My God—you don't think Keith was murdered?"

"I don't know," said Wade. "But with your permission I'm going to call up the local police head—and I think, doctor, it would be best to perform an autopsy."

They carried Rutledge's body back to the hotel, and on the way Coe talked jerkily to Wade.

"It's hellishly tragic," he said. "Keith's father was going to retire next month. Keith would have been the head of the firm."

Wade's face showed sudden interest.

"There'll be fewer partners to divide the profits now," he said. "You might figure it that way, eh, Coe?"

A startled look came into Coe's eyes.

"You don't mean—why it's impossible."

"Nothing's impossible where there's big money at stake," said Wade. He spoke from his long experience with crime and criminals.

BUT Sullivan, the local police chief, seemed to agree with Coe. Sullivan was a slow-moving man with a sagging face and fishy eyes. He shook his head and smiled patronizingly when Wade hinted that Rutledge's death ought to be investigated.

"A detective on a vacation is like a sailor on shore," Sullivan said. "One tries to find water—the other looks for crime. The trouble with you, Hammond, is that you can't stop your imagination from working. Rutledge isn't the first man to die of sunstroke on a golf course. I've always claimed golf was too strenuous."

Wade lowered his voice and spoke harshly.

"All three of Keith Rutledge's partners stand to benefit by his death. One, I don't know which, probably has hopes of being the head of the firm now that Rutledge's father is going to retire. There's a murder motive for you, Sullivan."

Sullivan waved a superior hand.

"You city dicks are always looking for trouble. You'd expect to find murder at a Sunday School picnic. Leave this case to me."

"How will you handle it?"

"Shadow the three suspects. Watch 'em close. It's been my experience that if a man's guilty he always shows it."

Wade shook his head.

"I've met killers so cunning and self-disciplined that you had to trap them before they'd show their hands."

"Leave it to me," repeated Sullivan. "You may know a few police tricks but I know human nature. I'll have a chat with each of 'em—and maybe poke around in their stuff a bit. If one of 'em's guilty he'll get sore and give himself away."

"Go easy," warned Wade. "Remember that you don't know what you're up against."

Sullivan tapped his pocket pompously. A bulge showed where an old-fashioned Colt reposed. "There ain't a criminal going that can't be cured with a dose of lead," he said.

Wade didn't feel right about letting Sullivan handle the case. But the local police head seemed to resent his interference. And Wade's card from the city police commissioner didn't carry any power here.

Coe, Jacobson and Lennox had called off their golf match. The death of Rutledge seemed to have cast a pall of gloom over them. The hotel clerk told Wade that they'd arranged to go back to the city as soon as the doctor had performed his autopsy and the body could be shipped.

The doctor's name was Sterling. Wade was one of the first to talk with him after he had finished his gruesome work. Sterling had a serious expression on his face.

"I'm beginning to think there's something queer myself, Hammond," he said. "I found traces of a neuro-toxic in the blood. It belongs to the same class as snake venom, I think."

Wade knew something about poisons. His police work had brought him into contact with them. There were some like Kombe that a man could swallow without harm; but a fraction of a grain if taken into the blood through a scratch caused death.

The exact nature of the poison made little difference to Wade now. What he wanted was to find out how it had been administered and by whom.

He left the doctor's office and went back to the hotel. All afternoon he hung around the office and the wide veranda.

Coe, Jacobson and Lennox were not in evidence. They seemed to be sticking to their rooms. He knew that Sullivan was interviewing them.

It was toward evening that Wade, just finishing a cigarette and watching the sea fog roll in, heard a noise that brought him up in his chair with a start.

The sound had come from the office.

He heard the clerk call out excitedly. Then another voice sounded—a voice that was babbling and inhuman, and which seemed to carry with it a note of stark terror.

He leaped up from his chair and ran forward—flinging the door of the office open. And he gasped at what he saw.

Sullivan was staggering across the office floor. His face was a strange livid color and one arm was stretched out before him. There seemed to be something he wanted—something he was trying to say through teeth that contracting jaw muscles had clenched shut.

He moved toward the desk, making motions with his arm.

"Pa-aaaaaa—"

A long, hideous sound like the bleat of a sheep came from his livid lips. The desk clerk stood like a man paralyzed, a look of horror on his face.

Wade jumped forward. He understood the significance of the sound Sullivan had made.

"He wants paper," Wade shouted. "Quick—give him a pad and pencil."

THE desk clerk moved to obey Wade's order. But it was too late. The poison in Sullivan's blood was acting already. He staggered, reeled, then collapsed on the office floor and his body went rigid as Rutledge's had done.

Wade bent over him; tried to make him talk, but could get no answer. Sullivan was beyond speech and would soon be beyond aid. The pallor of death was upon him now.

Wade shot a question at the hotel clerk then.

"Which rooms are Coe, Jacobson and Lennox in?"

The clerk looked at his register.

"Twenty-one, twenty-three and twenty-eight," he said in a shaking voice. "Sullivan must have been up there. He came running down the stairs just now."

Wade nodded. He made a dash for the elevator, which the policeman in his haste had neglected to use.

He reached the second floor, walked down the corridor and knocked at the doors of the three men, one after the other. They all answered him, and he asked the same question of each.

"Was Sullivan here?"

"Yea, about an hour ago," said Coe. "What's the matter?"

"He came to my room before that," said Lennox.

"He left mine at five-twenty. That was over a half-hour ago," said Jacobson. "What's wrong?"

Wade didn't answer. He knew that one of the men was lying; but which one? His face was inscrutable as he looked at them. He had never had a more baffling case. Sullivan had stumbled on something, and had paid with his life. But he might have come from any one of the three rooms. Wade's expression suddenly went hard.

"I'm not going to mince words," he said. "Two murders have been committed. I know that. I'm talking to the killer right now. One of you is he; but I don't know which one. I'll find out, though. You'll all stay here till this thing is solved. If necessary I'll get a search warrant and go through all three of your rooms."

With that he turned on his heel and left them standing there.

Sullivan was dead when he got downstairs. Wade had handled many murder cases before; but never one like this—never one in which he was so close to the killer and yet so far, and in which he was in such complete doubt as to how the murder had been committed. His mind had formulated and rejected a dozen theories.

"I'm taking charge," he said to the desk clerk. "Coe, Jacobson and Lennox are to be kept in this hotel—for a week if necessary. Get in touch with Sullivan's office and have two constables come out. They'll guard the doors."

The clerk obeyed and Wade went to his room, which he'd made homelike by bringing a few of his own belongings with him. The skin of a leopard, shot in Guatemalan jungles hung on the wall. Some ivory figurines he'd picked up in a bazaar in Hong Kong were on a table. A couple of gold-ornamented Turkish daggers were crossed above the mantel. They reminded him of his world travels and of the adventures he had had.

He paced the floor thinking and smoking cigarettes. He'd expected to have a quiet vacation, and here he was involved in a fantastic murder case. Either Coe, Lennox or Jacobson might be guilty, but he must find some way to trap the right one.

He saw them at dinner, all eating at the same table. Constables guarded the exits, but they were allowed the run of the hotel. They stared at Wade curiously. The other guests shunned them.

He had a talk with each after dinner, but learned nothing.

All three still seemed skeptical about the idea of murder.

"You're jumping at conclusions, Hammond," said Coe. "You're making it damned embarrassing for us. It's bad enough to have our partner killed."

"I'm thinking of Sullivan, too," said Wade grimly. "He was a hard-working police officer doing his job as he saw it. There's a saying, 'it doesn't pay to kill a copper,' and one of you is going to find it out."

HE went back to his room, mulled over the thing some more, and then went to bed. It was possible that, acting on Sullivan's theory, he might wear the killer down, shatter his nerves by keeping him cooped up. The partners would grow suspicious of one another. The murderer might betray himself.

He lay in the darkness of his room thinking. He could hear the slow wash of the surf far away, and from time to time the distant mournful note of a ship's foghorn. He began to doze off; then suddenly he sat bolt upright in bed. It seemed to him that he had heard another noise. The sound of a closing door—his own.

A faint light was coming through the transom. Wide-eyed, he stared around the room, but could see nothing except the familiar objects; his dresser, the table, and the big chair. Certainly no one was in the room with him.

But a tingling sensation crept along his spine. Had that door opened softly and closed again while he dozed, or had he dreamed it? And what made the feeling of menace so deep?

Then he turned his head again and listened. There *was* a sound in the room, an eerie, ghostly scratching that made his scalp prickle.

He rose higher on the bed and looked down on the floor. For a moment fingers of fear held him in the iciest grip he had ever known.

A ghostly white something moved across the floor. It was a living thing, a small animal; white as a graveyard wraith. He saw a snakelike body on short legs, a head with a pointed, ratlike nose. The creature looked up, baring its teeth at him, and he saw tiny red eyes looking at him, bright and sinister as coals of devil's fire. The snakelike body undulated. The thing was coming toward him— and he knew then what it was.

A ferret, an animal closely akin to the weasel family, domesticated and trained to hunt rabbits. He had used one himself once. They were loyal to one master, vicious to the rest of the world. They could give a man a nasty bite, though a harmless one. But this ferret was no ordinary beast. It was linked up with murder—was the tool of a sinister human fiend. Those bared animal teeth held some deadly secret.

And the thing was creeping nearer the bed every second; getting ready to spring up and attack him. He knew now what had been hidden in those bushes when Rutledge had been bitten. He wasn't sure why they hadn't found it there when they had searched. But he had a theory as to that now that he had seen the size of the animal.

Death was close at his elbow. One bite of those vicious, snapping teeth and he, too, would go staggering out of the room, babbling like an idiot, trying to tell what had happened before the fingers of eternal silence choked the breath in his throat.

His hands were moving along the quilt, getting under the edge of it. His body was tensing. And then the ferret sprang, a murderous white streak of sinew and muscle.

He felt its weight on his feet through the bedding. He saw it crouch there a moment and glare at him, then move forward toward his head and shoulders, led on by the blood lust and the sight of bared flesh. Its master had trained it well.

But as it sprang a second time, Wade's hands under the quilt swept up. He rolled the edge of the heavy cover over, caught the ferret before it could get him. He felt its warm, squirming body under the fabric. His hands pressed in, clutched the quilt closer, forced it around the animal, and squeezed for seconds till there was no movement left in that snakelike shape.

Sweat was dripping off his face when he finally relaxed his grip. He opened the quilt cautiously and looked at the dead body of the animal whose teeth had killed two men and had almost snuffed his own life out. He pried the ferret's jaws apart and saw how the tusks on each side had been tipped with some sort of brownish, gummy substance. Poison—put there by human hands!

HE got up shakily and smoked a cigarette. He had passed through the most terrible few seconds of his life.

A plan began to take shape in his mind.

He dressed quickly, stuffed the body of the ferret in his suitcase and slipped out into the hall.

"I've got to make a trip to the city," he said to the desk clerk. "I'll be back in a couple of hours. There's something I want to get."

His trim sport roadster was in the hotel garage. He got it out and made quick time to the big town. He did what he had to do quickly, and, before the hour was up, was on his way back to the seaside resort, the suitcase still in the car with him.

When he reached the hotel he made a strange request to the clerk.

"Send a boy up to wake Coe, Lennox and Jacobson," he said. "Have them all meet me in my room, number thirty-four."

Wade went back into his own room and switched on a corner light. Then he pulled the small table to the center of the room and set the suitcase on it.

Jacobson was the first to arrive. He looked worried and bewildered. Coe came next, slightly sullen at being roused out of bed. Lennox's face showed surprise and curiosity. When they were all inside Wade locked the door and put the key in his pocket. He looked at the trio grimly.

"A strange thing happened tonight," he said. "While I was dozing someone put an animal—a ferret—in my room. The thing attacked me, but I caught it before it could bite me and put it in that suitcase. It explains the mysteries of the murders, gentlemen. The animal has poison on its teeth. I wonder if any of you know anything about it?"

Coe shuddered and turned pale.

"You mean you've got the animal in there—alive?"

"Yes," said Wade.

"A ferret with poisoned fangs caused the deaths of two men. Someone put it in that clump of bayberry bushes knowing that Rutledge would hunt for his balls there and get bitten. The animal was retrieved by the same person."

WADE tapped the suitcase again; then suddenly swore under his breath. His foot had apparently stumbled against the table leg. He swayed, seemed to try to balance himself, and all at once the table went over. The suitcase slid off, struck on one corner, and the top flew open.

Wade's voice rose in a hoarse cry of warning.

"My God! He's got out. Careful—keep back!"

A sinuous, snakelike body on stubby feet had climbed over the edge of the open suitcase.

Coe, Jacobson and Lennox had backed against the wall. Wade joined them, looking at the ferret with apparent terror.

"Unlock the door," cried Coe. "We've got to get out of here."

Wade started for the door; but the ferret turned, and Wade pressed himself back against the wall.

"It will attack the first man who moves!" he cried harshly.

The animal pointed its head toward them and showed its teeth in a snarl.

"Something's got to be done," said Lennox. "Let's get it back in the suitcase."

"Don't move," cried Coe. "Hammond's right—it will bite anyone who stirs."

"We've got to take a chance," said Lennox grimly.

The ferret had moved away from the suitcase. It still seemed dazed. Lennox edged around it and picked the case up. Coe grunted in approval.

"Good work," he said, "but go easy."

Wade Hammond, too, was edging forward now.

"Drop it over him, Lennox," he said.

Lennox attempted to do so. He was almost over the animal now. Then suddenly the ferret turned with a snarl. Like a streak of white lightning it made for Lennox's ankle. The broker stepped back with a cry, and in that instant the animal fastened its teeth in the man's leg.

Wade caught the suitcase from Lennox's hand and dropped it over the ferret's body, breaking its hold. Lennox stood in the middle of the floor, swaying, his face a deathly white. Coe and Jacobson crowded up to him.

"Quick, the key," said Coe. "Maybe we can save him. Get a doctor."

Lennox seemed utterly dazed. Sweat stood out on his forehead.

"I'll go to my room," he said. "Get Doctor Sterling here at once. He may be able to give me something."

He stumbled out into the hall while Coe rushed downstairs.

"You were a fool not to lock that suitcase," growled Jacobson. "Why didn't you kill the animal?"

Wade didn't answer. He was watching Lennox. The man was walking unsteadily along the hall. He disappeared around the corner and went down the stairway to the floor below.

"He's going to his room," said Jacobson. "Let's go with him."

"Wait!" said Wade, and there was a strange ring to his voice.

He didn't follow Lennox for a few seconds, not until the broker had had time to get out of sight. Then he started forward. When they reached the floor below Lennox had gone into his room and the door was shut. But Wade jumped forward and threw it open.

Lights in the room were on. Lennox was standing near the dresser. He had something in his hand; a gleaming metal syringe. He had the point of it in his arm and was squeezing the plunger home.

His hand flew out and he tried to conceal the thing in his drawer. Then he saw he had been too late. Wade had caught him at it.

"Dope," said Lennox huskily. "It's a bad habit of mine. I take it when my nerves go back on me."

"Let's see that hypo!" Wade's voice was like the crack of a whip.

He reached for the syringe, but Lennox drew his hand back. Then he saw the expression of disbelief in Wade's eyes and his lips parted in a snarl. His right hand dived into the bureau drawer and this time when it came out there was a flash of blue metal. But once again he was too late.

A gun had appeared as if by magic in Wade Hammond's hand. There was a stabbing report, a puff of acrid smoke, and the automatic in Lennox's fingers clattered to the floor as his arm went limp. His face was contorted with rage and pain.

"You'd have shot me, wouldn't you?" said Wade. "You've played your cards rather badly, Lennox. The antidote in that syringe wasn't necessary. I killed the ferret that you let loose in my room. The one that bit you just now was quite harmless. I hired it from a pet shop. But you thought it was yours; thought it wouldn't turn on you and that you could get it back into the suitcase. Then when it did turn and bite, you lost your nerve—and thought only of the antidote you carried with you in case an emergency ever did arise.

"You were pretty cool, Lennox, carrying the ferret around in your golf bag the way you did and pretending to help us hunt for it. But there's some trick that will trap almost every murderer—no matter how original he is—and you certainly fell for mine."

Wade Hammond had planned a quiet evening at home. But a victim of the insidious Cobra changed those plans into a nightmare of stark terror. For Wade Hammond met a dying man with gay ideas—a living man with drab ideas—and a nightclub hot-cha dancer with mixed ideas.

Fangs of the Cobra

THE strident ringing of the doorbell brought Wade Hammond around in his chair with a jerk. He thrust a lean finger into the book he was reading to mark the place and stared across the den of his snug bachelor apartment.

His eye wandered past cabinets filled with curios, primitive weapons and pieces of pottery—mementos of his many travels. Stuffed heads of big game, shot in the far corners of the earth, stared back at him from the walls.

The doorbell sounded again. It was continuous this time, as though someone, out of patience, were holding an angry finger on it.

He shut his book with a snap, wrapped his silk-tasseled dressing gown around his tall figure and strode to the door with long, quick steps. His movements were as poised and precise as those of some fast-running, well-oiled machine.

He stopped beside the door, touched the button operating the electric lock in the vestibule below and waited. The button would spring the catch and afford his visitor admittance.

The ringing ceased abruptly, but seconds passed and no one came up the stairs. Wade's long, lean face with its thin mustache line grew alert.

As a special investigator of crime, acting sub rosa in homicide cases, the ringing of that doorbell had often presaged a visit from Inspector Thompson, or from some stranger asking his help. Who could it be now, he wondered.

He waited another half minute, and a hard look came into his eyes. He had enemies in the underworld, friends of criminals he had sent to the electric chair. A time might come when some assassin's hand would reach out for his own life.

He crossed quickly to a table, opened a drawer and drew from it an automatic in a worn leather holster. It was a weapon that had been with him on many adventures when, as a newspaper correspondent and soldier-of-fortune, he had prowled the out-trails of the world. He drew back the safety catch and slipped the gun into his pocket. A moment later he opened the corridor doorway and went down the apartment house stairs.

It was raining outside. He could see the glow of a streetlight on wet pavements, hear the moaning lash of the wind. Somewhere a taxi honked dismally.

The night switchboard operator wasn't in sight. No one was visible through the glass of the vestibule door. But he opened it cautiously and stared out, then drew in his breath in a hissing gasp.

On the floor of the vestibule a human figure lay sprawled. The starkly pale face of a young man stared up at him; eyes wide, bloodless lips moving incoherently. He bent closer and stared in amazement. On the young man's face, stamped there with some sort of dark ink, was a hideous design—the head of a snake with open jaws and sharp fangs.

The young man made a gurgling sound in his throat and lifted one trembling arm. He pointed back through the doorway toward the street—and Wade understood.

He leaped across the man's body to the front of the vestibule and looked into the night. Far down the block the red tail-light of a car was disappearing. As he watched, it was swallowed up by the rain-swept darkness.

He ran down the steps, crossed the pavement and stooped down. Tire tracks showed faintly where the water had been pressed back from the asphalt. The rain was obliterating them. There was no time for him to make a photo as an expert from the Bureau of Criminal Identification might have done. But he recorded the markings on the sensitive film of his brain. He would recognize them if he saw them again.

He turned back into the apartment building, running long fingers through rain-wet hair. The figure of the young man was still there, slumped flatter now. The staring eyes were closed, the bloodless lips still. Wade felt one of the stranger's hands, held it for a moment, and nodded to himself. There was no pulse beat. The young man was dead. Then he saw the bluish markings near one of the veins on the young man's wrists—and prickles of horror crept along his scalp. He bent closer and stared more intently. The markings had been made by the fangs of a snake!

IT was fifteen minutes later that a headquarters' car arrived in answer to his summons. In the meantime he had gone through the dead man's pockets and had established his identity. A wallet showed that his name was Thomas Bailey. A business letter indicated that he was employed by the Zeddler brothers, bankers who owned the controlling interest in the Central Savings Bank.

Wade straightened up as Detective Murphy of the radio car patrol came through the door with the tails of his wet slicker flapping around his legs. Outside, a cop named Sullivan sat at the wheel of the police cruiser chugging at the curb.

Murphy said: "What is it, Hammond, what's the trouble now? Have—"

He stopped speaking as his eye fell on the dead form of Bailey. His big face assumed the alert expression of a terrier watching a rat hole. "Who's the guy and who bumped him?"

"That's what I'd like to know," said Wade softly. "He was coming to see me. He must have had something to tell. But somebody got to him first. Look at his face, Murphy!"

Wade heard the big dick's sharply indrawn breath.

"It's a snake's head, Hammond—what the hell—" his voice trailed off.

Wade's voice was harsh. "There are marks on his wrist where a snake's teeth went in, Murphy. Telephone the medical examiner, and let Thompson know about it. I've found where he worked. I'm going up to get a coat and hat. You can leave Sullivan here—and when I come down we'll pay a visit to this man's bosses. They may know something about him."

All cars were the same to Wade Hammond. He sent the slim-bodied police cruiser roaring through the night streets till Murphy beside him gripped the top of the door for support.

"Take it easy, Hammond—the pavement's wet."

Wade's only answer was to send the car whizzing around the tail end of a lumbering milk truck. He spun the wheel, straightened out and went roaring down a long avenue. He was seeing the darkly despairing face of young Bailey as though it hung on a curtain before his eyes. He was seeing also that strange mark on his forehead and the disappearing tail-light of that mystery car.

The long avenue widened till handsome residences showed on either side. Elm trees dripped water from branches arching overhead. Wade slid the car in to the curb and leaped out.

"Here we are, Murphy. This is where the Zeddlers hang out."

The house that they entered was large and built of brick, and a sleek butler opened the door. Wade nudged Murphy.

"You do the honors," he said. "I'll watch—and get the lay of the land before I begin asking questions."

The big headquarters dick opened his slicker and let the butler see his badge.

"There's been a murder," he said. "We want to talk to your bosses."

The butler's eyelids flickered and it seemed that his face grew a shade paler.

"Mr. G.C. Zeddler is ill upstairs. Go into the drawing room. I'll speak to his brother, Mr. A.J."

Murphy snorted and muttered under his breath.

"Why do these rich guys use all the letters of the alphabet, Hammond?"

"That's another mystery, Murphy."

WADE lit a cigarette and smoked in silence till a step sounded in the doorway. A thick-set, broad-shouldered man entered. He had yellow eyes like a cat's and he stared at them sharply.

"What's this I hear about a murder?"

"I'm from headquarters," said Murphy showing his badge again. "Did a young man named Thomas Bailey work for you?"

A.J. Zeddler gave a visible start. He drew a nervous hand across his chin.

"Yes, we employed him as a secretary. Why, what's happened?"

"He was found dead. Somebody bumped him off."

"Good God!" The exclamation on Zeddler's lips seemed genuine. Wade stepped closer and spoke quietly.

"I found him in the vestibule of my apartment, Mr. Zeddler. There was a mark on his face—a snake's head. Do you know anything about it?"

It was almost as though someone had struck Zeddler in the face. His heavy features paled and he stepped back.

"The Cobra!" he said. "Yes—I know. I got a threatening letter yesterday. Here, I'll show it to you—wait a minute."

He left the drawing room with hurried steps. Wade turned. Murphy was standing silent, looking around. Rain beat a monotonous tattoo on the windows opening on the lawn. There were French doors between them with a balcony beyond.

Wade edged forward to look out, and as he did so he gave a sudden start. Murphy behind him cried out harshly—for at that instant the lights in the room had winked out.

It was surprising, spine-chilling. They stood in utter darkness except for the faint glow from the corridor outside—and Wade was suddenly conscious of a draft of cold air on his face. It was like the touch of dead fingers and, as he realized its significance, his blood seemed to freeze. Someone had opened the French doors to the balcony!

In the brief second that he listened there was the stealthy sound of movement in the room. He sensed that he was silhouetted against the light of the corridor doorway and he stepped aside with a sudden constricted feeling in his throat.

Someone made a grab for him then. Fingers of steel clutched his arm. He glimpsed dimly a ghostly, horrible shape moving down toward his wrist. Death seemed to be in the room with him. He twisted, struck out, and breath hissed through his teeth.

Murphy called out to him, hoarse with anxiety.

"Are you all right, Hammond? What's the matter—what's happened?" He heard the big dick's footsteps pounding toward him. He could not seem to speak; those steely fingers were reaching for him again.

A sense of nausea gripped him as though the danger that faced him was unspeakably loathsome. His balled fist struck a human body and he heard a grunt.

Then he heard Murphy leap upon the unseen attacker, a snarl in his throat.

"What the hell! Here—hands up—"

Murphy's words ended in a choking, terrible cry. It was a cry that seemed to freeze Wade Hammond's blood. He heard the sound of bodies struggling; heard breath whistling through clenched teeth and a man making smothered, ghastly noises in his throat.

HE reached for a match paper, tried to light one. But something knocked it from his fingers. He drew out his gun and fired blindly at the spot. The shots seemed to rip through the darkness of the room like the reports of a cannon and the walls beat the sound back deafeningly into his ears.

"Murphy! Murphy!" he called.

He heard the French doors slam, heard someone go out.

Walking unsteadily, he crossed the room, groping for a wall switch. His feet bumped into something, something soft and yielding and the skin of his scalp tightened in horror.

He found the switch beside the door, pressed it and flooded the room with light. He saw then that there was another switch over by the French doors. But his eyes swung from it to the floor. Murphy lay there, his face contorted and his eyes fast glazing. He tried to speak, tried to move his lips, but no sound came from them. On his forehead was the hideous mark of the Cobra and he was clutching his left wrist tensely, clutching it where tiny bluish marks showed on the skin.

Wade ran to his side, stooped down. But Murphy's head fell back. The poison in his veins seemed almost as quick in its effect as a bullet fired from a gun. The death rattle sounded in his throat.

Wade rose and ran to the French doors, gripping his automatic in his hand. He flung them open, stepped out onto the balcony and felt the chill lash of rain in his face. A streetlight spread ghostly radiance across the wet grass of the lawn; but he could see nothing, no movement, and the water would destroy tracks. For seconds he stood there, trying to pierce the darkness while the rain beat against his face. Then he turned back into the room.

He saw A.J. Zeddler enter and give a gasp of horror at sight of Murphy's body.

"What is it? What's happened?" the banker said.

He held a card in his trembling fingers and on it Wade saw some words printed and the mark of the Cobra's head.

"He came here," said Wade harshly. "He got Murphy. Where's your telephone?"

Zeddler jerked his thumb toward the outside hallway, and Wade ran across it, brushing by the butler who was standing white-faced near the door. He found the phone in the closet, called headquarters and turned in a report of the second murder. Zeddler was at his elbow when he came out. He spoke huskily.

"Doctor Vail, our family physician, will be here any minute to attend my brother who is ill upstairs. It's possible he can do something for that man in there."

Wade shook his head.

"Murphy's beyond help now. The Cobra struck quickly, but it was me he was after. Murphy died saving my life. He was as fine as they come."

As he stopped speaking, the doorbell rang and the butler, trembling still, opened it.

A TALL man with a pink face and a clipped blonde moustache stood in the threshold. He entered with a black case in his hand and looked from one to the other, seeming to sense their strained attitudes.

"Doctor Vail," said Zeddler huskily. "This is Hammond, of the police. There's been a murder here—a detective killed. And our secretary, Bailey, was killed tonight, too. The Cobra's been at work."

A shadow drifted across Vail's eyes.

"What about your brother? Was there any noise when all this happened?"

Zeddler started as if he remembered for the first time that there had been shots.

"Yes—good God! Go to George quickly."

The doctor turned and took the stairs three at a time.

"What's wrong with your brother?" said Wade.

"Heart trouble. He's been ill for days. Doctor Vail has been in constant attendance—just keeping him alive."

Wade nodded and left Zeddler. He prowled through the rooms on the lower floor until a siren outside told him that the police had arrived. An instant later steps sounded on the porch.

He went into the hallway to greet Inspector Thompson, owlish head of the homicide squad, who entered with three men and the assistant medical examiner. In brief words he told what had happened and saw the strained look that came over the old inspector's face at mention of Murphy's death. Behind a blunt exterior Thompson hid a soft heart.

He turned, giving crisp orders to his men, then entered the drawing room to view the dead man, with A.J. Zeddler at his heels. Wade, without asking permission, ascended the stairs and moved down a hallway toward a door that was slightly ajar and through the crack of which he saw a glow of light.

At sound of his steps Doctor Vail suddenly appeared. His face was grave and he put a finger to his lips.

"Tonight's events may have serious consequences for my patient," he said, speaking in a hoarse whisper. "Mr. Zeddler is very low. I'm sending for a nurse."

Wade looked past the doctor toward a bed where a man lay. He heard stertorous breathing and saw bluish lips in a white face. But the man in the bed suddenly opened eyes which fixed themselves upon him and beckoned with one pale hand.

Wade entered the room, walking up to the bedside.

"Are you a detective?" asked the sick man.

"Unofficial," said Wade, "but I've helped the inspector more than once."

"Whoever you are," said Zeddler, "find this fiend who calls himself the Cobra. He sent my brother a threatening letter demanding money. And tonight I heard a man cry out downstairs followed by the sound of shots. What was it?"

Wade glanced at the doctor and Vail answered for him, lying adroitly.

"Nothing much, Mr. Zeddler. A detective your brother called in to investigate the extortion letter accidentally discharged a pistol."

The sick man lay back with a weary sigh and Wade turned toward the door. Then his eye was suddenly caught by something on Zeddler's bureau. It was a small thing, a paper of matches, but printed on it was the name of the Jungle Grove, a well-known nightclub. What member of the Zeddler household, he wondered, patronized that gay resort. Could it be that the sick man on the bed had been there? With a swift movement he pocketed the matches.

He went downstairs and spoke to Inspector Thompson, but the chief of the homicide squad shook his head in discouragement.

"We can't find anything, Hammond. No tracks—no clews. A man came through those French doors—but who was he and where did he go?"

"You've got me, chief." Wade's voice was low and his eyes were bright. He wasn't ready yet to formulate any theory. The whole thing was a mystery.

TWO interesting things occurred within the next twelve hours. The medical examiner turned in a report that snake venom of super-strength had been found in the blood of both Bailey and Detective Murphy. And at four o'clock in the morning of the night that the murders had taken place, Doctor Vail and the attending nurse announced the death of G.C. Zeddler.

His brother, A.J. Zeddler, was like a broken man when Wade arrived to make an exhaustive search of the grounds by daylight.

"George will be buried tomorrow," Zeddler said. "At his request he has not been embalmed and the services will be brief and simple." His voice suddenly took on a metallic harshness and he leaned toward Wade with blazing eyes.

"The Cobra is as responsible for George's death as though he had injected a dose of his foul poison into my brother's veins. Are the police imbeciles that they cannot find him?"

"We're doing what we can," Wade said.

He saw that the banker was close to the breaking point. The man's whole body was quivering; and yet he had the feeling that Zeddler might be holding something back—some secret information perhaps.

Wade saw the funeral notices the next day. The body of G.C. Zeddler was to be interred in the family mausoleum in Cypress Vale Cemetery.

Wade picked up the French type telephone in his apartment, and with a frown of concentration on his face he called police headquarters.

"Hammond speaking. It might be a good idea, chief, to have a man shadow A.J. Zeddler. He won't talk, but I think he's got ideas about the Cobra."

"Just what do you mean?"

"That's all, chief. Keep an eye on him—it can't do any harm."

Smiling grimly at the inspector's profane rejoinder he hung up. He spent three hours reading up on poisonous reptiles and their venom. At four that afternoon he called the Jungle Grove Night Club to see when it opened. At seven he presented himself at the door and drew the blonde hat-check girl aside. He pulled from his pocket the match paper he had taken from Zeddler's bureau and showed it to her. Her eyes were cold and she snapped her gum against pearly teeth, then parked it under the hat counter.

"Don't expect me to get excited over that, mister. They swipe lots of 'em here."

Wade grinned.

"Do you know the people who come in here?" he asked.

"Yeah, why?"

"I mean do you know them by name?"

"Some of 'em."

"Did you ever see one of the Zeddler brothers—the bankers?"

"Did I? Say—" The girl suddenly froze up on him and assumed a dead pan. "Who the hell are you, mister?"

Quietly Wade pulled out his wallet and displayed his special investigator's card signed by the police commissioner himself. As quietly he selected a crisp five-dollar bill and slipped it into the girl's fingers.

"Gee!" she said.

"Which Zeddler was it?" asked Wade.

"The younger one. 'George,' she called him."

"Who?"

For an instant the girl hesitated, looking at the five-dollar bill.

"It's real money," she said. "What the hell! I mean Marlene Lunt—you know, the hot-cha girl who has an act here. That old bird was crazy about her. He used to come to see her often."

"When did he come last and what time does she go on?"

"About a week ago. Her act doesn't begin till ten. Anything else you'd like to know?"

"No, sister. You've earned that five dollars. Just keep quiet and look pretty."

She unparked her gum again, and Wade sauntered off. He got Marlene Lunt's address from the telephone book and sped to it in his roadster. It was a swanky apartment; but again Wade showed his special card and the superintendent admitted him. Miss Lunt didn't know she had a visitor till Wade buzzed her door.

She looked startled and not too pleased when he pushed past her into her apartment. She was a smoky-haired brunette with a voluptuous figure and eyes that could do things.

"Who are you?" she asked.

Wade stared around her apartment and saw a wardrobe trunk and three suitcases all packed up.

"Going away?" he asked.

"Yes, to the country."

Wade walked over to a table and picked up three steamship booklets setting forth the delights of European travel. He held them up.

"You were thinking of the water, weren't you?" he said.

"I changed my mind."

He moved up to the wardrobe trunk then and placed his finger on a big label that said: *S.S. Berengaria.* He looked at the clock. It was Saturday. The ship sailed at midnight.

The girl, Marlene Lunt, had suddenly turned pale. Her fingers shook as she lit a cigarette, and she started across the floor toward a desk. There was something feline and sinister about the swaying of her lithe hips and the sidelong glance she shot at Wade.

He stepped forward and caught her hand just as she drew a pearl-handled revolver from a drawer and tried to turn it on him. He twisted it from her fingers. She backed away panting, and breath hissed from between her teeth.

He caught her suddenly, thrust her into a closet and turned the key in the lock.

"Don't make any noise," he said. "Nobody will hear you anyway. I'll be back later."

FOG was creeping over the city as he went outside. It was almost as thick as the fog of mystery that surrounded the murder of Thomas Bailey and Detective Murphy.

Wade called up headquarters.

"Any news of A.J. Zeddler?" he asked.

"No. A man's still on the job shadowing him."

Wade hopped into his car and drove toward the banker's house. There might be some way to make Zeddler talk. If not, a fantastic idea was forming in Wade's mind, a murder theory—but there were pieces missing. Someone must know the answer.

He parked his car down the block, and a man moved out of the shadows and hissed at him. It was the headquarters dick assigned to the case.

"Keep out of sight, Mr. Hammond. Zeddler's just coming out now—getting into his car."

It was true. Ahead, in front of the house, the broad-shouldered figure of A.J. Zeddler was getting into a big limousine. But there was no chauffeur. Zeddler was taking the wheel himself.

Wade drew the detective, whose name was Van Brunt, back into the shadows.

"I'll handle this from now on."

He waited until the limousine rolled out of the drive and purred down the street. Then he caught Van Brunt's arm and pulled him forward. They sprinted for Wade's car.

Wade sent it forward with silently meshed gears, and for blocks he kept Zeddler's car in sight.

"Where the hell's he going?" whispered Van Brunt.

Wade didn't answer. His eyes were bright, staring ahead. They moved out of the city, out where houses were scarce and where there were lots of trees. Then Zeddler's car stopped in the shadows by a high wall. The lights flicked off.

"It's Cypress Vale Cemetery," Van Brunt said hoarsely, and Wade nodded.

He turned off his own lights and climbed out. Ahead a key grated in a lock and the massive iron gate of the cemetery swung open. Zeddler's broad-shouldered form disappeared through it.

With Van Brunt at his heels, Wade followed. Their rubber-soled shoes made no noise. They kept in the shadows. Zeddler didn't know he was not alone. After a time Wade spoke softly.

"You stay here, Van Brunt. Come if you hear shots."

He glided off into the darkness and his face grew tense. A faint light had shown for an instant far ahead. On all sides of him the ghostly white shapes of gravestones rose. He picked his way among them toward the light that seemed to have no right to be there at this dark hour. It was ten o'clock and the cemetery had been closed since six.

Then he saw Zeddler again. The man was crouching now, creeping forward toward the light, his stocky form bent over like a great bear. There was something gleaming in his hand.

And Wade saw now where the light came from. It was from the partly open door of a huge mausoleum. Prickles of horror ran up his spine. He was not sure what ghoulish work was going on inside.

HE waited, fingering his own automatic; and he saw Zeddler close to the mausoleum's door. Then the door opened wider and Zeddler went inside.

Looking beyond Zeddler, he saw a man with a dark handkerchief over his face prying open the lid of a coffin. The man was intent, bending over. But he rose as Zeddler spoke.

"Who are you and what are you doing?"

The banker's voice was hoarse, his whole body was trembling. The man with the handkerchief over his face stared with the cold ferocity of a killer. Then Zeddler cried out and swayed like a drunken man.

For the lid of the coffin moved aside and a figure rose from it to a sitting position. It was the figure of Zeddler's brother, G.C. Zeddler, whose death certificate had been made out twenty-four hours before. His face was pale now and contorted but he was alive.

A.J. Zeddler rushed forward furiously.

"What does this mean?"

He made a fierce clutch for the man in the handkerchief, but the man stepped back and drew something from behind him. Wade gasped in horror.

On the man's right hand was a glove in the form of a Cobra's head. The jaws worked with thumb and forefingers; sharp fangs showing, and before Wade could move he had plunged the fangs into the elder Zeddler's arm.

With a choking cry, A.J. Zeddler staggered back. He tried to speak, failed and sank to the floor writhing. And at that moment the man sitting in the coffin spoke.

"You've killed him, Vail—you've killed my brother. I didn't intend that. You're a murderer!"

"Yes!" the single word hissed from behind the handkerchief, the snake's head on the man's right hand flashed out. But before it reached the figure in the coffin Wade's gun barked twice.

A cry of pain and fury came from the lips of the masked killer. The arm with the snake's head glove fell limply, crimson dripping from it. He backed into a corner, glaring at Wade. The handkerchief fell away and Wade saw the blond features of Doctor Vail. Then, with a movement so quick that Wade could hardly follow it, the doctor thrust his left hand between the snake's jaws and pressed them shut with his thumb.

A horrible, mirthless smile spread over his face. He looked at Wade, swaying slowly. Then his knees buckled under him.

The younger Zeddler was like a man stricken dumb. Then words came:

"I didn't plan for any killings. God help me, I didn't. It was Vail who did it. He would have killed me, too. I see it now. I'm a thief, but not a murderer. And see—here's the money. I can return it all."

Zeddler's voice rose wildly as he drew a satchel from between his legs in the coffin and held it up.

"The bank was failing—it would have crashed. I took the money from the vault—the last half million. I was going to leave America and go where no one would ever find me. Vail was paid for the part he played; the drugs that made it seem I was dead."

"What of Marlene Lunt?" said Wade sternly.

Zeddler, moaning, covered his face.

"You know about her then. She was beautiful—her beauty maddened me, drove me to crime. She was to meet me on the boat tonight. We were going away together."

"I know it," said Wade softly. "It's funny, Zeddler, what small things will sometimes trip up a criminal. That match paper on your bureau, for instance—I couldn't figure why a man with heart trouble would be going to the Jungle Grove. It made me investigate—started me on the right track.

"I hear Detective Van Brunt coming now. You'll stay in prison a long time, Zeddler. It's too bad you didn't put all that brainwork into building up your bank. But I'm glad the depositors aren't going to lose that half million anyway.

"And I'm glad, too, there won't be anymore biting with that Cobra's head. Vail had distilled venom stuck in the fangs. He killed your secretary when the young man grew suspicious and came to me. It was Vail's car I saw disappearing that night. And when your brother began to figure things out and came here, he killed him, too. He was a murderer at heart with a sense of the dramatic—and there's no telling how many more people he might have killed if he hadn't been stopped."

The Fiend was amuck in the Faville mansion, garroting, shattering skulls. Never had Wade Hammond such need for a swift coup. There was beautiful Judith Leith, spirit crushed, grieving. There was Rand Faville, glaring hate at his cousin. There was Attorney Stubbins, wringing his hands. Death menaced them all, that hell-born night. For when Hammond found the tiny vial of an enslaving drug, he knew that more than an insensate brute was loose in those horror halls, knew that a wily brain had devised an enticing—

Murder Bait

THERE was menace in the darkness all around Wade Hammond. It whispered in the shadows along the pine-clad slopes of Granite Ridge. It sounded in the mournful clatter of loose shutters on the old Jute Faville mansion. It brought a quaver to the voice of young Rand Faville, heir to the Faville fortune, as his trembling fingers clutched Wade Hammond's arm.

"There," he said. "That's where I saw him. He was dead, I tell you—sitting against those stairs with a knife in his neck and blood running over his shirt. And now—now he's gone!"

Teeth chattering behind pallid lips, Rand Faville pointed to a flight of steps leading to a stoop at the rear of the old house. His flashlight made a wavering circle of luminescence as his fingers shook. But no one was by the steps now. They showed up black and rotted, with a withered tangle of last year's weeds around their base.

Wade Hammond shrugged impatiently. The reflected glow of the flash cast ruddy highlights on his lean, hawklike face. His lips were a grim line paralleling the higher line of his close-clipped, military mustache. His eyes were grim, too. He had accepted Rand Faville's wild story with mental reservations, had come to the old house against his will, knowing that Faville was a flighty specimen of decayed gentility, whose alcoholic imagination might have invented the bleeding corpse.

He half suspected Faville of some shady purpose in wanting to visit his uncle's house at night. For Faville had been closemouthed about his motives when he'd asked Wade's help. On the trip from town he'd thrown up a barrage of flattery which seemed deliberate to Wade.

"You're a manhunter," he had said to Wade. "You've sat in on murder cases before. You've got nerve and guts. You haven't lived soft the way I have. I can't go to the police—yet; but you can help me because you're unofficial and will keep mum. I'll explain what it's all about later."

His flattering words had contained an element of truth. Life hadn't made Wade Hammond soft. He'd chosen the hard spots deliberately. Exploration. Soldiering under fortune's flag in China and the banana republics. Press work in distant countries where a well-oiled automatic was just as important as a typewriter.

Then a period of crime study when, as a freelance investigator, he'd helped crack over a score of weird murder mysteries. This had won him the respect of the city's homicide head and a special card from the commissioner himself.

Faville, a fellow member of a club which collected dues from Wade but didn't see him often, had asked his aid. Faville was talking murder now.

"You'll think I'm lying," he said, "but he was there—with the knife stuck through him like a skewer. It was horrible!"

Wade Hammond stalked forward, snapping his own flash on and stabbing its beam at the steps. He frowned abruptly and bent down, for there was something on the rotted boarding—a pool of liquid that glittered darkly, sinisterly.

He reached out a tentative finger, and Faville spoke explosively, his words choked with horror.

"Don't touch it! It—it's blood!"

But Wade had already drawn a smear of the red stuff on his skin. He raised it to his nose, sniffed, frowned again. Faville backed away as though from some loathsome thing.

"I was right!" he croaked. "That was where he was—and that's his blood."

Wade Hammond shook his head slowly. "Not blood!" he corrected grimly. "Red paint. What sort of a gag is this, Faville?"

"Paint!" There was stark disbelief in Faville's voice. Wade, watching him keenly, saw that he wasn't acting. He held his finger forward and Faville gingerly sniffed, then nodded.

"You're right, but I don't understand it."

"Neither do I," said Wade.

He swiveled his eyes suddenly as the lights of a car showed down the ridge. They glinted through the pines, made weirdly interweaving shadows. The car was traveling fast, grinding up the hill.

"Someone's coming!" Faville said.

The car stopped close to the spot outside the gate where Wade had parked his own roadster. A voice called out of the darkness:

"Hello, there! Is that you, Rand?"

Faville called an answer, and a moment later a man came striding into the radius of their lights. He was thin and birdlike in his movements, with bright eyes under a bulging forehead. Except for his silvery gray hair, he had the look of an overgrown baby. He stopped at sight of Wade, turned to stare at Faville.

"What's all this, Rand? I got your message. I came as fast as I could. But what are you up to, boy—and who's this gentleman with you?"

"Wade Hammond!" said Faville nervously. "Meet Stubbins, Wade—our family lawyer."

The lawyer tapped a spatted foot irritably. "You haven't answered my question, Rand. What's this gruesome story of finding a corpse? Why have you brought a detective to your uncle's house? And what are you doing here at this time of night? Surely you don't believe that report of the hidden will?"

Rand Faville looked sly suddenly. He shot Stubbins a warning glance which Wade was obviously not meant to see.

"You mentioned it yourself," he said huskily.

"Mentioned it, yes! But only as the foolish gossip of servants. I didn't give it credence, and didn't expect you to, either. Come, Rand—you'd better leave this place! It appears to have gone to your head, made you so excited you don't know what you're doing or saying."

Rand Faville's eyes narrowed and his mouth grew sullen. "I'm free, white, and twenty-one," he snapped. "You're not my guardian any more, Stubbins. I'll do as I damn well please!"

Greed replaced the look of fear on Faville's face. He turned resolutely toward the empty house. "Corpse or no corpse," he said, "now that I'm here, I'm going to take a look. I brought Wade Hammond along just to be on the safe side in case of trouble. I—"

HE stopped speaking abruptly and lifted his head to stare at an upper window of the house. Then he pressed Wade Hammond's arm with clawlike fingers and spoke in a hoarse whisper.

"Look! Isn't that a light?"

Wade Hammond was staring also. One of the paned oblongs above the rear porch roof seemed slightly lighter. There was a wavering, ghostly quality about it, as though someone were hurrying away with a glittering candle or a flashlight cupped in the hand. The eerie glow faded as they watched. Faville spoke in a croaking gasp that was filled with fear again.

"Maybe it's Ole—the halfwit my uncle let stay on the place. We kids used to call him the Fiend, because his mouth was big and his teeth long. Uncle thought he was harmless, but I was afraid he might be prowling around. I thought it might have been he who killed the man I saw."

The light had disappeared now. The house was bleakly dark. The pines moaned softly above the roof. Stubbins, the lawyer, was standing alert and tense, his thin nostrils dilated.

"Rand may be right," he said. "It may be Ole, unbalanced by Mr. Faville's death. If so, we'd better take care."

Young Faville started to answer, but let his lips hang slack. For a sound cut like a spear thrust through the darkness, a scream shrill and terror-laden, muffled by the damp walls of the house as though murderous hands were garroting a human throat.

Faville gasped. His face had drained of color. Stubbins' thin features had gone white also. His forehead seemed to bulge below his hat. Faville took a key dazedly from his pocket. He gathered his frightened faculties and stumbled up the steps toward the rear door, waving the key before him. Wade and Stubbins followed.

Faville's intent was apparent. He tried to put the key into the lock, but his trembling hands wouldn't function properly. Wade snatched the bit of metal from him and jabbed it into the hole in the door.

The scream was repeated as they entered. It was louder, closer, followed by a hollow thud and a panicky clatter of feet on boards. Then sudden silence descended, as though the place were peopled with ghosts holding some dread and secret carnival of their own, and fleeing now before human intruders.

Wade heard the tense breathing of the others, heard the hollow drumming of his own heart. He tiptoed forward into a kitchen, passed through it into a dining room, and saw a flight of stairs through an open door beyond. It was a big house, and his flash played over dusty, ancient furniture that had been neglected since its owner's death.

He moved close to the stairs, saw a hallway opening on his right, and paused again as another noise sounded. It was faint, yet precise, like someone tapping softly at intervals on wood.

He turned his light into the hall, lifting it slowly as something on the ceiling caught his eye.

A dark, wet spot showed on the peeling paper. It was spreading, as some liquid seeped down from the room above. The faint tapping came again, and Wade understood now what it was. Drops of the dark liquid were falling in the hall.

He heard Rand Faville close behind him suck breath through tightly-clenched teeth, heard Stubbins gasp in panic. He jerked forward, stooped and bent over the splashing drops. He touched one with his fingers and straightened quickly.

It wasn't paint this time. It was blood, warm and fresh! The old house held some unknown horror. Faville gave a smothered whimper. He crouched and turned as though he wanted to run. Wade pushed by him and headed for the stairs. But as his foot touched the bottom step, movement glimpsed between doors two rooms away caught his eye. A white face had reflected a beam of light for an instant. Wade Hammond whipped his gun out, pivoted, and lunged through the intervening doors.

He covered space quickly and tensed to a stiff-legged stop. A lock grated just ahead of him. A brass chain rattled, then suddenly jerked taut. Wade heard a terrified exclamation. He crouched and his stabbing flash picked out the cringing figure of a girl standing close by the big front door.

She had pulled it open and the old-fashioned safety chain connecting it to the frame had barred her way. She was fumbling with the chain, trying desperately to yank it loose. Wade Hammond reached her in three strides and grabbed her arm.

She was good-looking, well-dressed and artfully made up; but the synthetic red on her lips and cheeks only accentuated the livid paleness of her skin. Fear made her speechless, and as Wade drew her away from the door he said:

"Trying to give us the slip, weren't you?"

Her eyes probed beyond the lens of the flash, traveled over his lean, muscular body, peered into his intent face. She gripped his arm suddenly, pointing toward the floor above.

Wade nodded and led her quickly back to the room where Faville and Stubbins stood. Faville gasped as she came into the circle of his flash.

"Judy! What—why are you here?"

There was a moment's tense silence while the girl stared back at Rand Faville. Wade broke in with a quick question.

"You know her then, Rand?"

"Know her! She's my cousin, Judith Leith."

THE GIRL spoke suddenly in a husky whisper.

"Never mind about me! Clark Randall's upstairs. We were attacked. He's dead, I think!"

"Randall?"

"Yes, he came here with me. We were—" She choked and pressed a terrified hand to her mouth as the sinister dripping drew her gaze to the spot on the hallway ceiling. She trembled, said: "Please! Somebody go up and see!"

Wade Hammond took the stairs three at a time. The spreading crimson on the ceiling told him where to look. There was a hall directly above at the left of the stairs, corresponding to the one below. In the center of this, the sprawled figure of a man lay.

He was young, well-dressed, handsome, but disfigured now by a bone-shattering blow that had smashed the side of his head. Blood was coming from this, trickling through the uneven floor boards of the old house. He was dead, with a short length of heavy pipe beside him.

Wade Hammond stared and shuddered. Feet sounded in the hall behind him and Lawyer Stubbins came gasping up. He stared at the dead man with bulging eyes.

"Randall!" he husked. "He was an actor, a friend of Judith Leith's. This is terrible!"

Faville and the girl were climbing the stairs also. Wade jerked his eyes toward another stairway farther on that seemed to lead down. He moved toward it, gripping his gun, till he felt a draft of cold air sweeping up against his face. He stood there tensely as Faville's voice sounded.

"It was Ole, Hammond! Judith says so. She saw him. He's—turned killer!"

"Yes," Judith Leith gasped. "Yes—I saw him! I spoke, but he didn't seem to know me. He attacked Clark with a piece of pipe. He was coming for me when I screamed and ran. My uncle's death must have affected him. He looked like a fiend."

"He must have run down those stairs and out the side door," said Faville. "It was he who killed the other man—the body I saw outside."

Judith Leith gave a nervous start at that. She shot Faville a glance and shook her head. Wade was watching closely, and she caught his eye. Suddenly she dropped her own gaze and her fingers twisted her woolen dress.

"No!" she said. "No! Don't—even think about him. He's only a dummy!"

Stunned silence followed her words till Wade Hammond spoke. "A dummy!"

Judith Leith pointed to the dead man then, keeping her eyes averted, staring fearfully at Wade.

"Yes—it was Clark's idea. I—wouldn't have thought of it, I guess. We hoped—" She stopped, still tensely twisting her dress, then continued brokenly. "We brought it with us and set it up—to scare Ole away. Clark stuck a knife in its neck, splashed red paint on it—and made it look as realistic as he could. It was a stage dummy from the mystery play Clark was in. But—it didn't work. Ole came, anyway."

Rand Faville was hanging on his cousin's words. He spoke now with pent-up indignation. "Thought you were being pretty cunning, eh? You figured it would scare me, too, I guess—and give you plenty of time to search the house. That's what I get for being a fool and blabbing what I shouldn't."

"Stop!" said Stubbins hoarsely. "For God's sake, stop quarreling. We're—in the presence of death. A man's been murdered, and the killer's still loose."

Faville shot Judith Leith a venomous glance, pulled a gun from his pocket, and fingered the safety catch.

"I'm glad I brought this with me! We've got to get Ole now. Maybe he's still outside. Let's go hunt for him, Hammond!"

Wade considered a moment and shook his head. "We can't leave Miss Leith alone. You stay here. Keep that gun ready. Ole may come back. I'll take a look. Where does he hang out?"

"In a shack down behind the garage. You'll see a path. Follow it, but look out!"

Wade Hammond didn't answer. He turned and clumped down the stairs behind him, holding his flashlight in his left hand, his automatic in the other. He was a dead shot, and if he caught sight of Ole, he would shoot to kill. The man had been nicknamed the Fiend, and now was living up to his name. But Wade wondered why he'd suddenly become a killer.

The night was inky black. What stars had shone before were now obscured by scudding clouds. The sense of menace Wade had felt earlier in the evening deepened. Something was going on he didn't understand.

Yet the girl, Judith Leith, had seemed honest. Her story torn from fear-blanched lips had hung together. Wade gathered that there was supposed to be a will hidden somewhere in the house. Rand and Judith as legal heirs of old Jute Faville were both interested in it.

Judith had brought Clark Randall with the dummy to scare Ole off and give her time to search unmolested. Evidently Rand had mentioned the story of the hidden will to her. And now Ole, the Fiend, had appointed himself the murderous guardian of the will, presiding over the old house like an evil spirit.

WADE HAMMOND gripped his gun and stabbed the black shadows with his flash. His ears were alert for any sinister sound. The moaning of the pines made a deceptive background. He turned every few seconds and swung his light in an arc to ward off possible attack from the rear. He probed the trees and bushes ahead for secret ambush.

There was no sign of Ole on the grounds around the house. Only the black, straight trunks of the pines, and the denser woods beyond. Wade searched for tracks and saw places where the pine needles seemed to have been disturbed. But no clear footprints were visible.

He swung toward the right, moved down a slight declivity, and saw the ghostly bulk of the old garage. He approached it cautiously, but it was padlocked, with no loose boards that might constitute a hidden entrance.

He saw the path behind it then, and walked along it, into the deeper shadow of the woods.

The matted needles in the path had been disturbed recently. He stopped presently and swung his light to center on a gleaming reddish smear that his quick eye caught. He bent, touched his finger to it, and sniffed again. Once more he caught the unmistakable odor of paint, turpentine, and linseed oil.

The weird dummy, that Judith Leith and her friend Randall had set up, had obviously been dragged or carried along here. The mad monster, Ole, had perhaps run off with it.

Wade saw a spot then where the bushes beside the path had been recently stirred.

He moved cautiously through it, gripping his gun with steel fingers; eyes and muscles alert. Suddenly he stopped and stared.

What appeared to be the figure of a man was lying on the ground before him. A horrible, grotesque figure with a gaping mouth, crimson-soaked shirt, and knife skewered into the neck. No wonder it had fooled Rand Faville and sent him scurrying back to town for help.

Prepared as he was, the dummy was so lifelike that Wade Hammond felt a twinge of horror. A piece of the nose had broken loose, however, showing that the ugly puppet was plaster and not flesh as it appeared. Wade shuddered and turned away. Who, he wondered, had flung the dummy here? Ole or someone else?

His probing flash picked out a lighter spot just beyond the plaster dummy's feet. He stepped around them, stooped, and picked something up. It was a large-size linen handkerchief, uninitialed, but wadded and covered with streaks of red paint like that on the dummy's shirt.

Wade stared at it intently, and stuffed it in his pocket, frowning. A linen handkerchief. It shed new light on the dummy's presence here, made Wade's thoughts more somber.

He went back to the path and continued along it till his light showed a log cabin huddled against a bank. There was a lopsided chimney stuck at one end. Wood was piled near by. There were tracks all around it.

Wade's automatic jutted forward. He crept cautiously nearer, stopped suddenly and called out.

"Ole! Open the door! You can't get away!"

He held the flashlight centered on the cabin's rough front, waiting for a response which did not come. There was only the constant, eerie murmuring of the pines overhead, which seemed like whispered mockery.

He walked forward resolutely and pushed against the door. It was unlocked and opened with a squeak of rusty hinges. A brief inspection showed him that the cabin was unoccupied.

There was a bunk piled high with dirty blankets. A chair. A low table, a row of shelves littered with stores of food. This was Ole's cabin obviously, but the halfwit killer was not at home. A row of books on religion and mysticism caught Wade's eye. In his better moments Ole evidently read. Or else someone had given him these books, which he kept as mere souvenirs.

Then Wade took something off the lower shelf. It was a small empty vial, uncorked, and with a pungent, bitterish smell at the open mouth. He scratched about on the shelf and found three others, all the same size, one with a tiny label on it. There was printing on this: *Mescaline Sulphate Dilute.*

Wade was no chemist, but he'd had a wide experience with crime. Mescaline came from the buttonlike flower buds of *Anhelonium Lewinii*, or mescal cactus—one of the wickedest and most insidious habit-forming drugs on earth.

A liquor, he knew, was sometimes brewed from it, responsible for ninety percent of the violent crimes in the Mexican quarters of certain localities in the Southwest. He'd had an experience once with a Yaqui Indian who'd run amuck on a mescal drink.

It could turn a normal, decent man into a dangerous criminal. What had it done to the abnormal brain of Ole? No wonder he hadn't recognized Judith Leith as one of the kids who had played around Jute Faville's estate. Somehow Ole had got a measured supply of this narcotic.

Wade turned and hurried out of the cabin. He'd seen enough to begin to understand. Ole must still be back at the house somewhere, perhaps waiting to kill again, thirsting for blood, now that the powerful drug had cankered his brain. Wade retraced his steps to the Faville mansion in long-legged, jerky strides. It had become a place of death, a spot to get away from quickly.

He found Faville and Judith Leith, Stubbins and the dead man, just as he had left them. The cousins had obviously been exchanging bitter words again. Rand Faville had a hard look on his face. His eyes were gleaming. Stubbins was nervous, tense, Judith Leith defiant. He met their concerted gaze coolly.

"I didn't find him," he said. "He's still loose, possibly prowling around the house."

RAND FAVILLE snorted. "The way Judy yelled was enough to scare Ole away. He's probably gone."

Faville seemed to have gathered courage during Wade's absence. Once again the look of greed was uppermost in his eyes. He licked his lips, said: "We know what we're up against now. It was the dummy that got me—something I didn't expect to find. I can handle Ole even if he does show up. I'm going to take a look around."

"We're all going to leave this house," said Wade. "You've got to think of Miss Leith—even if she is your beloved cousin. She's in danger, just like the rest of us."

Faville allowed himself a sneer. "I'm surprised, Hammond. Don't tell me you're getting cold feet."

"At least I'm not scared of a dummy," said Wade softly, and saw Faville flush with anger. Then the other became stubborn.

"I'm going to stick," he said. "You know what it's all about now, Hammond. Judy's showed her hand clearly enough. No will has turned up since Uncle Jute's death. It's going to make a legal mix-up that may take years to settle. There are rumors that Uncle Jute left a will hidden in the house. He was always slightly eccentric, and it may be true. I foolishly told Judy and she's tried to doublecross me."

"Liar!" said Judith Leith bitterly. "I wouldn't have hidden the will if I'd found it. But I didn't trust you. I knew you wouldn't play fair if you should happen to find it first. You've squandered one fortune already, and would try to grab all of this. I've got a right to share it, and the courts, as you say, will hold the estate up if the will isn't found."

"Very well," said Faville harshly, "I'm going to hunt for it now."

"Some other time!" warned Wade. "Daylight would be better. Remember, there's a killer loose."

He stared at Faville sharply, but Faville shook his head.

"Take Judy away if you want to. I'm going to stick—and Stubbins here will help me. It's in his interest to find the will."

Wade Hammond shrugged. "Go ahead, then—hunt! I'll give you half an hour. But if you can't find anything by then, I'm going to leave and take Miss Leith with me. We can't let Clark Randall lie here all night. The police will want to know about this, and grab Ole."

"The police!" said Faville heatedly. "That's just it! Nobody will find the will after they get here. They'll pry into everyone's business and hold things up."

He pulled Stubbins' arm, and together they turned and descended the stairs. Judith Leith stayed close to Wade, who followed to the floor below. Faville found a candle, lit it, and with Stubbins beside him, went to the big library in the front of the house.

"It's utter foolishness," Stubbins was protesting. "That story the servants told had no basis in fact, I'm certain."

Faville ignored his words. He began searching as the minutes ticked by. Wade Hammond, quietly guarding the girl, kept his eyes and ears alert, wondering where Ole was. He saw Judith Leith dart fearful glances into the open doors of other rooms.

He felt her draw as close as she could, holding her trembling body near to his. Once she asked him in a low voice if the time wasn't up. But when Wade volunteered to call the search off and go, she shook her head.

He spoke to her reassuringly then, trying to take her mind off the horror of Clark Randall's death. He patted the automatic in his hand, looked at his watch again. Twenty minutes had gone by.

Suddenly a crash sounded from the front of the house where Faville was. The sound of a violently breaking window. Bedlam seemed to break loose then. The crash was followed by a hideous, apelike bellow of rage, then a cry of sheer terror. A table fell over with a bang.

A door slammed shut, the door of the library. Wade heard Faville's gun blast two shots in quick succession, heard the shuddering cry of horror repeated. Judith Leith cowered back as Wade lunged forward, his own gun thrust out.

The sound of the breaking window and Faville's shots meant only one thing to Wade. Ole, the Fiend, had crept up to the house, broken a sash, and entered. He was trying to kill again.

Then he heard Stubbins calling frantically. "Ole, Ole, stop! You can't kill Rand. You can't—"

WADE'S shoulder struck the library door and jarred it open. His light swept the room, centering on the grisly drama being enacted there.

Rand Faville had fallen evidently under Ole's first attack. He had been close to the window. Ole, a blond giant of a man, eyes wild, unshaven, and hair in disorder, crouched near the sashes he had smashed. His great fists, hanging at his sides, were bleeding. His lips were skinned back from his long teeth. He was more simian than human.

Faville was dead beyond all doubt, his head twisted horribly to one side. Stubbins, his nostrils quivering, had had the courage to dash forward and snatch up Faville's fallen gun—the gun that Faville had been unable to use as a protective weapon, because of shattered nerves and faulty aim. Stubbins was lifting the gun to Ole now, cursing under his breath.

Ole stood dazedly for a moment. A strange look swept over his ugly face, then flaming anger came. He gave a sudden, gurgling bellow of rage and lunged toward Stubbins, his great hands spread out.

Wade Hammond's gun swung up; but he didn't need to use it. The weapon in the lawyer's hand gave a single, spiteful cough.

Ole clutched at his chest; stared down at his fingers in surprise, gazing stupidly at the crimson that showed between them. He stumbled on a few steps, collapsed in an ungainly posture at Stubbins' feet, lay still.

The lawyer let his pistol hand hang lax. He moved jerkily back, face working, staring wide-eyed at the man he'd killed. He didn't speak for a moment, then said hollowly:

"That ends it! I had to kill him. He got poor Rand. He was like a raging demon. He must have been waiting outside the window, waiting to murder again. He would have killed us all."

Wade was silent an instant. He bent down over the body of Rand Faville. The neck as he had feared had been broken by a twist of Ole's hand. He went to Ole next, stooped, and stared at the fingers that had swung the pipe to smash Clark Randall's skull and had snuffed out Faville's life. He looked at Ole's eyes, noting the enlarged pupils that indicated Ole's drugged state.

He crossed to the window then, peered out and fingered a piece of the shattered frame. Ole had smashed the whole thing inward. Wade turned suddenly, curled his finger, and raised it to his lips. He muttered under his breath.

"I've cut myself, Stubbins—right to the bone. Lend me your handkerchief—quick!"

It seemed an incongruous request in that murder room, but the lawyer fumbled in his pocket and shook his head.

"Sorry! I didn't bring any with me. Wait—maybe Miss Leith has one."

Still holding his finger, Wade advanced on the lawyer and abruptly spoke. "I just wanted to test you, Stubbins—see whether you had a handkerchief! I found this outside and thought it might be yours. Men as careful about their dress as you generally carry one."

The lawyer stared at the paint-smeared square of linen in Wade Hammond's hands. His expression remained blank.

"It isn't mine," he said. "Where did you find it? What's the big idea?"

Wade didn't answer. Instead, he gave another quick command. "Let's see your hand, Stubbins—the right one!"

Surprise and fear leaped into the lawyer's eyes. He spluttered: "Why—what—" He lifted his hand, stared at it dazedly, then suddenly thrust it behind him. "What's the meaning of this? How dare you order me—"

Wade had reached forward and grabbed the man's wrist in a viselike grip. He raised it while Stubbins protested and fought, while his face worked and his skin turned deathly white.

"You must be mad! You—" he choked.

"Look at your fingers," said Wade harshly. "You wiped your hands, but some of it stuck under the nails!"

"Some of what?"

"Paint," said Wade. "Paint, Stubbins—and you pretended that you hadn't been here before tonight."

"I haven't! I haven't! What are you driving at?"

"JUST this," said Wade quickly. "You should have been more careful when you took the dummy away from the back steps. You thought, too, apparently that it might scare Ole—and you didn't want him scared. When Rand left his crazy-sounding message, you came here quickly and pulled the dummy down. You hurried to get the stage set for what you wanted done, then hid out along the road, and when we passed, you followed, making it appear that you had just arrived."

"It's a lie!" screamed Stubbins. "I don't know what you're driving at."

"I do," said Wade. "That paint on your nails is a dead giveaway, man! There's none on Rand Faville's hands, or on Ole's. It was you who moved the dummy—and I see now where Ole got his dope. You fed it to him, got him in the habit of using it—to become your slave and killer."

Stubbins stepped back, his eyes blazing, the paint-smeared fingers of his right hand crooked. Judith Leith stood in the door, wide-eyed.

"Murder bait!" said Wade harshly. "That's why you circulated the story of the hidden will, pretending you didn't believe it yourself, but knowing the heirs would. Murder bait, to lure them back to this house secretly where Ole, under your influence, could kill them. Deny it if you can!"

Stubbins made a snarling sound in his throat. The gun that he had taken from Rand Faville whipped up, the same gun he had shot Ole with to cover up. But he wasn't quite quick enough. For Wade had been expecting some such move.

The net of circumstantial evidence was too tight. Stubbins was desperate, ready to turn killer himself, seeing a chance to murder both Wade and Judith

Leith and blame it on the mad Ole.

Wade's bullet caught him in the center of the shoulder. The blasting gun in the lawyer's hand dropped, spouting flame. He reeled backward and cried out, then collapsed in a faint, while Judith Leith gasped.

Wade stood still a moment, eyeing the lawyer grimly. Suddenly he stooped and went through Stubbins' pockets. In the coat, his fingers closed over a bunch of papers. He drew them out, selecting a wide envelope. He studied the contents of this eagerly.

It was a legal paper, a will—the last will and testament of Jute Faville. Wade thumbed through the folded sheets intently and suddenly spoke aloud.

"In the event of the deaths of my legal heirs," he read, "Judith Ellison Leith, and Rand Augustus Faville, I bequeath the income of my estate to the following institutions as endowment funds, to be disbursed under the direction of my good friend and attorney, Nelson Stubbins."

Wade triumphantly flipped the document shut and turned to Judith Leith.

"A lifelong job was all that Stubbins wanted! A soft berth for himself with plenty of secure pay. The will was never hidden. It was given into his hands. He had it all the time—and was going to make sure that it didn't turn up till you and Rand were dead.

"Then I suppose he planned to 'find' it in the house, maybe tonight. That's what he carried it for. And he might have got away with it eventually, except for that paint under his fingernails. Your dummy, Miss Leith, didn't scare poor old Ole off, but it caught the criminal who used him as a murder pawn."

Like an animal from the black depths of the jungle came the Sloth. And with him, a beautiful, exotic woman. The one obstacle to his greatest criminal ambition was Private Investigator Wade Hammond. And the mad murder march of the Sloth caught Wade Hammond in the law's own trap.

Scented Murder

CHAPTER I
The Perfumed Murder

THE car that slid to a stop before the block of shut-up houses had the long low lines of a hearse. The man who climbed from it was dressed in funeral black. The paper-wrapped parcel under his arm was shaped like a miniature coffin.

He glanced once along the silent street, turned and crossed the sidewalk with the peculiar, stiff-legged shuffle of a jungle animal.

A handmade key gleamed in his fingers as he stood by a basement door. The key, and the lock opening he thrust it into, both had the form of crosses. But there was nothing saintly about the man.

He looked more bestial than human as a dusty bulb inside sprayed light upon him. His skin had a ghastly, bluish tinge. His eyes were small and glittering under scraggly brows. His big nose tapered forward like an anteater's. Moss-gray hair sprouted from his wrists and hands.

In a low-ceilinged room at the rear of the shuttered building, he put his parcel down. His long fingers undid the outside wrapping. He lifted the cover, parted gossamer layers of green tissue, and stared down at the cluster of talisman roses that lay inside.

Delicate fronds of fern set off the lustrous leaves and dewy petals. Fragrance eddied about the man's distended nostrils. He smiled, pressed an electric button, and paced the small chamber until footsteps sounded and the door moved softly open. He turned then and eyed derisively the girl who stood in the threshold.

She had lovely, exotic features, white as though they had been cut from Carrara marble. Her almond-shaped eyes were dark and preternaturally bright. Yet they appeared to be unseeing.

She, too, was dressed in black, the only color about her being the vivid slash of her red lips that lay like a wound across her face.

She did not smile. She stared at the man with a dazed sort of fixity and spoke in a husky whisper. "You rang for me?"

"Yes, Benita." The man's voice was a caressing purr. He reached out, gathered up the flowers, went over to the silent girl.

Her hands lifted mechanically and grasped their slender stems.

Her nostrils quivered at the scent. Her lips parted in a vacant smile. The roses' odor seemed to break through her trance and bring back memories of a former, happier state.

"You are very kind," she breathed. "I haven't seen flowers like these for—many days."

"Weeks!" corrected the man softly. "Weeks, Benita. Your memory is growing—a trifle blurred."

He stood and watched intently as she bent her head to smell the flowers. An evil, humorless smile distorted his ugly face. "You like them? You find them—attractive, eh?"

"They are lovely. You are very kind. I want to thank—"

With a slithering rush of feet the man moved closer. His hairy hands darted out abruptly. His face was a snarling mask of cruelty.

"Idiot! I didn't get them for you! I only wanted to see—how you'd react."

Ignoring the look of a hurt child that crossed her face, he snatched the roses from her. His left hand flashed out, smacked against her cheek. She recoiled.

"Go back to your quarters, Benita. Stay there until I ring."

"Yes, master."

Sphinxlike again, obedient as a slave, the girl turned and moved away. When the door shut behind her, the man snapped a brass bolt into place. He turned, set the roses in a vase and eyed them. Then he shuffled to a cabinet filled with a strange assortment of bottles, boxes and odd-appearing apparatus.

He took a perforated respirator out, fitted the snoutlike thing over his bestial nose, clamped it around his head with elastic bands. He picked up a small atomizer, unscrewed the top and set it on the table. He selected a bottle of colorless, odorless liquid. This he poured carefully into the atomizer's mouth, replacing the screw top. With the rubber bulb in his right hand he approached the roses again.

He bent forward, eyes malevolently bright, and sent a thin mist from the atomizer's nozzle over the salmon-tinted petals. The oily liquid settled in a thin, invisible film. When the flowers had been sprayed thoroughly, he put his atomizer and bottle away.

He kept the snoutlike respirator on, tucked the roses back in their tissue-lined box, and set a small electric fan overhead in motion. This connected with a ceiling vent.

As the air of the room cleared of the oily spray, the man bent over a small desk. He drew from a pigeonhole a bit of paper with a signature on it. He studied it for seconds, then selected a blank visiting card and wrote:

To Vicki Condon
With kindest regards
from
Wade Hammond

His long fingers blotted the forged writing. He placed the card in the nest of tissue on top of the talisman roses. He closed the lid, wrapped the box around with paper, tied it, and wrote Wade Hammond's name again on the upper, left-hand corner. In the lower right, he put the address of Vicki Condon.

He waited a full minute before removing the respirator from his nose, then pressed the electric signal button once more—two long rings, a short and another long.

THIS time a man came to the door which he unbolted—a huge, bearlike person with monstrous hands, a neckless head, and a blotched and bloated face. He towered above the other like a giant, yet stood dumbly as a slave stands before a master.

"Come in here, Jaquin! Listen to what I have to say."

The long-nosed man's voice rasped with steely harshness now. He tapped the box of flowers.

"Take this to the corner drugstore, Jaquin. Phone for a telegraph messenger, and wait outside the store until he comes. Give him this box. Tell him to deliver it at once to the address I've written on it. Shadow him, make sure the parcel reaches its destination. When he comes out, follow him for several blocks and then—"

The speaker's right hand described a peculiar spiral motion in the air. His eyes blazed up balefully into those of the taller man.

"You understand, Jaquin?"

The giant did not answer, but his neckless head bobbed up and down, and one great hand duplicated the motion which the other had made. He took the box of flowers.

"You know the penalty for blunders, Jaquin?"

The big man tensed and whitened, opening his mouth twice like a gasping fish, but remaining silent. Out in the street he moved quickly, soundlessly for one of such huge proportions. He went to the drugstore, made his telephone call, and waited for the messenger. When the boy arrived, he gave the parcel of roses into his hands and muttered his instructions.

The uniformed messenger set off, and the man called Jaquin followed. Like a silent, skulking bear he kept the messenger in sight till he neared the steps of the palatial Condon home.

Two sharp-eyed detectives were on duty here, lounging beside the massive steps. They stopped the messenger at once, examined the box, conferred, then handed it back to him and let him pass. The messenger quickly rang the bell, delivered his parcel and turned away.

Inside the big house a party was in progress. Guests were assembled in the mansion's music room. A vivid brunette in a striking yellow dress stood by a grand piano singing. Another girl beside her caressed the instrument's ivory keys in soft accompaniment.

The girl in yellow had just begun her song. The gray-haired maid who had taken the roses and signed the messenger's book stood undecided. She tiptoed uncertainly to the door of the lighted room, tiptoed away again. The music might last for many minutes. Miss Condon and her guests would not welcome interruption.

Yet the lightness of the box and the florist's label told the maid that here were fragile flowers. Left enclosed they might soon wilt. The maid consulted with the family butler. "Open them," he said. "I'll get a vase. We'll give them to Miss Condon later."

The maid unwrapped the roses as the song of her mistress floated through the ancient house. She drew the green tissue away as the solemn-faced butler returned. Before she thrust the long stems into the vase's mouth she raised the bouquet for one appreciative sniff.

Then a faint, stifled cry came suddenly from her lips. She coughed and strangled as the vagus nerve, close to her larynx, contracted. Blood rushed into her face, mottling the skin. A leaden pallor quickly followed.

Her hands, writhing upward to her quivering throat, opened and let the flowers cascade at her feet.

She swayed, stepped back, cried out again—and the frightened butler let the vase of water drop. It struck the parquet flooring with a resounding crash as the maid's body sagged and toppled over.

CHAPTER II

Killer's Threat

TWO miles away in a modernistic apartment far downtown, Wade Hammond, freelance investigator of crime picked up a French-type phone. He scowled at the excited voice that squawked in the receiver.

"Terrant speaking. There's hell to pay at Oswald Condon's place. A maid just keeled over holding the bunch of roses you sent. Looks like a bum heart, but the folks are scared after the extortion threat that was handed Condon yesterday.

Better drop up if you can spare the time."

"Right, sergeant. I think I *had* better. You're talking riddles. I didn't send any roses."

"Sure you did, Hammond. They're for Miss Condon. Your name's on the paper. There's a card from you inside."

"Vicki Condon's a swell kid, sergeant. I've met her a couple of times, and like her. But I haven't reached the stage where I hand out presents. I tell you I didn't send those roses. It must have been somebody using my name."

"Yeah?"

"Yes—and don't touch them, sergeant, or let anyone else either. Understand? Stick close by the corpse, but keep away from the roses. Better give the inspector a buzz. I'm starting up right now."

Wade Hammond made rubber tires screech as he sent his fast roadster roaring through the evening streets, heading toward the avenue where the Condons lived.

He knew them slightly, as he knew many members of the city's upper crust. But theirs was a different world from his. He'd traveled the rough roads of adventure in the far places of the earth; worked for the press in spots so hot that a news hawk had to pack a gun. More than once, he'd horned in on murder cases that had baffled the police. He'd won a special card for himself signed by the commissioner—and had gained a lot of enemies in crookdom, criminals who would like to have his blood.

A siren moaned along the Condon block as he braked in front of the big house. A black car filled with headquarters men slid to a stop. Thompson, head of the city homicide squad, was among them. He knew there was something up when Hammond called.

They climbed the steps together, Wade, tall, military in his bearing; the inspector smaller, his owlish eyes bright behind his rimless glasses.

Inside the house, they found the maid just where she'd fallen, with Sergeant Terrant standing guard. Quiet had settled over the place. Vicki Condon and her guests stared from the music room door with fear-blanched faces. Condon himself, portly and worried, paced the hall. The butler stood like a frightened ghost behind him. Neither the body nor the flowers had been touched.

Wade Hammond bent over the fallen maid, while the others waited. This had become his case, if case it was. Even Inspector Thompson was grimly silent. Wade touched the leaden skin, rolled back the eyelids, pursed up his lips.

"Something corrosive," he said. "Cyanide maybe. I wonder—" He picked up one of the roses, sniffed, and felt a nauseous tension in his throat. He thrust the flower away. "Strong stuff, but it doesn't smell. You'll have to send them to the lab, inspector. And tell Gortz to watch his step."

"You mean those posies have got poison on 'em—and killed the maid?"

"Right. They're plastered with it."

Sergeant Terrant was fumbling in his pocket. He took out something small and white and passed it over to Wade.

"That's the card, Hammond. There may be fingerprints. I wouldn't have touched it if I hadn't thought it was yours."

Wade held the card by its squared-off edges, frowned at the inked writing that was a duplicate of his own. It was his signature to a dot, penned by a master forger's hand. Condon spoke hoarsely.

"This—this is a murder then! If Vicki had opened those flowers she'd have been the victim. That man who called up yesterday demanding money wasn't just a crank!"

"No," said Wade grimly, "he was a killer, not a crank."

Somewhere in the rear of the hall a telephone tinkled. The trembling butler turned toward it, moving like a mechanical man. He was back in a moment, nodding to Wade.

"A gentleman wants to speak to you, sir."

Wade eyed the others and swore under his breath. He stalked to the closet where the phone was kept. A voice that brought vague unpleasant memories spoke softly in his ear. A voice that combined the purr of a jungle cat and the sinister buzz of a desert rattler.

"Greetings, Wade Hammond!"

THERE was a moment of silence. Wade reached back into his memory. Suddenly, he spoke a single word. "Volbo!"

"The Sloth, if you prefer! I hope the roses are becoming to Miss Condon's corpse. She must look lovely with them. The police, of course, have arrived, and you with them. Condon realizes now the folly of ignoring my demand. He called me a crank when I spoke to him on the phone. He said he would pay me nothing, yet he took the precaution of having detectives patrol his place. I had to teach him a lesson. I've improved since we last met, Hammond."

Laughter gurgled over the wire; a sound so hideous that it might have issued straight from the mouth of hell. The barbarous, unearthly laughter of the Sloth. Cords in Wade Hammond's neck stood out. His grim composure left him.

"Vicki Condon is alive and well, you heel!" he shouted. "You've only succeeded in slaughtering a harmless maid. You—"

He bit off his words as a snarl came from the receiver, a cry of fury. Then the Sloth resumed his purr, tense with the rage he could barely control.

"Probably you're telling the truth. You would do that. But what you say only means greater gain for me. You're slated to die, Hammond. I've had it in mind to take care of you for years. But I'll attend to this Condon business first. Tell him that the amount I ask is doubled. Not fifty, but a hundred thousand now. Tell him that, to prove myself, I'm going to grab his girl alive before twelve tonight. I'll hold her till every cent is paid, then maybe—"

The laughter gurgled again, shrill with bravado.

"Before midnight, Hammond! You think I'm mad—but we'll see. Neither you nor all the police can stop me!"

There was a ring of conviction in the threat that made Wade Hammond tense. The receiver clicked up with the brutal laughter still sounding. Wade turned into the hall and faced the inspector.

"The killer is Michael Volbo. They call him the Sloth because of his funny looks. You've heard of him, inspector?"

The inspector nodded. "We've had him mugged for two years at headquarters. He's wanted on a dozen counts. He isn't a man—he's a living devil, a paranoiac criminal, but as smart as Satan. I'd rather meet a tiger."

Hammond said: "I know about him. He's a top-class forger. I helped get him once out on the coast on a murder charge. Nailed him red-handed. But he broke jail before the trial. My name figured in the thing. Volbo knew it—and he never forgets or forgives. He's dropped out of sight for a couple of years. Only the devil knows what he's been doing. The rumor was that he was dead, but I never believed it. That kind don't die natural deaths. My guess is that he's turned up again because his money's running low."

"And now," added Hammond, "he demands a hundred thousand—and boasts that he's going to kidnap Vicki before midnight and hold her till the money is paid."

Inspector Thompson emitted an angry snort. "He's mad—nutty. He can't do it! We'll throw a cordon around the block. We'll land him in the chair. Terrant, trace that call!"

Wade shrugged. "It's no use, chief—the Sloth would've thought of that. And I'd advise that we don't take any chances.... Vicki, you'd better get out of town. The Sloth may be nutty as the inspector says, but he's smart as sin. He'll risk his life to pull this job."

Condon was listening. He agreed at once. "Vicki can go to our place in the country. I'll get the commissioner to provide an escort. We'll keep her under lock and key till this crazy killer's been caught."

But Vicki Condon shook her head. Her voice was firm. "It's stupid. I won't go. I'm going to stay right here, dad, with you. I'll be as safe in this house as anywhere. How do we know this man they call the Sloth isn't just trying to scare us? He probably expects I'll do that very thing—run out of town, and thinks he'll get me that way. He might."

Wade Hammond had his black pipe in his hand. He stuffed shreds of brown tobacco in the bowl. There was truth in what the girl said. But, on the other hand, there was the Sloth—a criminal who would stop at nothing. Nobody knew what mad plan he had in mind.

"You'd better go," he persisted. "You've seen the sort of thing he does."

She shook her head. "I tell you I'm going to stay here with dad. This Sloth hasn't an army, has he? He can't get me in my own home with police all around. It's crazy to think he can."

Condon laid a hand on his daughter's shoulder. "All right, Vicki. I shan't try to force you. You may be right."

The inspector nodded, spoke with sudden briskness. "Who brought those flowers? Has anyone tried to trace them?"

"A telegraph messenger," the butler husked. "I saw him at the door."

"Get every telegraph office in town, Terrant! Find out which messenger delivered the box, and have him questioned. Look up the florist's label. We've got to get busy. You seem to be lying down on the job, Hammond. It isn't like you. This man's got you buffaloed."

Wade Hammond shook his head as he struck a match. Smoke curled from his lips as he spoke. "It may interest you to know, chief, that there is no florist by that name in this city. It's a San Francisco firm. The Sloth brought the label with him. Just another of his little jokes! And I don't think you'll learn anything from the messenger. The Sloth is thorough. He would have seen—"

He paused, and turned at a sudden commotion by the door. The cop stationed there let someone in, one of the plainclothes men who had been outside. He was breathing hard. His face looked pale and strained.

"They've just found a kid a coupla of blocks away, inspector—a telegraph messenger! There's finger marks all over his throat. His neck's broke clean in two. He's dead!"

CHAPTER III
THE SLOTH ATTACKS

A GASP of horror came from Vicki Condon's lips. She shrank against her father.

Wade Hammond turned on her fiercely, scowled through a cloud of smoke. "You see what kind of devil we're dealing with! Now—do you still want to stay here?"

"Yes, yes. I'd—be afraid to leave. This is the safest place. The police will catch him when he comes."

"You bet we will," said Thompson. "The man's crazy to make such a threat. He's talking through his hat. We'll get him sure if he shows up. Have those roses wrapped up, Terrant. Send them to Gortz. Get the commissioner on the wire. Let me speak to him. We'll scatter men all around the block." He turned to Vicki Condon. "You'll stay in one room till this is over, miss. There'll be two of my men with you constantly. You'll be safer than you would be in a fort. Don't even think about it."

Wade Hammond shifted the bulge under his coat where his automatic was strapped in a shoulder holster. His voice was low and grim. "With your permission, I'll take a look around the house, Mr. Condon."

"Go anywhere you like," said Condon. "I wish the night was over. If—if anything happens to Vicki—I'll never forgive myself. You say this criminal wants a hundred thousand. Why don't I get in touch with him? Why don't I pay! I'd rather hand over all I've got than risk Vicki's life."

"It's too late now," said Wade. "You don't know the Sloth. His ego's hurt. He won't take your cash till he's had his try at making a snatch. He wants to prove he's tough."

"But surely he can't succeed!"

"No," said Wade, "surely not." He tried to put confidence into his words, but it was as though something cold lay along his scalp. Volbo wasn't working alone. There was no saying what sort of evil helpers he had, or what fantastic plan was in his mind.

Headquarters men arrived in two big cars. They were deployed over the house as though a siege was expected. Others were set around the entire block. The commissioner had acted quickly on Thompson's suggestion. Armed men were posted in every door and areaway along the street. Cops were stationed at its end. But Wade was still uneasy.

It was almost eleven now. A tenseness descended on the house. At Condon's request, and at their own inclination, Vicki's guests had gone—along with the body of the maid.

Two plainclothes men with tear gas bombs and riot guns were posted in the front hall. Two more were in the cellar, two in the attic. Others were watching all the windows. Thompson, impressed by the Sloth's uncanny craft, stayed on the job himself.

He looked at his watch as eleven-thirty came. Wade stood nearby, smoking his black pipe. There seemed nothing he or anyone could do but wait. The inspector's voice grew rasping.

"It's just a bluff. He wouldn't have the nerve! No crook would. He can murder women and kids, but when it comes to a snatch like this, facing a lot of cops, he hasn't the guts."

His head jerked up abruptly as he finished speaking. He made a desperate lunge for the door. Somewhere in the house there had come a crash. It was followed by a series of piercing cries.

"The basement, chief!" said Wade. "Down—quick!"

Wade had his automatic in his hand. He ran for the basement stairs as a woman, a maid in the kitchen below, screamed:

"Fire! Fire!"

Wade reached the stairway bottom first. A muffled explosion sounded, and a sudden mushroom of flame that sent burning drops of liquid over the whole basement front. Fiery globules fell on Wade's suit. He beat them out, heard the detectives in front give howls of agony. They came running back, driven by heat, clutching their faces. One spoke between clenched teeth.

"It came through the window—a bomb. It's burning like hell itself."

Wade Hammond could see that. Flames were sweeping back to the stairway. The front basement room had become a roaring furnace as some sort of flammable chemicals fed the flames.

He turned and ran up the stairway, bolted through the hall, lunged by the armed headquarters men around the door. They had already flung it open, shoved the snouts of their riot guns out; but there was nothing in sight to shoot. Detectives were milling in the street outside, looking for a target, talking, cursing.

Another muffled explosion sounded in the basement of the Condon home. A second container of explosive liquid seemed to be inside the first. Wade dashed back into the house, saw the butler running for the phone to put in an alarm. Smoke was filling the whole house now, pouring up. The servants had left the quarters below in panic. The flames were making fearful headway. Inspector Thompson, white with rage, voiced Wade's thought. "Everyone's got to get out. This place is going up."

"The girl!" said Wade harshly. "Don't forget that all this is a kidnap trick. When you leave this building, post every available man around her."

Thompson nodded, barked swift orders. A group of six men pressed around Vicki Condon, guns in their hands.

"Wait," said Wade. "The fire engines are coming. Don't go out till you have to."

The seething flames gutting the inside of the house seemed to mock all efforts to quell them. They were like the ghoulish laughter of the Sloth. Condon's face was as white as death. Vicki stood tense and silent, her eyes black with fright. Shrieking, clanging fire engines roared into the street. Police and detectives shouted.

"Make them understand that Miss Condon is to be considered first," growled Wade. "Get her out—now."

The detectives moved forward in a group, the girl in the center, her father close behind her, Wade Hammond going ahead. He marshaled other men along the steps. Cops and firemen on the walk outside stood back. A closed headquarters car was at the curb, ready to whisk Vicki Condon away. Only magic, it seemed, could effect a kidnapping now.

Vicki looked dazed with fear and wonder as she moved out on the steps. Night air played with the dark hair wisping around her face. Light from the flames silhouetted her figure. Her skin was deathly white.

WADE HAMMOND, eyes alert, gave a sudden cry. The others followed his gaze that lifted upward. Something had appeared on the coping of a roof across the street. Wade paused in amazement as a shadow streaked down from the black sky, with a serpentine hiss.

Vicki Condon gave a piercing shriek. For a moment she seemed to struggle with the ring of detectives holding her. Then her plunging body knocked two of them aside. She went down the steps, feet asprawl, silken legs dangling, arms waving out. She was strangely silent now.

Wade caught a glimpse of her face. It was purpling, strangled. He saw then the snakelike thing around her neck. But the force that propelled her forward out of the detective's grasp lifted her on swiftly across the street. Wade made a desperate dive, missed the shadowy, hissing thing, fell to his knees. Vicki Condon was jerked into the air.

He turned and raised his gun, but didn't fire. A huge, ungainly figure was hunched over the coping of the roof, pulling swiftly upward with brawny arms. He didn't shoot because Vicki Condon was already off the ground; because he saw what the man was doing.

The giant figure above was pulling up, hand over hand, a slender black line fastened around the girl's white neck. He had roped her as a man might rope a heifer. If the line dropped now she would be dashed to her death on the pavement below.

Wade sprang across the street with a crowd of detectives following. They, too, understood the incredible plan that the Sloth had used to effect his snatch. He'd shot some kind of incendiary cartridge through the basement window from the roof across the street. He'd fired the house, driven the Condons out, roped the girl. The man above wasn't the Sloth, but he was the Sloth's agent, acting under his orders, doing the manual work.

"Get up on the roof of every house on the block!" Wade called. "Get the firemen to use their ladders."

He reached the door of the house across the street, saw that the house was locked and empty. These were old-time residences along this street. Some of them were closed and boarded. The Sloth had planned with uncanny cunning.

"Surround the house!" Wade barked. He lunged away from the door, leaving detectives and firemen pressed into service, to batter it down with their axes. He entered another doorway where frightened people stood, watching the fire, wondering at the excitement, and mounted a stairway three steps at a time. He came to a hall, turned, climbed more stairs to the roof. These were residences. There would be no fire escapes in back. But there was no telling through which house the Sloth would descend. The roofs were on a level.

He came to an attic at last, tore up a ladderlike flight of stairs. He undid the hooks of a skylight door, heaved up against it, and swore. For it did not yield. The Sloth had placed some sort of fastening outside.

Sweat streamed down Wade Hammond's face. He hurled his shoulder upward till it felt numb. Still the door wouldn't budge. Cries came faintly to him. Engines' sirens. The sounds of the men still battering at the other door below. The whole block was in a bedlam.

He drew out his gun and blasted wildly again and again, putting bullet after bullet around the skylight's edge. Something gave then. With a rush of straining muscles, he lunged up into the night air.

A hulking shape crouched on the roof beyond. Flame lanced toward him. The girl was nowhere in sight. The slender line that had roped her was curled at the big man's feet. He seemed to be guarding his master's retreat. Wade leaped forward, flattened himself, and fired back.

He knew his shots found a mark. His aim was sure as death. The giant grunted, bellowed with rage. But at the third shot Wade's gun clicked emptily. He had used up most of his magazine blasting at the skylight door. He flung the weapon at the big man's head, leaped at him with bared fists.

The man, wounded, put up a huge arm to fend off the flying gun that struck him. He howled again, tried to fire straight at Wade. Wade Hammond was upon him then. The man was hurt, struck in the arm and chest, but still not out. Apelike fury seemed to drive him on. Wade tried to drop him with a single, savage blow, so he could reach the second skylight door. It was through this the girl must have been taken.

But the giant man locked bleeding arms around him. With a mighty heave, he pulled Wade Hammond toward the edge of the roof.

For a moment, they fought like madmen, their bodies close to the edge, wavering over the street in the eerie light of the flames from the Condon home. Death faced them both. Then Wade Hammond, with blood pounding in his temples, pulled back and struck a jabbing blow. The big man toppled, cried out, and tried to drag Wade with him. Wade caught the coping, dropped to his knees, as the giant's body slipped from sight.

He heard the gruesome *spat* as it struck on the street three floors below. He stared over the roof, saw that, mercifully, no one was at the spot. The body was sprawled like a giant spider under the glare of the fire.

Wade turned back to the skylight door. He heaved at it, found that it was bolted on the inside. He could still hear the men with axes breaking in below. The Sloth had had time to reach the bottom of the house. Wade ran to the rear coping and saw dim movement at the end of the vacant court. Cops were swarming into the courts on either side—too late.

He returned to the skylight up which he had come, ran down blind with anger. The Sloth had made good his fantastic threat—kidnapped Vicki Condon.

CHAPTER IV
Death to Wade Hammond

DETECTIVES were breaking down the door in front when Wade Hammond reached the street. He saw why it had taken them so long. The furniture on the bottom floor was wedged against it. The Sloth's helper had worked fast to prepare the way for the snatch.

Wade ran with the others out into the court in back, through which the Sloth had gone. High board fences on either side formed barriers. A garden door into the yard of the house at the rear had been his exit. That, too, was locked. It took them more than a minute to batter it down. The house on the other side was also shuttered, empty. The Sloth had used it in his getaway.

"It's no use," snapped Thompson. "That devil tricked us. He's got us going and coming."

A detective came running up with something in his hand, an envelope with writing on it.

"Here's a note for you, Mr. Hammond. We found it out in the street in front."

Wade Hammond grabbed it, tore it across the end, drew a sheet of paper out. Thompson, with sweat streaming from his face, stared over Wade's shoulder.

My Dear Hammond:

I'm doing you an honor. Knowing your trustworthiness, I've elected you to act for me in the collection of the money. It's late, but Condon is rich and influential. Ask him to get you the hundred grand in unmarked bills, and take them to your apartment.

A girl of mine will arrive not later than one-thirty. She's very charming, and quite obedient to my wishes. She'll guide you to where I am. Your own car will serve the purpose nicely. Of course, no dicks must follow. I'll be watching along the route. If a police car keeps yours in sight, Vicki Condon will die unpleasantly. Be sure of that.

Two o'clock is the deadline. If you don't come with the cash by then, I'll give the Condon girl another bunch of roses—personally.

I look forward to our meeting, Hammond. The girl's life is in your hands. You are too fine a gentleman to turn her down—unless you've grown yellow. But let me remind you of my promise in our talk tonight. I'm delighted at the prospect of your visit.

The Sloth.

Thompson was white around the lips. "It's a trap!" he rasped. "He'll murder you if you go. You haven't a chance. You can't do it. We'll nab that girl when she comes to your place and make her talk. We'll get the truth out of her."

"It won't work, chief. I haven't seen the girl, but the Sloth must know he can trust her not to squeal."

"You're going then?"

"Sure—there's nothing else to do. I'm partly to blame for getting Vicki into this. I should have been more tough and sent her out of town. And I can't turn down an invitation like the Sloth has sent me."

"Then some of us will have to trail you."

"Don't be funny, inspector. You see what the letter says. The Sloth would spot you in a minute."

"Damn! There must be something we can do. You haven't a chance alone."

"If you want to follow about twenty minutes after I leave there may be a way," said Wade. "But don't try to keep me in sight."

Thompson swore fiercely. "How the hell can we trail you if we don't see you, Hammond?"

"Oil," said Wade succinctly. . . .

He was pacing his apartment alone an hour later. There was a fat satchel on the table, holding a hundred thousand in well-worn bills. It had been a job getting that much together late at night. But Condon's prestige with the head of a certain bank had done it. Securities had changed hands. A vault had been opened. A sleepy teller had counted out the cash. Condon had seen to the details with a pallid, twitching face.

And now, Wade Hammond was alone, waiting for the Sloth's girl to come. He stared around the familiar apartment with its mementos of his travels. He wondered if this was to be his last look at the old place.

The Bengal tiger that his Mannlicher rifle had felled in Bihar state was no more savage than the Sloth. The cobra from the Punjab, mounted in a glass case against the wall, lifting its mottled head, was no more deadly. The Sloth would expect him to try to shoot his way out. The Sloth would be prepared. It was almost futile to take a gun. He would surely be disarmed. The Sloth was gloating, waiting with a monstrous appetite for murder.

But Wade's hands were steady as he sucked at his black pipe. The smoke felt cool and good against his tongue. His eyes were thoughtful. He'd made some few secret preparations for what impended. A can of oil with a small nail hole in it was wired beneath his car. Its slow trickle would leave a line of drops. He'd roused a friend who owned a florist's shop to make a purchase of roses. The thought of them made Wade smile thinly. Buying the flowers was a mere gambler's play. But all his life Wade Hammond had been a gambler against odds.

He looked at his watch. Ten minutes past one already. The Sloth's girl ought to arrive any moment now. He went to the window, stared out, and saw a figure on the other side of the street. It was a girl, alone, dressed in black, and apparently looking for numbers. She disappeared under the shadow of his apartment. A moment later his buzzer sounded.

Wade Hammond was tense as he crossed to the door and threw it open. He was curious as to what sort of person this emissary of the Sloth's would be. Some tough gun moll perhaps, an evil creature of the underworld whom the Sloth had got into his power.

But a breath of tasteful perfume met his nostrils. A slim girl in sheerest black, beautiful and pale and delicate stood in the door.

"Are you Wade Hammond?" she inquired softly.

He nodded. One look at her pallid skin and dilated pupils told him the story. She was doped, the slave of some habit that had broken her will. She wasn't vicious obviously, only weak, yet probably more submissive to the Sloth than any criminal would have been. "Mr. Hammond, you are to come with me."

Her vivid lips, forming the only color in her face, moved as though she were a child speaking a part. Her mind was functioning within certain limits only. Treatment in some sanitarium where they cured the drug habit was what she needed. She, too, was patently a victim of the Sloth.

Wade Hammond spoke gently. "Sure," he said. "I've been expecting you. You lead the way—I'll follow. My car's downstairs. Everything's ready."

SHE spoke only a single sentence before they reached his roadster. She walked beside him staring straight ahead, her eyes focused far away. Only once she turned them to his with a faintly troubled look.

"I smell roses!" she said.

"Yes, I had some in my apartment. Do you like them?"

She didn't answer, but her mind, like a forgetful child's, seemed to be grappling with some memory that bothered her. In his car she settled herself beside him. Her black-gloved hands folded in her lap, her pale face turned straight ahead.

"Go to the right," she said. "Take the avenue north. I'll tell you when to turn."

Again it was as though she had carefully memorized some piece. Wade Hammond glanced behind. No police cars were in sight. Inspector Thompson had kept his word. But a thin stream of oil glistened in the center of the street, a simple ruse, but one that in time would surely bring the police to the Sloth's den. If Wade should be killed, if Vicki Condon should still be held or murdered after the bills were delivered, then the police could fall on the Sloth's hideout en masse.

The girl told him where to turn again. Her gloved hand lifted. She pointed like an automaton. They made a wide circle of the city and Wade Hammond frowned. They were doubling back he knew, going over the same ground twice. He wondered if the girl was lost, then saw that this was part of a deliberate plan. The Sloth had coached her well. Somewhere along here he was watching. Wade was glad he'd told the police to keep far behind. They hadn't begun to trail him even the second time over the same route.

The girl pointed in a new direction now. Her voice was like a sleepwalker's. The Sloth's evil will had made her mind mechanically obedient. But the trickle of oil behind would guide the police even through the circling maze they had traveled.

Then the girl breathed fast and spoke more quickly as though in panic of something that had almost slipped her mind. "Stop on this block—behind that parked car ahead. It's empty. It's there for us. We are to go in it from this street on."

Wade Hammond's fingers clenched. He ripped out a silent, bitter oath. The Sloth had anticipated that he might leave some trail behind him. The Sloth's mind worked like a master chess player's, figuring out his opponent's move.

For a brief instant, Wade considered the possibility of transferring his can of oil to the parked car ahead. He gave it up. The Sloth had left the car there for the very purpose of outwitting him. A spy might be watching to make sure that all was well. A wrong move now would rob Vicki Condon of any chance for life she had. The Sloth would order her death as callously as he had done with the messenger boy.

Grimly, Wade left his roadster at the curb, and walked with the girl to the car ahead. She seemed to notice nothing, had no inkling of the fierce thoughts that filled his mind. She was a human robot, fulfilling her criminal master's will.

In the new car, a cheap stock model coupe, they circled into the suburbs, then came back.

"Hurry—it's almost two o'clock." The girl in black knew, too, the significance of time. "Hurry! Or the master will be angry."

To her it was only fear of the Sloth's anger; fear that she might displease the dread being who ruled her life. To Wade, the seconds passing by were dark with an aura of death. His hands were strained on the black rim of the wheel. His face was set.

"Are we almost there?"

"Yes, it's only a little farther now. Drive swiftly, and we'll make it just in time."

Her eyes, he saw, were riveted on the clock on the car's panel. The lighted dial held her gaze with mesmeric fascination.

Three minutes to two, and the girl said suddenly: "Right here!"

It was a street of ancient rundown houses. A street where the city's onward rush had left a backwater of poverty and gloom. These had been costly dwellings once. The few that still were occupied were sordid rooming houses now. And the spot where the girl had told Wade to stop was before a mansion that was empty, boarded up. But she took his arm, pulled him across the pavement quickly into the black shadow of a stoop. A door of wrought iron with heavy steel behind it rose in front. In the dimness, Wade saw a keyhole that was shaped strangely like a cross.

But the girl took no key out. She touched a button behind a piece of molding along the frame. She waited tensely beside Wade. He fingered the satchel of money, cast a brief look along the street. Now, even if he died, no cars would come. The place of his death, the Sloth's hideous secret, might remain concealed forever.

THE door opened softly, operated by some hidden spring inside. A rush of damp air struck his face. There was no light, but the girl in black drew him aside with her. The door moved again, clicked shut, and a dim bulb along a dusty hallway took on a sudden glow.

"You are to wait here," said the girl. "I am to leave you now. It is the master's wish." She moved away, and another voice sounded, coming from unseen lips.

"Yes, you are to wait, Wade Hammond. To follow her would mean instant death. A dozen bullets would fill you before you could take two steps."

There was only a blank door down the hall in front of Wade. But there were small slits in its middle plank. Faintly he saw something round and black.

The Sloth's laughter sounded. It was his voice that had spoken. The girl disappeared through an exit at the side. A lock clicked shut behind her.

"Stand where you are, Wade Hammond. Hold your hands out from your sides—straight. Now, Matsu, search him. Remove his gun. Hold yours against his spine down low. That is a good place to shoot—in case he moves."

Wade started slightly at the whisper of steps behind him. The Sloth continued in his evil purr:

"You did for Jaquin, Hammond. I thought you would. I had to lock him out, knowing his loss was worth the price. Matsu behind you is a more intelligent aide, one of a very agile race."

Wade stuck his arms straight out as he had been ordered, holding the satchel of money. Turning slightly, he saw the sinister, wrinkled face of the yellow man behind him. The big automatic in his clawlike hand was steady. Its muzzle spelled blasting death if Wade so much as stirred. He spoke with sudden malice.

"Your precautions compliment me, Sloth. You crouch like a rat behind an armored door."

There was no answer till the yellow man had found Wade's gun and taken it from him. Then a lock clicked, the door in front jerked open. The Sloth stood in the threshold with a German-type automatic rifle in his hand. Its muzzle had been sawed off. It was as wicked a weapon as Wade had ever seen. The Sloth's eyes blazed with the venom of a snake about to strike. His blue-veined face was hideous.

"Each foolish word brings you nearer death. Understand that I am going to kill you, Hammond. Understand that you are beaten, outwitted. You'll cry for mercy before I'm finished."

"You're being melodramatic, Sloth! Let's admit you've got the drop on me. But I've been in tight spots before. I never whine for a card that isn't in the game."

"You'll whine when I kill the Condon girl before your eyes."

An unholy smile twisted the Sloth's thin lips. Wade Hammond struggled to fight the tumult of emotion that made his temples throb. He tried to make his voice sound even, cold.

"I thought perhaps you'd free her—and keep your word for once."

The Sloth's laughter was a gloating, horrible sound. "The girl must die to break your nerve, if for nothing else. She hardly matters. It's you I'm thinking of. I want to see you sweat. Your manner is insulting."

Veins in the Sloth's high forehead stood out like unwholesome fruit about to burst. Again, the man's pathologic ego was upset. He wanted to cow Wade, make him grovel, crush him with horror. Wade spoke more softly.

"Here's your money, Sloth. Must I hold it? You'd better be sure I've brought the right amount. It is a fortune you have here."

"A fortune!" the Sloth repeated the word. And greed slowly supplanted the look of fury on his face.

"Keep the gun steady, Matsu. Remember—shoot if he so much as moves."

The man behind Wade didn't answer; but the big automatic's muzzle pressed till it cut into his flesh. The Sloth came forward with his oddly shuffling gait, keeping the butt of the deadly rifle clamped against his body, its snout pointing straight at Wade. He held his left hand out and took the satchel of money from Wade's outstretched hand.

Its weight and bulk made his eyes grow brighter still with avarice, made him forget his malevolence for a moment. He lowered his weapon, set it on a table close to his hand, muttering and chuckling with a horrible glee.

He bent eagerly, undid the satchel's catch. He drew the sections at the top apart, and stared down with blazing eyes. Then suddenly he stiffened, gave a fearful cry—jumped away.

In that brief instant when the startling sound transmitted itself to the yellow man behind him, Wade Hammond moved. He dropped to the floor like a plummet, every muscle lax.

A gun roared so close to his head that powder flame burned him. A bullet clipped through his hair. He swept his arms backward, caught the yellow man by the legs, heaved, and catapulted him forward. The man shrieked and clawed, but went over Wade's head. The gun fell from the man's opening fingers. He bobbed up like a hissing snake. A fist caught him straight between the eyes, sent him reeling back. Wade Hammond stooped and swept up the gun before him.

Then he dropped again and rolled over twice as the Sloth's automatic rifle blasted. Soft-nosed bullets spattered the spot where Wade had been. Lead lashed at his feet, burning the soles of his shoes like red-hot brands. The sinister weapon bucked and clattered in the Sloth's hairy hands.

Then Wade fired twice. The Sloth screamed in a frenzy as lead slapped against his legs. There had been no time to aim. Wade dared not pull the gun any higher. The Sloth's rifle was swinging toward his chest. Again it clattered, sending its stream of hot death so close that air fanned Wade's cheek. Only the shattered leg that toppled the Sloth's balance had kept Wade from destruction.

Wade fired again, raising the muzzle higher. The third shot caught the Sloth above the heart. Only then did he let his rifle fall. He clutched at the table, pulled it over, and fell forward, staring at Wade with glazing, murderous eyes.

Wade Hammond straightened slowly. He felt dazed and weak. He glanced at the dead form of the Sloth, at the inert body of Matsu over by the wall. He righted the table, picked up the leather satchel, and stared down in it where the money lay.

The bills were hidden now by green leaves and salmon-tinted petals; hidden by the talisman roses Wade had bought and placed there, hoping to bluff the Sloth into thinking they were his own. It had been a gambler's desperate play. For the roses had given him the split-second chance of action that had saved his life.

Wade Hammond scoffed when word came that Borneo headhunters had come to the United States for victims for their bloody rites. Then he saw the headless corpse sprawled by the swimming pool, and remembered the tom-toms in the jungle. But something was wrong with the killer's picture, so Hammond set out to find—

The Murder Maker

WADE HAMMOND stood stock still in the open doorway of the stately Gresham mansion. Heavy, exotic incense eddied about him, filling his nostrils with a scent that was cloyingly sweet. With it there came a sudden feeling that he was close to some nightmare world of sinister mystery and terror.

Web-like draperies hung across the end of the ancient high-ceilinged hall. An ebony table was set between them, black as a monstrous spider. The walls were flanked with amazing curios. Kris and blowpipes from the Malay states, scarabs from Egypt. Spears from the Sambas and Landak districts of western Borneo.

More startling still was the huge brown-skinned man who stood in the threshold. He was wrinkled, mummified, inscrutable as a sphinx. The hair at the back and sides of his narrow skull was clipped short, leaving a weird topknot. There was a series of ridges in the center of his forehead, reaching down to his eyebrows, recognizable by Wade Hammond as the marks of a knife used long ago in some barbarous tribal rite. The corrugated scars had healed and hardened into a perpetual scowl.

The man intoned in a sing-song voice: "Mr. Gresham, he wait. You follow—this way."

Wade Hammond did so, moving after the brown-skinned servant down the long eerily ornamented hall. He passed a lighted room in which three people sat, got a glimpse of a dark-haired girl with two male companions. One was about the girl's own age, the other looked older, sharp-featured, with a bald head that caught a gleam of light.

The brown-skinned servant spoke again. "Mr. Gresham in here." He thrust open the door of another chamber, motioning Wade to enter. Wade stepped into a large square room that was a combination library and den. In it was a man who turned to face him—a man whose withered skin was the color of bleached-out leather, whose eyes had a wildness and glassiness in their depths and whose hands were visibly trembling.

"You're Hammond," he said in a husky whisper. "I'm Gresham—Sydney Gresham—and I'm glad you came so soon."

Wade Hammond, freelance investigator of crime, had never looked at a face that held such utter terror. But he was totally in the dark as to its cause. Gresham's telephone call, asking him to come at once, had been brief and mysterious. He waited for some explanation and saw Gresham give an apologetic shrug.

"There was no one else I felt safe to call on," Gresham muttered. "The police would hardly understand. But I've read about you in the papers several times. You've done some traveling, they say, and been mixed up in some odd crime cases. This is odd all right, and if you'll help me I'll be glad to pay whatever your trouble's worth."

Wade Hammond waved the offer down. It was a gesture he often had to make. Some of the homicide cases he'd worked on had brought him publicity. But he was a globetrotter, soldier-of-fortune and newspaper correspondent by profession, not a detective. The special card he carried, signed by the police commissioner himself, didn't entitle him to fees. It was a tribute to his daring and skill as a sub rosa investigator of off-the-trail crime.

He plucked a black pipe from his pocket, squinted down the stem, screwing his lean tanned face with its close-clipped mustache into a scowl. He rubbed the bowl against his hawklike nose, said irritably: "Shoot! Forget the cash. What's on your mind?"

Gresham didn't speak till he'd gone to the end of the room and carefully locked the door. On his way back he reached into a half-open safe and drew out a small black bag. He held it strangely, arm stiff, fingers clenched, keeping it away from his body as though it contained some loathsome or horrible thing.

He stopped in front of the table, set the bag quickly down. His fingers dipped into his coat pocket next, and took out a piece of crumpled paper. Still without explanation, he handed this to Wade.

There was a scrawled message on it, words that didn't seem to make much sense. "This will help you remember Calvert," it said. "You know what to do."

The writing looked illiterate or purposely disguised. The paper was a piece of thick and carelessly torn Manila. Gresham licked his white lips and shook his head, staring at Wade. "You don't understand, of course—but you will in a minute. That note and *this*—came in the mail late this afternoon."

He stooped and opened the black bag on the table. He started to reach in and appeared suddenly to lose all strength. "I can't! I can't!" he gasped. "In the name of mercy—you take it out and look at it, Hammond!"

Gresham, shutting his eyes tightly for an instant, shoved the bag toward Wade. There was a round paper bundle in it, a thing about six inches in diameter. Wade lifted it gingerly, turning it over and over in his hands. "What is it?" he asked with a sudden note of tenseness.

Gresham didn't speak for a moment, but he made an inarticulate sound in his throat; then abruptly raised his finger to his head and pointed, letting his hand drop back.

Wade Hammond's scalp began to prickle and there was a faint sensation of chilliness along his spine. The thing held gruesome suggestion in its shape, size and weight. He stared at Gresham and saw that the man was gripping the table, looking in fixed and horrified fascination at the bundle in Wade Hammond's fingers.

"Go ahead," Gresham croaked. "I—I've got to see. But—I can't do it myself."

Wade Hammond's hands felt suddenly cold and clumsy. He began untying the string, peeling off the paper. There were several layers of it. Through them he could feel the hard surface that lay beneath. He scowled suddenly and worked more quickly, removing the paper piece by piece. The last one came unrolled, and Wade let out a harshly explosive curse. Gresham choked up words.

"A coconut," he gasped.

All the color had left Sydney Gresham's face. He sat down in a chair limply with sweat oozing from his sallow skin while his eyes stayed fixed on the brown nut in Wade Hammond's hands, as though it were a symbol of some horrible thing he'd feared to see. Wade stared again at the scrawled message on the paper slip.

GRESHAM took a handkerchief out and began wiping his damp forehead. His eyes hadn't lost their look of desperate fear. "You'll think I'm crazy, Hammond, asking your help with such a thing!"

"What's it all about?" said Wade.

"It wasn't what I thought," husked Gresham. "But it's a threat—and it means death for me!"

Wade Hammond was silent, fingering the brownish nut. The eyes at the end had been punctured, the milk drained out. Plaster of Paris had been poured in to make it heavy again.

"You've heard of the Dyaks of Borneo?" said Gresham suddenly.

"Headhunters!" said Wade. "Sure, I was in the Sambas district once myself."

Gresham nodded slowly, fearfully. "Exactly—headhunters—and this man, Calvert, was my partner. We got permission from the Raja of Sarawak to prospect for metals. Calvert insisted on going up into the hills alone. I saw his head afterwards in one of their damned native temples, stuck on a pole, cured like a smoked herring. I couldn't get it back. When I got this thing and that message there I thought—" Gresham waved his hand toward the coconut and shuddered.

"This threat," said Wade. "I take it you know what the rest of the message means."

Gresham nodded again. He closed his eyes, ran a hand through his gray hair, and spoke as though in a trance. "The Dyaks are queer people, Hammond. You know as well as I do that headhunting still persists among them. Even the Dutch governors can't stamp it out.

"It's in the natives' blood. A man in the Illongotes tribe, for instance, must bring his bride three heads before she'll accept him. Preferably white men's heads. They must have heads for certain religious ceremonies. When once they mark a man for death his head goes up in value. The way they look at it, it gets to be more precious than gold. Voodoo-ism, you know. They won't stop at anything to hack it off."

Wade Hammond nodded. "Right," he said. "But I don't quite get the connection. You're not in Borneo now."

Gresham spread his hands in a hopeless gesture. "It doesn't make much difference. The Dyaks have secret societies backed by religious superstition. They're powerful, Hammond—powerful as hell itself. Ask the Dutch about them. Ask the British. Ask the Raja of Sarawak. Calvert and I were both marked men. We went places we weren't supposed to.

"We violated some of their heathen taboos, you understand. They got Calvert right away. Now, after twenty years, they've decided to get me. They want me to come back quietly and give up my head. If I don't—" Gresham spread his hands again and shuddered. "They'll murder me here and take it along with them."

"There aren't many Dyaks in America," said Wade dryly.

"There are two," quavered Gresham. "Servants in my house."

Wade Hammond nodded, smiling thinly, humorless as he twirled the brown nut in his hands. "I thought I recognized the breed in the old fellow who met me at the door."

Gresham leaned forward, tapped Wade on the arm and whispered hoarsely. "The one you saw was Bella Kassi. He came from Borneo with me and has been here twenty years. He's as good a house boy as any man would want and I can't believe he's anything but loyal. It's the other one, Ganak, his cousin, that I don't trust. He's only been here a few months."

Gresham rose and drew Wade with him. "Come, let's take a look around the house."

They went out into the high-ceilinged hall again, passing the racks of spears and Malay knives. Gresham glanced uneasily toward them. "Things I brought back with me, Hammond, and I wish now I hadn't. I'm going to get rid of them."

Voices floated through the door of the lighted room and Gresham jerked a finger in that direction. "Calvert's daughter June is in there with some friends. She's an orphan now and lives with me. I'm educating her. She calls me Uncle Syd. I won't let her know why you're here. We must try not to scare her. Be careful, Hammond, what you say."

Wade nodded and followed Gresham into the room. June Calvert was small and pretty, with features so clear-cut they might have seemed sharp except for their delicate youthfulness. Her eyes were a deep gray, cool and level under thinly drawn brows.

Keeping his voice casual with an effort, Gresham said: "This is Mr. Hammond, June. He's a collector of curios like myself." He turned to the two men. "Bob Sawyer, Hammond, and Mr. Smith, Miss Calvert's legal guardian."

In a swift glance Wade Hammond sized them up. Smith looked pompous, self-important. He was smiling, bobbing his shiny head. Sawyer, young and good-looking in a rugged way, had given an abrupt start at sight of Wade. He watched uneasily while June Calvert lifted her eyes to Gresham's face with an anxious frown.

"You look ill, Uncle Syd!" she said. "Is something wrong?" There was a note of aloofness in her voice, as though some intangible barrier existed between her and Gresham that nothing could penetrate. Gresham answered heavily, refusing to meet her eyes.

"I'm all right, June. I'm going to show Mr. Hammond around the house. You'll excuse us, please."

HE drew Wade quickly into the hall, said in a nervous whisper: "I'll go and get hold of Ganak. You wait here. Bella Kassi will know where Ganak is. I want you to talk to them both, Hammond, and see what you can find out. If they're mixed up in this business, I've got to know it."

Sweat beaded his forehead again. Deep-seated terror was in his eyes. He strode with jerky steps along the hall and disappeared. The house grew strangely silent. Wade's coming appeared to have put a damper on the conversation of those in the other room. A door squeaked softly somewhere, closed with a brittle click.

Wade Hammond fingered the shiny bowl of his pipe. His right elbow pressed the bulge beneath his coat where an automatic was concealed in a shoulder holster. Long habit made him always carry a gun. He was glad he had it now. This house was creepy, uncanny, a fit place for a murder. Gresham's strange story made him recall his own days in Borneo, the sweltering, sleepless nights, the tom-toms of headhunting tribes.

He lifted a match to his pipe, but dropped it quickly and turned. The web-like draperies at the end of the hall had bellied out as though wind had pushed them. A tall man slid through, rolling slant eyes at Wade—a man of the same breed as Bella Kassi, but younger and more vigorous. He, too, had a shaved head and ugly scabrous ridges in the center of his forehead, made more recently than Kassi's and drawing his face into a sinister scowl. His nostrils flared above thick, pouting lips like an Oriental idol's.

Wade Hammond watched in silence. The brown man glided by him, walking on flat grass slippers, treading softly, carrying himself in the easy way of a savage. He disappeared through the same door Gresham had taken. Wade tensed and started to follow; but thought better of it. This was Gresham's house. Gresham had asked him to wait.

Two minutes passed, and a shot suddenly broke the silence of the big mansion. A cry followed close on the heels of it, then a crash of breaking glass. In the drawing room June Calvert gave a shrill scream of terror. But the shot had come from the rear of the house, toward the kitchen. Dropping his pipe in his pocket and drawing his gun, Wade Hammond jumped that way.

He lost time in the hall, opening doors that led to closets, banging them shut again. He ran on swiftly. The third door he tried led to a pantry and he barged straight through it.

Gresham loomed in his way, running from the kitchen. There was a gun in his hand, too, and his pallid face was twitching.

"I shot him," he gasped. "I shot Ganak. He attacked me, tried to kill me. I don't know whether I hit him—but I drove him out the window. He's behind this thing, Hammond. I know it now."

Wade thrust out a steadying hand. He pushed by Gresham and entered the big kitchen. French windows opening on a back veranda were smashed. Gresham, white and shaken, spoke again from the doorway.

"I couldn't find Bella Kassi. Ganak ran into the garden, wounded, I think, though I'm not a very good shot. I scared him off anyway. We'll have to get him and lock him up. Shush—here comes June. Try not to frighten her."

But the girl was already taut with fear. She'd heard the shot and her small face was pale. She gasped: "Uncle, what's happened?"

Gresham spoke nervously, glancing sidewise at Wade. "You might as well know the truth, June. Something I've been half afraid of has happened. Ganak went wild. He tried to attack me with a knife. But you needn't feel afraid. We'll get the police."

Smith, the lawyer, had followed the girl into the room. He was no longer smiling and he spoke with snapping impatience. "I've warned you a dozen times, Mr. Gresham, told you those heathens shouldn't be in this house. It isn't fair to June. I hope this will teach you a lesson."

"Kassi's all right," muttered Gresham. "You know he's been here since June was a baby. He's like one of the family and I'd trust him to protect us. He's probably out after Ganak right now."

June Calvert spoke suddenly with deep terror in her voice. "We've got to warn Bob! He's outside somewhere, too, and Ganak might hurt him."

Wade glanced at her quickly and Gresham said: "What's Sawyer doing out there? I thought he was in the front room with you."

June Calvert hesitated an instant, then spoke with embarrassment. "He left right after you and Mr. Hammond came. He's been moody all evening. I don't know what's the matter, but something's on his mind. He said he wanted some air and went out the side door into the garden. He mustn't stay out if Ganak's turned savage."

Wade said quickly: "Don't worry, I'll get him. You get the police, Gresham. Ask for Sergeant Terrant and tell him Wade Hammond wants him to come with a couple of men."

WADE took a small flash from his coat and stepped through the smashed doors into the darkness. Gresham called after him: "For heaven's sake be careful. We don't want any more trouble."

Ten feet from the house and Wade Hammond paused. A cigarette end was bobbing in the gloom just ahead. He waited a moment, clicked on the flash, and its beam showed up young Sawyer, striding toward the house, frowning.

"What's all the racket?" he asked.

"One of Gresham's brown men made some trouble. He's on the prowl now. Better get into the house."

As they neared it, June Calvert called out from the doorway. "Hurry, Bob—please. Ganak's gone wild. He attacked Uncle Syd, and the police are coming to get him. I was so afraid for your sake. Ganak may be out there, hiding in the dark."

"The police!" Sawyer echoed the word queerly, again swinging his eyes to Wade. He pointed and said accusingly: "We've got a detective here now, June. This man's Wade Hammond. Maybe you don't know about him, but I do. He's always getting himself in the papers."

Wade studied Sawyer's face keenly. The man looked frightened, strangely disturbed about something. He appeared to resent Wade's presence. Wade stepped closer and abruptly touched Sawyer's arm. "You've got something on your coat—there at the elbow."

Sawyer jumped away and began brushing his sleeve angrily. "Powder," he mumbled. "Came from June's compact. It was on the arm of the chair. I stuck my elbow in it." To Wade, Sawyer's explanation seemed needlessly lengthy.

June Calvert was staring. "Why, Bob," she said, "you had it there when you came. The powder I use is pink. That's white, like plaster."

Red mottled Sawyer's face. He glared ungallantly at the girl. "Make me out a liar, June, if it gives you any pleasure. What about it anyway? Where's Mr. Gresham?"

"Getting the police," said Smith. "He's learned his lesson. This house will be rid of those wild men now. Come back to the front room, June, and stay there till the police arrive. I'll see that you're safe." He pulled the girl with him in a proprietary way. Sawyer went with them and Wade Hammond followed. At the door of the drawing room he abruptly touched Sawyer's arm. "I'd like a word with you."

Sawyer looked stubborn. "What is it you want?"

Wade collected his thoughts a moment, said with sudden decision: "You're pretty much at home in this house aren't you, Sawyer?"

"Yes, I've come here since June was a kid. I live down the street. Now she and I are engaged—but what's it to you?"

"Nothing," said Wade, "except that I want to ask a few questions and show you something queer."

He led Sawyer to the library at the side of the hall, opened Gresham's black bag, and pointed to the coconut.

"That's why I'm here, Sawyer. It was sent to Mr. Gresham with a funny sort of threat. There's plaster of Paris in it. Wrapped up, it looked and felt like a man's head."

Bob Sawyer laughed strangely, his eyes avoiding Wade's. "Sounds like somebody was kidding," he said.

"Gresham didn't think so. He believes it's a threat of death."

Sawyer's face grew pale at Wade's words. He started to answer, but tensed into silence as a siren wailed outside. They both turned and went into the hall.

Smith came out of the drawing room rubbing his hands. "The police!" He opened the front door and let Sergeant Terrant and two cops into the house. "Mr. Gresham!" he called.

Gresham appeared in a moment, still shaken with terror. "You tell them, Hammond. Explain just what's happened. Then, let's see if we can't get Ganak rounded up. I'm worried about Bella Kassi. He was here when you came. Now he's disappeared completely."

Terrant and Wade Hammond had often worked together. Wade buttonholed him now and explained things quickly. Terrant nodded and scowled. "It's just like you, Hammond. You drag me up from headquarters just to hunt a crazy Filipino."

"Not a Filipino, sergeant," Wade said. "A Dyak whose folks back home collect heads. Get your guns out and your flashes. We'll scour the grounds. But don't shoot unless you have to."

They filed outside quickly, spreading as they reached the lawn. Wade was still puzzled by young Sawyer's manner, sure that he knew something about Ganak he wouldn't tell. Sawyer had a flashlight and had come along, too.

The grounds around the house were big. The gardens formed an elaborate maze. There were a dozen places where a man could hide. But Gresham had said that the two servants had probably gone to the old carriage house in back, converted into a garage. Wade Hammond strode toward this, until a shout stopped him.

He whirled and ran toward a spot where Sergeant Terrant stood with his light. Sawyer ran up, too, and a cry ripped from his throat.

"It's Kassi!" he said. "Kassi—and he's dead!" He stooped lower, gasped, and shrank back in horror. Wade Hammond felt his own spine grow cold. For the headless body of a man lay at Terrant's feet. The wrinkled hands, the thin figure, showed that it was Kassi. A blow had severed his head from his emaciated neck, and the head had disappeared!

His eyes swung to Sawyer. The young man was trembling, his face deathly white. Sergeant Terrant looked at Wade, his stolid front shaken. Wade snapped an order: "Come on to the garage, sergeant. We've got to find Ganak. Send one of your men back to protect those in the house. You come with us, Sawyer!"

Sawyer's combativeness had left him. There was fear in his eyes. He looked at Wade strangely, followed along. But the garage and the rooms over it were dark and deserted.

THEY circled back through the gardens, guns in their hands. Terrant said grimly: "He's probably run off with that blasted head. It's the sort of thing, Hammond, I'd expect you to be mixed up in. I can fight regular crooks, but I'll need a good drink after this!"

There was a swimming pool in the garden. Wade passed and flashed his light on the ground. "Somebody's been here—there are tracks."

"I walked around it," husked Sawyer, "when I came out to smoke."

Terrant circled the hedges, gun jutting from his hand. The other cop was twenty feet away. Sawyer slouched close to Wade. They neared the house, left the path at the end of the gardens, with shrubbery still about. There was deep shadow behind the kitchen. Bob Sawyer suddenly screamed.

Wade Hammond saw it, too—a figure creeping forward. For one nightmare moment he seemed to be in the jungles again. Seemed to hear tom-toms beating, feel the sweltering heat. For the savage figure was Ganak, with a huge knife in his hand.

He ducked as Wade fired, and came straight for Bob Sawyer, lips curled back from his teeth. Sawyer, still screaming, turned and ran. Bushes spoiled Wade's aim. But he leaped through an open space and intercepted Ganak's murderous advance. The brown man was so preoccupied in getting Sawyer with his knife that Wade slipped behind him.

Instead of shooting he brought his gun muzzle down with a crack behind the brown man's ear. Ganak toppled forward with a gibbering cry. Terrant and the cop came up on the run. Sawyer stood trembling, close to the point of collapse.

"He tried to kill me," he gasped.

Terrant laughed harshly. "You're telling us. If Hammond hadn't got him he'd have had your head, too."

Wade Hammond's flash was centered on Ganak. The Dyak was still breathing, but completely knocked out. Wade suddenly swore and stooped down on the grass. He lifted the long knife that Ganak had carried, let the beam of his flash play along its blade.

"Funny, sergeant," he snapped. "There's not a sign of blood!"

"A neat chap," said Terrant. "He cleans it between kills. But he won't lop off any more heads. This isn't Borneo. He'll know that when he gets in the chair. Put the bracelets on him, Barney. We'll carry him out to the car. I'll send the wagon for what's-his-name—Chassis!"

"Kassi," said Wade, "and we've got to find his head. But hang around, sergeant. There's a lot I want to know."

"You're a hard guy to satisfy, Hammond. What is it now?"

"This knife hasn't been cleaned, Terrant. There's rust on it still. Leave Ganak with Barney, here. Let's go look at Kassi's corpse. Come along, Sawyer!"

They strode in silence to the spot where the dead man was lying. Wade bent and stared at the headless neck. He whistled suddenly, straightened his head.

"There's something damn funny! Look, sergeant—a knife didn't do this. It was some sort of cleaver—and there's not enough blood."

He looked up at Bob Sawyer, who was biting his lips. Wade grabbed at his coat sleeve and stared at the white powder that was still in the weave. He sniffed at it, said sharply: "I don't like to hound you, Sawyer, but that looks like plaster of Paris, as Miss Calvert said. And you've been acting funny. I've got a theory, Sawyer, that it was you who put that coconut in the mail. Suppose you come clean. A Dyak who's only been in this country a few months wouldn't think of such a trick."

"What the hell!" barked Terrant. "I don't get any of this."

But Bob Sawyer apparently did. His face was twisted, frightened. He gasped: "You can't pin anything on me, Hammond. I'm not talking—understand! I saw Ganak running loose with that knife."

"Come in the house," said Wade harshly. "You'll be glad of the chance to talk before I get through. You'll stop being a fool."

Gresham and Smith met them at the kitchen door. They heard the news aghast, but Smith rubbed his thin hands.

"It's a good thing it happened. With Kassi dead and Ganak in jail this house will be civilized again. I won't have to worry about June."

Wade Hammond went and got the black bag and the coconut. To June Calvert's frightened queries he said: "Keep out of this, please. You'll know about it later."

He returned to the kitchen and took the coconut from the bag. Terrant glared at it scornfully, said: "Hammond's going to do a trick." Bob Sawyer closed his lips and shrank away.

"Trick is right," growled Wade. "You're going to remember this nut a long time, sergeant." He knocked the end of it against the wall, broke a piece off, and exposed the plaster of Paris. He abruptly approached Sawyer and rubbed it on his coat. The mark was the same as the one already there.

"You fixed this thing up and sent it to Mr. Gresham. You wrote that note.

What was it you wanted him to do?"

Sawyer shook his head. "I told you I wouldn't talk."

"Okay," said Wade shortly. "But when I prove that Ganak didn't kill Kassi, you're going to be in trouble. This isn't headhunting stuff. This is a white man's murder. A white man killed Kassi."

"Murder!" Sawyer, trembling violently, spilled the word from his lips. He looked at the brown nut, and suddenly nodded. "You're right—I sent it—but I'm not a murderer. I only wanted to remind Gresham to do what he should. He's got all of June's money—that her own father left her. He promised Calvert he'd take care of her till she was eighteen, then turn the money over to her. She's twenty-three now, and he hasn't done it yet. She doesn't even know about it, but Kassi did. He told me."

Terrant interrupted, glaring at Sawyer. "So you bumped off Kassi, hoping to get the cash yourself, trying to blackmail Gresham. This other bird, Ganak, was after you for killing his pal."

"Wrong, sergeant," said Wade, "over there stands your murderer." He pointed toward Gresham, and suddenly drew his gun. "None of that, Gresham—keep your hands in sight. You shot one man tonight—don't try it again."

"Shot!" Terrant gaped at Wade. "That man outside was killed with a cleaver."

Wade ignored the comment, said: "Keep him covered, sergeant, while I look around."

He turned and surveyed the kitchen, walked suddenly to a door at its end. He jerked it open, revealing a closet. He stooped, pointed to a red stain on the floor.

"Gresham shot Kassi because he knew too much. He killed him and kept the door closed till he had a chance to take the body outside. Ganak didn't attack him. He made that story up. He carried Kassi out and sliced off his head while I was talking to you, Sawyer, in the front hall. He had to do that to hide the mark of the bullet. I don't know, but I imagine we'll find the head and the cleaver out there in the pool."

"But Ganak!" the sergeant growled. "I saw him chasing Sawyer here with my own eyes."

"Sure," said Wade. "Ganak's only a savage. He hasn't been here long. He can hardly speak English. Gresham told him that Sawyer had murdered Kassi, hoping to get Sawyer out of the way. With Kassi and Sawyer both gone, no one would know about the money.

"It was pretty clever if it had worked. With Sawyer dead the knife would have had blood on it. I might never have guessed, and I couldn't question Sawyer about the plaster of Paris. Gresham himself knew what was up as soon as I opened the nut. Up to then he thought it really was Calvert's head. You thought you were only sending him a reminder, Sawyer. It was more than that. You didn't know it, but it was a *murder maker*."

Wade Hammond owed a hot lead debt to the killer who struck at his best friends—but when he went to pay it, he found himself face to face with a grinning ghoul. And he learned that his corpse was wanted for the devil's brew.

The Grinning Ghoul

CHAPTER I
DISCIPLE OF DEATH

THE pale, big-eyed girl in the karakul coat leaned forward tensely and lifted the limousine's speaking tube to her trembling lips. She said in a strangled whisper: "Stop."

The car rolled in toward the curb and the girl turned to stare back fearfully along the squalid waterfront block. The big car came to a standstill. The poker-faced chauffeur alighted and held the door open for the girl. She paused as though to gather courage before thrusting her slim legs out. There was a questioning look in the uniformed man's eyes which she ignored. She lowered her head, stepped from the car and said in a tone of flat command: "Wait for me here."

Her heels made a brittle clicking sound as she hurried away. Wind struck her when she reached the corner, pressing her clothing tightly against her slender, supple body.

She clenched her teeth so as not to shiver, held her beaded bag close to her side and came to a stop at a spot halfway down the block in front of a vacant store. Here she stood peering in excited fright in both directions, straining her face into the gloom till a scrape of footsteps sounded.

The girl made out a figure coming toward her. It was a slouching, stooped-over, ragged man, moving as though the wind were driving him aimlessly before it.

He came near, peering at her with a show of cunning. He had a wizened face and huge ears that thrust out startlingly from the sides of his narrow skull. He stopped, fumbled a moment in a baggy pocket, and pulled a frayed cigar butt from it. "You wouldn't have a match on you, would you now, lady?" he said in a whining voice.

The girl opened her bag at once and drew a small box from it. "Here—take them all," she said.

The man made no move to accept her offer. Instead he turned, nodding for her to follow, and the girl hesitantly obeyed.

At a dark opening between two rundown buildings, the large-eared stranger paused. He pulled a square of black cloth from an inner pocket of his coat. The girl stood submissively while he tied it over her face and head.

He took her hand roughly then and led her after him into the blackness of an alley. He didn't speak. He guided her through a maze of passages and crisscross alleys, descending a flight of stairs at last, making her step into a creaking elevator that rose slowly up the black shaft of a deserted building. He led her along a corridor where echoes whispered, into a stuffy chamber. He removed the cloth from her face and disappeared abruptly.

THE girl blinked in the dim light of the room and shrank away. A man wearing a long cape and with a black hood over his face was coming toward her. Only the gleaming pupils of his eyes were visible. The girl stifled a cry of terror and the man spoke softly.

"Quiet, Valerie. Behold your dear departed brother!"

"Brian," she whispered.

The man bowed low, said mockingly: "Again you recognize the voice of the dead!"

"Why do you wear that terrible hood? Take it off! Let me see you!"

A note of grating harshness came into the man's voice as he answered. "A murderer learns the wisdom of distrust. Even you, dear Valerie, aren't above suspicion—though my face has changed considerably since you last saw it and I doubt if you'd know me now."

"I don't understand how you lived at all," the girl said, shuddering. "I thought you'd been burned to death."

"Along with the other prison rats who roasted in their steel-barred cages. That's what I hoped everyone would believe."

"You hoped? You don't mean that you, Brian—"

"Let's not go into that! The money—did you bring it?"

The girl nodded, keeping her eyes away from the black-hooded man before her. She opened her bag again and took out a big packet of bills. "I sold the block of securities as you asked—but at a sacrifice. They only brought twenty thousand."

"That will do for the present," the hooded man said. "My wants are much simpler than they used to be. And when I need money, you, dear sister, will bring me more. You won't begrudge the dead, I know, considering that you have full enjoyment of the deceased man's estate."

The girl uttered a sound like a sob. "Don't, please, Brian—don't talk like that! I'll always get you the money you need, as I told you yesterday when you phoned. But you're not going to stay here, surely! You'll go back wherever you've been hiding all these years."

The hooded man gave vent to a harsh peal of laughter.

"I'll go back—but first I've work to do. Come here, Valerie, I want to show you something."

The man walked to the end of the room and snapped on a shaded light. Under its slanting glow the pictures of four men leaped into view. One was gray-haired, with round, bland features. The second had an aggressive chin and sharply penetrating eyes. The third was hawk-faced and ruggedly handsome with a thin mustache line above a powerful, grimly humorous mouth. The fourth was elderly, white-haired, and had the look of a servant.

"Do you know who these are, Valerie?" The hooded man's tone was bitter, accusing. The girl stared in wonder.

"One's Judge Willis, who sentenced you, Brian. That other's Ross, the district attorney who prosecuted you, and"—the girl passed over the picture of the mustached man with a shake of her head, speaking again when her eyes centered on the one with the snow-white hair—"that's Meigan, who used to be your butler!"

"Correct!" said the hooded figure. He tapped a finger against the face of the mustached, hawk-faced man. "Wade Hammond, Valerie, the newspaper correspondent whose interest in my walking stick helped to send me to prison for life."

"Why do you keep their photographs, Brian?"

"Why?" The hooded man echoed her question and laughed suddenly in a strangely harsh manner that deepened the paleness of her face. "These are the gentlemen," he said sardonically, "with whom I have business. Judge Patrick Willis, elegant ornament of the bar. Ross, now prosperous head of the city's largest law firm. Wade Hammond, freelance investigator of crime, and Meigan, my estimable old servant who was so willing to testify to his master's unruly temper!"

"He didn't, Brian—the police had to drag it out of him—after you beat that janitor to death."

The hooded man's eyes blazed. He crouched forward and glared at the white-faced girl till she shrank away. "We won't talk of that, dear sister! You asked me why I'm remaining close by, and I've told you—pressing business with these worthy gentlemen."

The girl was silent a moment, seeming to read some horrible meaning in his words. She spoke in a frightened whisper. "But the police, Brian—they'll trap you if you stay around!"

"The police!" The man uttered the words in a savage snarl. He brought the two gleaming holes that were his eyes close to the face of the girl. "The police will never find me, Valerie. I've taken precautions, as you know, even with your visit here. And you'll say nothing to a living soul about what I've said, or of your knowledge that I'm alive. You've a loving husband and a beautiful baby daughter, I'm told. For their sake and your own you'll be as silent as the grave, Valerie!"

The girl put a hand to her trembling mouth.

"You're not threatening me, Brian! You couldn't do that!"

"Not as long as you keep quiet. If you should talk—" The man left the sentence unfinished, and turned away. He pressed a button and the shuffling footsteps of the ragged man sounded again. "Good night, dear sister, and thanks so much for the money. The dead are always appreciative of gifts."

After the girl had been led away, the cloth over her head once more, the man removed his hood. He looked at himself in a mirror for a moment, stared at the shockingly hideous face that gazed back at him—a face that was a mass of livid, crinkling scars; the nose almost gone, the scalp and eyebrows hairless, the lips burned to inflexibility and set in a fixed and terrible grin. He passed a clawlike hand across the awful features, laughed slowly in deep chuckles that bubbled madly from his lips and made his nostrils flare like a Chinese devil's.

He gathered up the four portraits, went through a door to another, smaller room. Here he counted the money that his sister had brought him, put it away in a small safe, and stared about him with a show of pride.

THE room looked like a small, compact laboratory. Row upon row of thick-glassed bottles ranged a shelf. Another held metal boxes, canisters and tubes. A third had glass jars filled with brownish powders, bits of bark and crystals that sent out opalescent gleams.

Here were the fruit of years of travel in strange and distant lands. Death long ago had brought misfortune to the "Man with the Grin." Death held his interest now. Each of those silent, harmless-looking receptacles ranging the shelves was an instrument of death. Here were bizarre poisons, vegetable, animal and mineral, that couldn't be found anywhere else in the whole United States. Dried sap from the upas-tree of the Malay Archipelago. Kingo, the deadly African drug that makes frenzied, raging beasts of men. Tincture of calabar. Venom from the fangs of the fer-de-lance, the bushmaster, hammerdryad, and a dozen other snakes. Toxic substances gathered from witch doctors in jungle villages.

The Man with the Grin walked through a door into a room from which animal howls issued. He studied a half-dozen cages in which animals writhed or dozed. He returned to his workroom and busied himself making delicate distillations, grinning over a boiling retort which contained a brownish liquid. Many hours later, after painstaking work, he loaded a tiny hollow dart with a substance he handled with rubber gloves.

No light entered the somber chamber, but day had long since come when the man set forth. He was dressed in shabby clothes but carried a walking stick. He looked like a shambling ugly tramp who had suffered some awful accident.

He rode uptown in a subway, seated himself on a bench beside a reservoir lake in a park and waited. There was terrible patience and purpose in the way he sat, looking out across an open space toward a bridle path beyond. He appeared to doze along with a dozen other bums on the benches around him, but his heavy-lidded eyes never lost their watchfulness. At four in the afternoon he ambled through some bushes, avoiding a patrolling cop, and took up a position beside the path for equestrians.

The thudding hoofs of horses sounded as several men cantered by. The eyes of the Man with the Grin were bright as he peered along the leafy roadway. He crouched back among bushes when a single horseman came into a view. A large, striking-looking man with bland features sat astride a sorrel thoroughbred. He rode with the ease and grace of a born equestrian despite his weight.

In a moment he came opposite, and the Man with the Grin, concealed in the thick bushes, raised his cane. Slowly he pointed its end, in which a tiny hole was visible, at the velvety flank of the horse. He pressed a stud in the cane's end and a faint hiss sounded.

The horse gave a muscular twitch of its sleek skin as though a fly bite had annoyed it. It twitched its tail and jerked its head around. The bland-faced rider soothed it calmly and the animal cantered on.

The Man with the Grin pressed forward stealthily through the bushes to watch.

In a moment the horse began to dance with the mincing steps of a circus pony suddenly jogging to music. The rider took a firmer grip on the reins and tried to calm it. The horse's mincing grew faster and it gave a frightened whinny. It turned in a circle, flicking its tail, drumming its hoofs on the dirt while its eyes showed flashing whites. The man now was unable to control it.

Abruptly the sorrel began to buck and rear. It arched its back like an untamed bronco, dropped stiff-legged, sunfished back and forth. Even the skillful rider couldn't keep his seat at this unexpected frenzy. At the fourth buck he was flung over the animal's head, landing dazedly in the dirt.

The sorrel's eyes were red as fire now. Foam flecked its mouth. It stared at the man in the road before it, gave a horrible, high-pitched scream and lunged straight forward just as the rider started to lift himself up. The man kneeled, frozen, too scared and surprised to move. The horse reared, a foam-flecked monster of destruction, and brought its sharp hoofs down on the rider's back. There was a hideous crunching crack. The man went down in a writhing heap. Madly the horse continued to rear and trample till the figure of its rider was no more than a silent, crimson-stained scarecrow. It kept on bucking and screaming till a white-faced policeman ran up and put an end to its frenzied movements with a shot between the eyes.

· · ·

CHAPTER II
Killer's Challenge

WADE HAMMOND, press correspondent, world rover, and freelance investigator of crime, stared somberly at the morning paper spread before him. He sucked at his black pipe, sipped his breakfast coffee, and read the story at the top of the front page.

EMINENT JURIST KILLED BY MADDENED HORSE

The Hon. Patrick Willis, resident of this city for many years, and judge in the criminal courts since 1920, met a tragic death late yesterday afternoon while indulging in his favorite hobby. His horse threw him suddenly, then turned upon him and trampled him to death.

Stebbins, a groom who cared for the beast, gave as his belief that the horse was frightened, perhaps purposely by someone along the bridle path. He recalled that a trampish stranger with abnormally large ears showed interest recently in the judge's equestrian habits, and hung about the stables asking questions until he was ordered away.

Close friends of the judge, however, place no importance on Stebbins' story. They agree with the park police that the tragic accident was the result of some pathologic frenzy of the horse. This is upheld by testimony of Doctor Ronald Hindus, veterinary, who states that the animal had a sudden cerebral attack akin to homicidal paranoia.

Willis had been an acquaintance and fellow clubman of Wade Hammond's; yet even Wade, alert for criminal plots, saw nothing markedly suspicious in the judge's death.

He passed on to the foreign news, then to the sporting section—until the snarling of the buzzer in the apartment's hall brought him abruptly to his feet. It was only a little after seven. Visitors seldom came as early as that. The mailman wasn't due for half an hour.

In long-legged strides he walked the length of the corridor and stopped before a square, inconspicuous box beside the frame of the door. His startling coups in combating crime had made him enemies in the underworld. Numerous attempts had been made to murder him. The box by the door was part of an electrical device that grim necessity had forced him to install.

He raised the cover, threw a switch, and an image leaped suddenly upon a silver screen—a miniature television portrait of the man who had touched the button in the vestibule three flights below.

The man was a stranger to Wade Hammond. He looked like a panhandler, judging by his unkempt clothes. But Wade's curiosity changed suddenly to lynx-eyed interest. For the man was dropping something in his mailbox! In doing this he faced the television receptor squarely, and Wade got a glimpse of abnormally large, grotesquely out-thrust ears.

In one and the same movement, Wade shut off the television mechanism and sprang across the hall. He jerked a blue automatic from a well-worn holster. Holding the gun ready he yanked open the apartment door and ran for the head of the stairs. He took them three at a time. In the street outside Wade got a glimpse of the man just turning the corner.

Wade raced ahead. He reached the corner and saw the man half a block away. For a moment he followed unseen and then the stranger turned his head. At once he began to run. Wade called to him to halt, and the man only ran faster.

He ducked sidewise like a scuttling rat, dodged into a doorway, and disappeared. Something glistened at once beside the frame. There was a flash, a barking report, and lead spanged close to Wade.

Wade flattened against the side of another building and moved nearer, risking the lead that spanged dangerously close again. Windows were squalling up in a dozen apartments. Frightened faces were peering down. Wade snapped a bullet toward the spot where the other's gun hand protruded and saw the gun snatched back. He pushed forward ten feet more and heard a sudden crash of glass. The big-eared man had broken the door behind him, was planning to make a getaway through the hall of the house he was in.

Wade threw caution to the winds and plunged ahead. He hurled himself into the doorway where the man had been, saw the smashed glass and a bobbing form beyond. He dropped flat as two bullets whined above him. He fired high purposely, not wanting to kill, and saw the man fling himself at another door in back. The door burst open and the man plunged through.

He slid down a flight of steps and ran like a deer across a yard. There was a tradesmen's alley on the other side. The man gave a spurt of speed and ran through this to the street beyond. Wade trailed him grimly, reaching the sidewalk only ten feet behind. The man turned desperately for one more shot.

A whistle shrilled at that instant close at hand. The patrolman on the block, who knew Wade by sight, came running up. Wade shouted an order but the officer was too excited to hear. He'd drawn his gun. When the big-eared man refused to stop, the officer fired straight from the hip, sending a bullet that doubled him up.

The man struck the pavement, sprawled and lay still. He was dead, a stain above his heart, when Wade Hammond came close. The excited officer was bending over him.

"I had to bump him, Mr. Hammond! He was trying to put the lug on you. He's a tough egg all right—look at them elephant ears! Who is he, do you know?"

Wade Hammond didn't answer for a moment. He was furious with the well-meaning cop whose shot had ended the stranger's flight—furious, and yet he couldn't speak—for the officer had only tried to save his life. He stooped, went through the man's clothing with expert hands, but found nothing to indicate the man was anything more than a homeless bum.

"Take charge of him, Murray," said Wade thickly. "I don't know who he is—he's your job now. But tell headquarters I said to have his pedigree looked up. Ask the inspector to give me a ring if anything's found about him."

The officer touched his cap. Wade turned away. His lips were still set. Dead men couldn't talk. There was nothing now except to see what the stranger had put into his box.

This proved to be a sealed envelope with no address. Wade returned to his apartment and opened the thing. There was a typewritten, single-spaced sheet inside. It said:

```
Dear Hammond:
    As a newspaper man with some ability in crime detection
you should be interested in the death of Judge Patrick
Willis.
    The press calls the thing an unfortunate accident—
but you should not.
    If you doubt it, have the animal's blood examined.
The exact nature of the drug that made the horse a
killer will be puzzling, but its presence should be
fairly easy to detect.
    For your information also, let me add that the judge
is only one of several who are soon to die. You yourself
are on the list. Richard Ross, who was formerly an able
district attorney in this city, will be the next to go.
To give the affair a sporting aspect, let me state that
Ross will meet his end before nine tonight. Knowing
your aptitude for crime prevention I trust that you
will do your best to save him.
```

There was no signature, but Wade stared aghast. This didn't sound like the ravings of a crank. It appeared to be the carefully thought-out message of a sinister and calculating brain.

In grim haste, Wade snatched up hat and coat and descended to the street again. This time he backed his powerful roadster out of its garage and whirled up a long avenue to the home of the city toxicologist, Doctor Bruno Gortz.

THEY found the carcass of the horse already loaded on a Department of Sanitation scow, waiting to be shipped off for incineration. Gortz drew a syringe from his pocket and thrust its needle point into a vein in the dead animal's neck. Wade Hammond began a grimly careful inspection of the whole carcass. He caught his breath at the end of two minutes, pulled a tiny bit of metal from the skin of the horse's flank.

It was no larger than a phonograph needle, but its end was hollow. Handling it gingerly, Wade passed the thing to Gortz. "Analyze that, too, doc," he said. "Call me at Attorney Richard Ross's and let me know what you find. I'll be at his office or at his home until nine tonight."

There was a chill along Wade Hammond's back as he turned away. The dart was grim proof that the murderous writer of the mysterious letter meant what he said.

Wade sped downtown to a modern twenty-story office building. He took an elevator to a luxurious suite which bore gilt lettering on its doors: "Ross, Hilary & Brown." He went directly to the office of the senior partner, where a thin man with a lean face and penetrating eyes sat behind a desk.

Richard Ross, in the role of district attorney, had spun deft webs of damning evidence that had snared a score of notorious murderers. He was a close friend of Wade's. Ross reached out a friendly hand to Wade Hammond, but his face was glum.

"You've heard of course about Judge Willis? Tough, wasn't it—and damned ironic, I'd say! He knew horses if ever any man did. He's ridden since he was a kid."

Wade Hammond nodded and drew the letter from his pocket. He opened it slowly, spread it out on Ross's desk. "Read that," he said.

He watched the other's face. Ross was a brave man, he knew. As a district attorney he had received many threats. Ross struck his desktop suddenly.

"It's crazy," he said. "It must be from some crank."

"I'd think so, too," said Wade, "except for things that have happened, and things I've seen. I looked over the horse with Gortz this morning. He's making an analysis of the blood for me now. There was some sort of dart in the horse's flank."

Ross rose from behind his desk and took a turn across the office.

"Any idea who this mad killer can be?"

Wade Hammond shook his head. "You and the judge and I," he said, "have all made enemies, Richard. The man has given us no clue here—except that he must have known the judge's habit. He might be any one of a hundred criminals that you helped to convict and the judge sentenced."

Ross answered with a sharp crackle that had often made witnesses tremble at the bar. "I can't be frightened by any such threat. If the man who sent that letter knows me as well as he apparently did the judge, he ought to realize that."

"I think he does," said Wade softly. "He's probably depending on it."

"Just what do you mean?"

"He knows you won't run away, Richard. He's counting on the fact that he can find you where he wants you."

Richard Ross let out a curse.

Wade Hammond rose and laid a friendly hand on Ross's shoulder. His tanned, hawklike face was grim. "The best protection for you is to do the unexpected, Ross. Leave town, drop everything and get out right away."

The lips of Attorney Ross clamped grimly. Stubbornly he shook his head. "I've got a big case on the fire, Wade. I can't leave it, and I won't. I won't run away any more than you would. But I'll admit the thing looks bad. So I'll take my briefs back to my house and stay there till after nine tonight, with a guard of a dozen men outside. Will that satisfy you?"

"It won't!" said Wade Hammond shortly. "Turn your place into a fort and I still won't be satisfied."

Ross was already filling a bulging satchel with briefs. "You can stay with me up to the fatal hour," he said lightly.

"You're right I'll stay with you," Wade retorted, "if you intend to be stubborn and stick around home."

Ross left instructions with his secretary that he would not return to the office that day, but could be reached at home. He picked up the phone, called headquarters, and asked that a special guard of a dozen detectives be placed in and about his house. He descended to the street, and Wade Hammond drove him directly home.

RICHARD ROSS, like Wade Hammond, was a bachelor. He lived in the big, old house he had inherited from his father. But where curios of all sorts lined the walls of Wade's apartment, musical instruments were Ross's hobby. He was an accomplished violinist, and played often in his spare time.

Detectives arrived shortly. Wade, at Ross's suggestion, took charge of them, ordering that no one in whatever guise or on whatever mission was to be admitted. He shut the blinds of all the windows. He had Ross send all the servants away till after nine o'clock.

There was a tingling, uneasy feeling along Wade Hammond's spine. While Ross bent over his briefs, Wade prowled like a cat around the house. He peered and poked into every cranny. When Ross reached for a jar of cigars, Wade snatched it from him. "No you don't, Richard! Don't touch anything in this house—understand? And I mean that literally. I'm going to make a trip out now for some supplies. We'll eat only what I bring in."

Wade left, went to a grocery ten blocks away, returned with a pile of canned goods, a box of cigars and toilet articles done up in cellophane. He even included a box of matches. He let the water run ten minutes from all the taps, and drank some himself before filling the pot of coffee.

The phone rang sharply just before lunch. It was Gortz.

"That was a job you handed me, Hammond," Gortz said. "The only stuff we've been able to isolate is trigonelline. That comes from Indian hemp, and it's no wonder the horse went crazy. There's something else mixed up with it that the boys can't label. If we find out what it is, I'll let you know."

Ross grumbled and grinned as they sat down for their lunch. "Canned stuff's all right," he said, "on a hunting trip. But it doesn't set so well at home. You're a hell of a cook, Hammond."

Wade Hammond didn't smile. His uneasiness had sharpened with Gortz's report. What Gortz had found verified the words of the letter. It was proof that the man who had killed Judge Willis had education and a cunning brain. There was no saying what fiendish method he had in mind to put an end to Ross. Wade Hammond spoke sharply.

"Your club might be safer than this. You could stay in a room there. I don't like it, Richard. This house is too big. There are too many things to think of."

Ross shrugged and shook his head. "Don't let it bother you, Hammond. We'll call his bluff. You've looked the place over thoroughly. Those dicks outside won't let anybody in."

Wade started to reply, then closed his lips grimly. He had had long experience of his friend's stubbornness.

Ross returned to his briefs. The detectives paced outside. Wade Hammond continued to prowl and the afternoon wore on. As evening shadows lengthened, Wade's sense of catastrophe increased.

Ross put down his briefs at last. He looked at his watch. "Six-thirty, Hammond. Two hours and a half to go." Ross began to pace impatiently, stretching his arms and legs. Wade stayed close, his brow drawn into an anxious frown, his nerves taut.

"I'm beginning to feel the suspense," Ross said suddenly. "I know now how a man must feel in the death house. I still think it may be a bluff—but that letter was damn businesslike!" He stopped and stared toward the musical instruments that ranged the wall—violins, violas, clarinets and flutes.

WADE HAMMOND drew out his black pipe and puffed tensely, thoughtfully. Ross walked suddenly to a corner of the room and lifted his violin case. "You don't mind, Wade. I'm a bit keyed up. Music always relaxes me. I'll knock off a few tunes."

Wade Hammond nodded slowly, then suddenly jumped forward.

"No, wait, Richard!"

"What the devil's the matter now?"

Wade took the violin case from his hands. "You haven't had it open yet today?"

"No."

"Stand back—I'll open the case."

He walked away from Ross, opened the case gingerly. He breathed with relief when only the violin showed.

Ross laughed shortly. "No bomb—no snakes! Here, let me have it." He reached for his fiddle, but Wade still held him back. He took the instrument out, examined every inch of it, paying particular attention to the rubber rest that went under the chin. He fingered the pegs and the bow, finally handed it reluctantly to Ross.

Ross took the violin lovingly. "Finest fiddle I've ever seen, Wade," he murmured as he tuned the strings. "With all the instruments I've collected, I don't think I've played on anything else for two years." He walked to a music stand, stopped suddenly and stared. His laugh was jerky.

"This is odd—only a coincidence, of course—but it sort of got me for a second."

He pointed with his bow to the face of the stand. A sheet of music lay open there—Saint-Saëns' *Danse Macabre*.

Wade Hammond scowled, drew in a hissing breath. But Ross shook his head. "Don't worry, it's my music. I play it sometimes, but I haven't touched it for a couple of weeks. The maid must have put it here when she was cleaning."

Wade Hammond stood tense and uneasy. Ross gave a nervous laugh. "Death!" he said. "This music seems appropriate—and here goes. Hope you don't mind, Wade. Tell me if it gets on your nerves."

CHAPTER III
Murder Music

GRIMLY, throwing his skill into it, Richard Ross drew the bow across the strings. His long fingers moved in the first jerky passage of the French composer's weird dance of death, the staccato notes that portray the clink and shuffle of skeleton feet.

Wade Hammond stood watching, tinglingly aware of the drama of the scene—a man playing a dance of death, while a death threat hung over his head. It was like Richard Ross, who had always been fearless and daring.

But tense as Wade was, he wasn't prepared for the thing that happened. In the first instant he hardly sensed the meaning of the sudden snap. He saw Ross leap back, heard him swear. Then he saw the gleaming thread of the metal E string that had broken close to the violin's nut. He saw the crimson streak like the line of a whip where the end of the string had cut Ross's cheek.

Ross put the violin down, laughed shakily. "It's nothing, Wade. I've had it happen a dozen times before. There's hardly a fiddler alive who hasn't been cut by a broken string. I—"

A sudden thickness came into Ross's speech. He turned his eyes queerly toward Wade, lifted his hand to his cheek.

"It feels—sort of numb. You don't suppose—"

Wade leaped to squeeze blood from the threadlike cut that the E string had made. But Richard Ross staggered back. He stumbled against the music stand and fell over with it. A sickly smile was twitching his lips. He spoke in a wheezing whisper.

"I get it now, Wade, old man—and you were right. I shouldn't—have touched the damned thing—the fiddle. String—poisoned. I—good luck, old man—and goodbye—"

Wade Hammond leaped to the side of his fallen friend. He loosened Ross's collar, felt for his pulse. He saw that life was fast leaking from Ross.

He picked the lawyer up as though he were a baby and made a swift dash for the door. Detectives stood back in open-eyed amazement.

"Don't touch anything," said Wade. "Don't let anyone in. Stay just as you are till I get back."

He ran to his parked roadster, laid Ross on the seat, and sent the long car roaring toward the nearest hospital. Interns came running out as he whirled up to the steps.

"Poison!" said Wade. "That scratch on his cheek. I don't know what kind it is—but in heaven's name do what you can."

Up in the white-tiled emergency room a doctor made a quick examination, pressing a stethoscope to Ross's chest. He turned somberly and shook his head. "Too late," he said. "This man's dead. What's his name, and who are you?"

For answer Wade Hammond flipped open his wallet and thrust his special investigator's card before the doctor's face. "Call headquarters," he snapped. "Have the medical examiner come. It's Attorney Richard Ross—and he's just been murdered."

Wade left the hospital with set, white lips. He returned to Ross's house and lifted the violin from the floor. The metal E string dangled like a tiny shimmering snake. Wade looked at the broken ends. There had been a small nick on the underside of the string just in front of the fingerboard nut. The vibration of the bow had made it break there at its weakest point.

It was ten minutes past eight. Fifty minutes still to go, and the murderer had achieved his awful end. Gortz would make an examination of the string as he had of the horse's blood; but another, different, quick-acting poison had obviously been used—planted there while Ross was out and without the servants seeing the intruder.

The phone rang as Wade walked toward it, planning to put all facts before Inspector Thompson, homicide squad head. He picked the instrument up, heard a muffled voice whisper in the receiver. "Good evening, Hammond!"

The voice was low-pitched, disguised obviously, yet it stirred vague memories in Wade's mind. "Who's this?" he asked.

"You'll find it hard to place me, Hammond. It's been a long time since we met. But you received a letter from me this morning—brought by a messenger who was—accidentally killed. Congratulate me on my victory in our little game with Richard Ross. Your flying trip to the hospital was evidence that my play won."

Blood beat hammer blows in Wade Hammond's temples. His knuckles circling the phone grew hard and white. He clenched his teeth against the fierce words that rose to his lips. He listened tensely as the strange voice continued.

"I won't introduce myself," it said. "There'd be little point in that. Shortly you will die. Perhaps, just before the end, we shall have the pleasure of meeting face to face. Meanwhile your puzzlement will be amusing."

Wade Hammond held in leash the tumult of fury in his brain. He made his voice harshly ironic. He said, "I'm not worrying who you are. I know you're a yellow, third-rate killer afraid to show his shadow. A slab is waiting for you in the police morgue. You'll be on it soon."

Wade laughed into the dead silence that followed his words, putting into it all the grating contempt he could muster. He spoke again in a tone of jeering insult. "You were afraid to give me more than a few hours to meet your play with Ross. You had the trap already set. Now you're too cowardly even to tell me whom you plan to murder next."

The silence continued for a moment longer. Then a voice choked with fury came from the receiver.

"Fool! Liar! I'm not afraid of you or the police!"

"No?"

"No! Meigan will die next! Meigan, a servant who—"

The voice ceased abruptly, as the man realized he'd been baited too far by Wade Hammond's scorn. Wade Hammond breathed a name: "Brian Suttner!"

THERE was no answer. The phone clicked up. Wade stood in taut-faced wonder. He knew now with whom he had to deal. Brian Suttner had killed a man in a homicidal fury and Wade had helped send him to jail for life. Meigan had been Suttner's butler and had testified at the trial to his master's fits of temper. There had been a prison fire, in which Suttner was thought to have died. But Suttner had returned with a raging devil in his soul, as though the flames of the fire had branded him with the marks of hell.

Wade Hammond clenched his fist. He remembered suddenly that Suttner had a sister, a Mrs. Valerie Elston now, who had inherited his money. Would she know that her brother had come back?

A sudden unpleasant thought occurred to Wade. Brian Suttner fancied himself the master player in a game of hideous death. Wade had forced a furious admission from him, at which Suttner's better judgment would rebel. If Valerie knew that her brother still lived, she, as a possible witness against him, had been placed in a position of mortal danger.

Wade didn't stop to give orders to the men. He flung down the steps of Ross's house to his roadster and whirled away.

He held the horn button down, cutting madly through traffic. He whirled up before a handsome brick-front house and leaped to the curb.

When no one answered the bell he pressed it again. Then he caught his breath and held his body tense. For a wild scream sounded. It came from somewhere behind the big front door. It held in it a note of quavering, ghastly terror.

Wade's face went white. He reached in his pocket, took out his skeleton keys. The lock gave quickly. He opened the door and plunged into the hall.

At once he stumbled and almost fell as his foot struck something. He looked down, cursed. The limp body of a maid lay at his feet. Her mouth was open. Her breathing was labored. There was a livid bruise on the side of her face. Wade drew his gun and ran toward the landing of the big front stairs.

He heard the scream again, cut off as though fingers had clasped across a throat or a blow had descended. It came from somewhere above. He took the stairs three at a time and reached a hall. A child was crying close by, moving restlessly in its crib. A door slammed directly in front of Wade at the end of the long upper corridor. He jerked the door open, stared down another flight of stairs to the servants' quarters, and flung himself sidewise suddenly as gun flame lanced below.

Bullets sped close to his shoulder, missing him by bare inches. He squatted, peered around the frame of the door and saw movement close to the stair bottom. He raised his gun for an answering shot, but instantly hesitated.

A weird, black-hooded figure with slitted eyes malevolently bright was carrying Mrs. Elston down. The hooded man was using the girl's body as a human shield. His gun was thrust around her, ready to spray death. It was Suttner, Wade knew, come to make sure that his sister didn't talk. He was taking her away with him to cover up his hideous trail of death.

Wade Hammond sent a bullet screaming close to the murderer's head. Flame flickered again as Suttner fired up the stairs. Lead gnawed the door frame at Wade Hammond's side. He risked a second shot, firing low, close to the level of the stairs, aiming at the killer's feet, briefly visible below the girl's skirt.

The nerve of Brian Suttner broke at that. Wade's shooting was deadly. Suttner dropped his sister suddenly, whisked out of sight around the stair bottom, raced thuddingly away. Wade Hammond leaped down the stairs as the door leading to the short kitchen hallway slammed shut.

He stepped over the body of the girl, ran to the door and found that it was locked. Bullets slashed through the panels in a savage volley as he started to probe with a skeleton key. He jumped aside and fired blindly. The fusillade on the other aide stopped. He heard running feet. Then another door slammed somewhere farther away.

Clenching his gun, Wade lowered his shoulder and hurled himself at the door. It shook but it did not give. He beat a panel out with the muzzle of his gun, reached through and snapped back the lock. But an auto engine growled into life in a street behind the house. He heard the car whine away, knew that the black-hooded killer had made good his escape.

WADE returned quickly to the girl. She had fainted. He picked her up, carried her to a couch in the living room and put her down. The maid in the hallway hadn't stirred. A dull thumping sounded from somewhere above. It was rhythmic, ghostly. Wade traced the noise, climbing the stairs again, and cautiously approached the door of a closet. He jerked it open, holding his gun ready.

Inside a man was pounding feebly with his heels against the floor. He was pale, bruised. The man was Douglass Elston. Wade got water and sluiced it over his face.

Elston sat up, opened his eyes, struggled weakly to his feet. "Valerie!" he gasped. "Where is she—and who are you?"

"Mrs. Elston's fainted," said Wade quickly. "She's downstairs. She'll be all right." He showed his badge.

"Do you know the address of a man named Meigan—a servant who used to work for your wife's brother?"

"Yes, but that man who came wasn't Meigan. He was a bandit, I tell you." So Valerie hadn't shared her secret, Wade decided.

"Give me Meigan's address!" Wade's voice was harsh, cutting into Elston's fear-stricken daze.

Elston went to a rolltop desk, fumbled through it, drew out a black book at last, said, "Here we are."

Wade made mental note of Meigan's street and number and turned away. He hoped that speed would spoil Brian Suttner's plans. He hoped he could save the third victim from being killed. But if the house where Meigan lived was Suttner's objective, Suttner already had a start.

Wade sped across town to the address that Elston had given him. He drew up before an old-fashioned residence in a rundown residential section. A plump, red-haired woman answered his impatient ring. Wade fired a question at her quickly. "Does a Mr. Meigan live here?"

The woman nodded. "That's my husband. He left a moment ago."

"Do you know where he went?"

"Yes, it's stamps again!" the woman said in an impatient tone.

"Stamps?"

She nodded. "My husband collects them, and a man with some to sell came just now. He got Tom to go back with him to his store to look them over."

"Is stamp collecting your husband's biggest hobby?" asked Wade abruptly.

Again the woman nodded. "It keeps him so busy now that he doesn't work. He's just like a kid about it."

Wade stared at her fixedly. "What sort of a man was this fellow who had the stamps?"

"He had scars on his face—looked as if he'd been in an accident. Wait. He left an address. He told me someone else might come along who'd be interested in stamps, too. I guess you're the man he had in mind."

Wade didn't answer. The whole devilish murder pattern was apparent now. Suttner used the hobby of each of his victims to bring about his death. Horses had been the judge's hobby—and a horse had slain him. Ross had been stricken down through his favorite hobby—music. Now a passion for stamp collecting was taking Meigan to his doom.

The woman returned with a slip of paper which Wade Hammond took. Now Suttner was using his hobby of crime investigation to lure Hammond to his death.

He thanked the woman and turned away. Suttner had thrown him a challenge which he couldn't ignore. To call the police would be futile on Wade's part. Suttner would be watching and would get away. If Wade hoped to meet the murderer face to face, he must go alone.

Speeding away from Mrs. Meigan's house, Wade suddenly stopped his roadster. His lips were grimly set. He entered a drugstore and made a purchase—a pint of pure grain alcohol, which he asked the clerk to put in a thin glass bottle.

He slipped the bottle into his coat. It seemed a strange thing to buy at such a time. He drove on through the night to the address that Meigan's wife had given him.

It was an empty store on a narrow, waterfront street. No light showed behind the dusty panes. His nerves tingled as he stepped inside the unlocked door. He was walking straight into the jaws of a trap.

THE store was narrow. There were empty shelves, a dusty counter, a door behind. Wade moved toward this. The rough, hard butt of his automatic was cold beneath his hand. He was ready to fight, but doubted if Suttner would give him any chance. If he lived through the next half-hour, wits, not bullets would save him.

He pushed open the door behind the store's counter, entered a hallway where his cautious feet made echoes. He stabbed his light along it, saw tracks in the thick dust at his feet. They led past two doors that opened to the left. They continued straight on toward a black cavern in the corridor that marked the bottom of a flight of stairs.

The tracks turned to the right onto the bottom landing. Wade followed while his sense of danger deepened. Suttner had him at a disadvantage now. Suttner could strike whenever he wanted to in whatever way he chose.

Wade drew in a sudden hissing breath as something came down out of the darkness of the stairs. He sent his light up, lifted his gun, but sensed in the instant he did so that it was futile. Smothering cloth descended over his head. Blankets tied together in a vast tangling square fell in folds that snared his arms with their smothering weight. He fired through the thick fabric, but tripped and went down. He lashed out fiercely with hands and feet, playing the role that Suttner would expect.

A blinding light glimmered before his eyes as a hard something struck his head. He toppled sidewise, sank into a vast black void.

He came to minutes later with the sound of Suttner's voice in his ears. Suttner was standing before him with the black hood over his face. Wade found that he was bound hand and foot in a heavy chair.

It was a small room that he was in, with shelves around the walls. There were rows of gleaming jars and bottles on the shelves. This must be where Suttner distilled his deadly poisons.

"Hammond," said Suttner. "We meet again face to face after all these years. You came—just as I thought you would."

Wade stared, silent, tense, his head aching from the blow he had received, and Suttner lifted the black hood from his own head and shoulders. The scarred and crinkled features, the hideous grin came into view.

"You see how the fire has changed me!" Suttner said harshly. He laughed then, like a gloating devil. He waved his hands toward the bottles. "All men have their hobbies—mine are these. Poisons, Hammond—poisons to create any effect I choose." He picked up a small brown bottle, held it before Wade's face. "Did you ever hear of the black poison that the Winnipeg Indians use? It turns a man's face yellow, copper, then black. It makes hair grow in unexpected places. I intend to try this on you. It is slower than some of the others."

"What have you done to Meigan?" said Wade hoarsely. His eyes were upon the hideous face of Suttner. He wondered now if he had overplayed his hand, lost the chance he had gambled on to win.

Suttner gestured toward the door behind which weird howls sounded.

"My place of experiment, Hammond. I have dogs in there. I try my poisons on them. Meigan is in an empty cage with an injection of rare toxin in his blood. He may take several days to die. Meanwhile he will have time to think how he betrayed his master."

Suttner's scarred face was twitching. "*Rhus Toxicodendron,*" he said again. "The black poison will do strange things to your skin. You will be uglier than I."

THERE was a coldness along Wade Hammond's scalp. Suttner had gone to a low table, the brown bottle in his hands. He drew the cork, lifted a gleaming syringe and thrust the point of it into the bottle's neck. Wade Hammond stared about him. The contents of his pockets were on a shelf nearby. His gun was there, his wallet, some loose coins and his keys, together with the bottle of alcohol he had bought on his way. Wade spoke abruptly.

"You're afraid of me, Suttner. You knock me out, disarm me, and even tie my hands and feet. Give me a smoke, Suttner—just one cigarette before you try your black poison on me."

Suttner was holding the syringe in his hand. A sudden gleam of malevolent cunning came into his eye. He put the syringe down, said: "You remind me that

I am a gentleman, and your host. You shall have your cigarette."

Wade watched him furtively. Suttner passed by Wade's own package of cigarettes lying on the shelf. He went to a small tin box in a cabinet and took one out, fingering it lovingly. He put it down a moment, approached Wade and loosened the rope around his right wrist.

"You can get it free now," he said. "Take your cigarette."

Suttner had picked up Wade's gun in his left hand. With his right he held out the cigarette and a match to Wade. The look of crafty malevolence still gleamed in his eyes. Wade Hammond was tense. He had caught the drift of Suttner's subtle cunning. This cigarette held some sort of poisonous torture. Wade spoke again, gesturing with his free right hand toward the shelf where his own belongings were.

"Another thing, Suttner! You speak of rare toxins and poisons that are your hobby—but I've brought you a poison that is as efficient as any. That bottle there, Suttner. Perhaps you'd like to know what it is."

Suttner smiled knowingly.

"Bluff won't work, Hammond. I examined everything I took from your pockets. Alcohol is all that the bottle contains."

"I thought you were smarter than that, Suttner. I didn't think you'd be fooled by appearances when it came to your own craft. There's a way of turning that alcohol into poison."

Interest showed on Suttner's face. Wade continued:

"I wouldn't have told you if circumstances had been different. I had a plan in mind. But—it hardly matters now."

"You are right—it hardly matters—to you. But I don't believe you, anyway. Light your cigarette."

Wade Hammond put the cigarette between his lips. But before striking the match he held his hand palm upward.

"If you think I'm lying, Suttner, bring the bottle here. Pour a drop on my skin."

Suttner hesitated, stared at Wade keenly, gripped the automatic in his fingers. "Fool, I'll call your bluff!" he muttered.

He picked up the bottle, uncorked it, sniffed at it, and approached Wade again cautiously. Standing at arm's length, he held the bottle's neck over Wade's hand, and spilled a few drops onto his skin, peering down tensely. "See, nothing happens! You are a liar, Hammond."

As quick as a striking snake, Wade Hammond moved. His hand flicked upward, knocked the bottle from Suttner's fingers. It dropped with a crash to the floor and alcohol spilled at Suttner's feet. Wade Hammond's fingernail slid across the match. As it snapped into flame he flung it downward.

There was a hiss, a glow of blue light. Suttner gave a terrified cry. He leaped away and alcohol flames crawled up his legs like twisting devils.

Wade Hammond desperately freed his other hand. The flames of the spilled alcohol were crawling toward him. He swung his body sideways in his chair and toppled it with him. Suttner was cursing, crying out, beating at the flames. There was a look of desperate terror in his eyes.

WADE pulled at the ropes that held his legs, loosed them with frantic fingers. He kicked out of the chair, plunged straight toward the flames where his gun, dropped from Suttner's fingers, lay. The metal was hot in his hand as he picked it up. Suttner, mouthing fury and terror, glimpsed his action and snatched up another gun. He blazed at Wade Hammond, and Wade fired calmly, sending two shattering pellets of lead into Suttner's arm.

Suttner dropped the gun, plunged toward Wade Hammond. He went down, screaming and cursing, with another bullet in his leg.

Wade pulled him away from the heat of the flames, drew him toward the side of the room. He spoke harshly:

"I was right, Suttner, alcohol to anyone else, but poison to you—because flame is the one thing you fear. I figured that out when I bought it, Suttner, and believed your vanity would give me a chance to try out the experiment. You wanted to meet me face to face so you could gloat. Well, you did—and I turned your own hobby of collecting poisons against you. I didn't kill you just now for only one reason. You're going to tell me what kind of stuff you used on Meigan so I can save him."

Tracks were cleared that night for the railroad magnate's special—but death caught up with the train. Death—and Wade Hammond. And when Hammond, reporter-detective, boarded that train, he ran up against wholesale murder. For a killer had vanished, leaving only corpses for clues. But when Hammond tried to track the murderer—he was heading straight for a berth in hell.

The Terror Train

CHAPTER I
Masked Murder

SLOWLY, stealthily, the crouching figure of a man crept through the aisle of the special train toward the private stateroom of J.P. Kelly.

His shadow bulked hugely. He stole past the doors of closed compartments, stooped and flattened himself against a lurching wall. A mask of gray gum rubber covered his face, giving his features a corpselike pallor. Behind it, his eyes were alive with menace. A gun with a silencer on it jutted from one gloved hand.

Up front, the train's big locomotive smashed the darkness with the lunging impact of a steel-mailed fist. Its headlight thrust a silver spearhead through the night. Its whistle screeched like a wild thing across the low Connecticut hills as it sped onward at a seventy-mile-an-hour clip. Even the night express had been sidetracked to let it pass. J.P. Kelly, maker and breaker of vast corporations, whose name was a byword in American homes, and whose flat-crowned derby and black cigar were familiar sights in half the capitals of Europe, had the right of way.

A dozen plainclothes men, alert and nervous, rode in the forward section of the car. Another nearby section was devoted to Kelly's clerical and legal staff. They, too, were tense, uneasy, grim.

Directly outside Kelly's door an armed guard was posted, a private detective from one of the biggest Boston agencies, specially hired for a special job. But, as he turned his head, unaware of his danger, the creeping, sinister figure of the masked man drew close.

Inside the private compartment, J.P. Kelly sat. He looked every inch what the newspapers dubbed a "man of iron." His big shoulders were sloped forward in a fighting hunch. His jaw was out-thrust, rocky. The fist that seemed made to grab and hang onto money was hooked around a fat cigar. A scowl creased his broad, low forehead, housing a brain which could figure out foreign discounts and compound interest down to the smallest decimal dot. He faced a younger, sharp-featured man who spoke with a touch of rancor.

"I don't quite get you, Mr. Kelly. Why bring in this fellow Hammond when you've already hired me and my boys to do the job? Too many cooks will spoil the broth, they say—and too many dicks will make a mess of the case and run your bill sky-high."

J.P. Kelly answered in a voice so soft it gave an impression of explosive power held in leash. "Wade Hammond doesn't take fees, Swinton. You ought to know that. He's a globetrotting newspaper man by trade. He dabbles in crime analysis only because he likes it. But he's rated as one of the smartest unlicensed detectives in the country. And I happen to know him socially. That's why I've wired him to meet the train."

Luke Swinton displayed a gold-toothed smile. "Give me a chance, boss, that's all I'm asking. I can look out for you okay."

"Maybe," said Kelly grimly, "but it won't hurt to have Wade Hammond in on it, too. I expect to step on a lot of people's toes when I testify against the bucket-shop* crowd before the Senate committee tomorrow. I didn't think, though, that it would be considered cause for murder and extortion. Hammond will do his best to get at the bottom of this thing. He'll try to find out who's making these threats against my life and demanding money. I got two warning letters, as you know, in Boston. And my nephew, Gerald Herd, received one in New York. I've asked him to meet the train at Norwalk junction along with Hammond. Hammond won't interfere with your work. See that you don't interfere with his."

Luke Swinton gave a helpless shrug. "You're the boss, Mr. Kelly. But I've nosed out crooks myself in my time, and I still can't figure why you need Wade Hammond. I—"

He stopped as a faint sound came from outside the compartment; a thud, followed by an eerie scratching as though a fingernail were being drawn across a panel. The door opened an instant later softly, and a harsh cry came from Luke Swinton's lips. His eyes bulged out. He leaped from his chair. Swiftly, mechanically, his hand streaked toward the lower right-hand pocket of his coat.

But the long barrel of the silenced gun in the door gave out a puff of vapor. The masked man stood behind it, his face corpselike, evil.

The sickening smack of the bullet against Swinton's flesh was audible above the dull cough of the gun. It struck Swinton just over the heart and seemed to hammer him back. His half-drawn gun dropped to the floor from nerveless

---

* A fraudulent brokerage.

fingers. His mouth opened and closed like that of a dying fish. Slowly his knees gave way beneath him, and he slipped to the floor in a crumpled heap beside the narrow table.

Kelly hadn't risen. He sat staring stonily at the masked murderer who had come into his stateroom.

The masked man was silent as he advanced. He left open the door behind him, and visible in the aisle were the head and shoulders of the detective whom he had shot before entering. The masked killer drew an envelope from his pocket and flung it in one gloved hand on the table before J.P. Kelly. With the other hand, likewise gloved, he pressed the trigger of the gun quickly again, turning the muzzle a fraction between each shot.

Again lead struck flesh in nauseous *spats*. Kelly's big body quivered. He gave a guttural gasp of pain. For a second he closed his eyes, then opened them to stare stonily once more at the masked, murderous figure before him.

Keeping the silenced gun thrust forward, the killer backed from the stateroom door and closed it.

For an instant Kelly sat in stunned, pain-racked silence. Then he lifted himself heavily from his seat, dangling two broken arms where the masked fiend's bullets had struck, and moved toward the door, his coat sleeves soggy with crimson.

Before he reached it he was thrown against the wall. The airbrakes of the special train slammed on. A giant force seemed to clutch and grind at its wheels as steel shoes gripped them. Someone had pulled the emergency cord and the train was stopping.

AT Norwalk junction Wade Hammond bent his face into the wind-driven mist and fumed. He had raced out of the city in his low-slung roadster. He had come like a servant to meet the special train in answer to Kelly's wire—not because he worshipped Kelly's money, but because he had a sneaking respect for Kelly as a man. Now the special was late, already five minutes overdue according to the schedule Kelly had given.

Wade scowled and paced and sucked at his black pipe.

He turned abruptly as the rumble of a powerful motor sounded and a long, high-priced car with the lines of a racer swung smoothly into the station drive. It whirled up to the platform and a young, eager-faced, dark-haired man leaped out. He walked up to Wade quickly, said in an excited voice: "I'm Herd—J.P. Kelly's nephew. You must be the detective he said was to meet the train."

Wade Hammond nodded. "Yes. Your uncle sent me a wire. Hammond's my name. Something seems to be the matter. I don't know just what."

A whistle shrieked far down the track, cutting through the night-time silence. A moment later the bright headlight of the special picked out Wade and Herd as it rounded the curve. Hammond stood beside the rails, tall and soldierly in his battered trench coat and turned-down hat. Light played over his lean, clean-cut face, his hawk nose, and the threadlike mustache close to the edge of his upper lip that added grimness to a faintly humorous mouth.

There was a debonair quality in his movements as he swung his shoulders and stepped back. Wade Hammond had seen adventure in the far places of the earth. In the Banana republics with their broiling, sweltering sun. In the white North, and in distant Malayan jungles. His press work had taken him into spots so hot that he had learned to pack a gun. His taste for lurid action had led him into many kinds of trouble. In recent years he had taken an unofficial part in some of the most bizarre homicide cases in the country.

The train began to grind to a stop and Wade and Herd strode toward it. Then they stopped abruptly. Even before the wheels ceased turning two men stepped down from a forward door. They lit stiff-legged on the cinders, turned their heads his way. One glance at their faces told Wade Hammond something was wrong.

He hurried toward them, recognized one as an agency man from Boston, a former police lieutenant by the name of Stull.

Wade came to a stop before them and peered into their fear-darkened eyes. "I'm Hammond," he said. "J.P. wired me to come. What's up? You men look scared."

Words came in a rush from Stull's trembling lips. His voice was croaking. "Plenty's up! Swinton and two of us are dead—murdered—and Kelly's been shot. Both arms broken. We've got to get hold of a doctor and notify the cops."

Young Herd gave a gasping cry, while Wade's tight face hid the surprise he felt. Kelly wouldn't have called him if there hadn't been something big afoot. But he hadn't expected this—wholesale murder. He drew out a bunch of keys, said: "Take these and use my car. It's over there. The station's closed and the village is on the other side of the hill."

Stull gave the keys to his younger colleague and the man sped off. There were beads of sweat on Stull's forehead in spite of the nighttime chill. He said in a trembling tone: "I'm glad you came, Hammond. With Swinton dead we don't know where we're at. Come into the car, and you, too, Mr. Herd. Kelly will want to see you."

CHAPTER II
Sinister Flight

WADE HAMMOND was silent as he followed the detective up the car steps. Fear, he saw, had gripped its passengers. It had become a terror train. The men he passed in the forward section looked dazed, nerveless. These were more private detectives from Swinton's office. Stull was the only one of them who seemed to have any self-possession left. He led Wade grimly on toward Kelly's stateroom.

Outside the door two bodies lay under a blanket. The floor was dark and wet with crimson. Stull shuddered, gestured toward one of the bodies, croaked:

"That's Hagan. Shot in the back—never knew what happened. Swinton was killed inside—right through the heart. We brought him out here. Joe Tracy's on the back platform, dead, too. The killer got him just before he pulled the emergency cord and jumped."

Wade barked a question. "Who was he? Any idea?"

Stull shook his head. "No. Mr. Kelly says he was masked. He must have been hiding on board, waiting to do his job when we pulled out of Boston. That's the only explanation. But it's beyond me. We searched the train before we started—and we haven't stopped anywhere along the line. All the way we've been hitting it up plenty, too."

"When did all this happen?"

"Not more than ten minutes ago, I guess. None of us knew a thing about it till the brakes went on and we heard Mr. Kelly call. Then I came and saw Hagan here dead."

Wade started to follow Herd into Kelly's stateroom, but stopped with a frown. Stull seemed a little vague about the time of the murders. It was an important point that would come up later. Wade thought he'd better check.

He stooped, drew the blanket away from Hagan's face, and looked at his lips. Wade Hammond was no doctor, but he'd watched enough medical examiners at work to learn some tricks. He felt Hagan's still wrist and nodded. There was some warmth left, and the last traces of color hadn't quite fled from the dead man's lips. Ten minutes was a pretty good guess. He examined Swinton and came to the same conclusion. He rose, stalked through the aisle to look at Tracy and verify his checkup. Stull dazedly followed.

The man who'd been posted at the train's rear platform was still slumped just as he had fallen; a look of surprise on his unmoving face, as though death were the last thing he'd expected.

"Through the heart, too," said Stull bleakly. "He tried to stop the killer from getting off and paid for it with his life."

Wade nodded, bent, and stared for a full five seconds. Then suddenly his fingers shot forward and gripped Tracy's wrist. A shudder passed through him. Tracy's flesh was perceptibly colder than Hagan's had been. The outside air of the platform wasn't enough to explain it. Tracy's lips were whiter, too, bloodless.

Wade lifted his eyes to Stull and spoke harshly. "You're wrong, man. Tracy here didn't get bumped off when that killer was leaving. He was shot first—even before Hagan got it!"

Detective Stull cursed and drew a big hand across his sweating forehead. "That changes things, I guess—and it beats me, Hammond."

Wade Hammond nodded, said: "Right! It changes things, and now I'm going to talk to Kelly."

He half expected to find the wounded banker in a state bordering on collapse. But J.P. Kelly was sitting in a chair in his stateroom, straight and grim, the inevitable black cigar clamped between his lips. "Hello, Hammond," he said. "You got here. Thanks."

Kelly closed his eyes in pain for a moment, but his jaw had a fighting tilt.

A girl with honey-colored hair and a marble-white face stood close to Kelly. She had torn up a bed sheet and wrapped it around his arms to staunch the flow of blood. An older man, hatchet-faced, his eyes dark with fear behind rimless glasses, was leaning helplessly against a table. Kelly nodded toward them both.

"Meet Miss Archer, my secretary, Hammond; and Walsh, my lawyer. Jerry, you've already met. Grace here's trying to play the part of nurse, and doing a good job of it. Walsh, get me another cigar and light it. Then all of you keep still while I talk to Hammond."

Wade came closer and stood by the end of the table, rubbing the bowl of his black pipe against the bridge of his nose. He watched Kelly snap off the end of the cigar that Walsh held out; watched the girl, Grace Archer, bend above the crude bandages on Kelly's arms. Herd stood helplessly by, concerned gaze on his uncle.

Hammond noticed that the girl's neck was rigid, her hands trembling violently, while the smooth round of her young cheek was as white as plaster. She was holding up like a thoroughbred, but she was scared.

Kelly breathed a mouthful of smoke and said in a harsh voice: "I guess you don't know exactly why I called you, Hammond. I couldn't say much in my wire. But take a look at that." He nodded toward a letter lying before him opened on the table. Wade picked it up. It said:

> What happened tonight will teach you a lesson, Kelly. You wouldn't listen to us in Boston. You forced our hand.
>
> Don't think we'll let you testify before the Senate. A lot of us don't like it—and if you try to go to Washington you'll never get there alive. That's final. The next time you'll get a bullet through the heart. And, because you've already made us lose a lot of money, you've got to pay. Stay over in New York. Get five hundred grand in cash out of your bank and go to your place in the suburbs. Stay there till we get in touch with you and tell you how to hand it over.

WADE HAMMOND put the letter down, and Kelly spoke. "A lot of folks," he said, "think I'm a hard man—a dollar chaser, a nickel squeezer, and all the rest of it. I admit I'm tough, but I play a straight game and stick to the rules. I've never tried to unload watered stock on the public, or rob widows and orphans. That's what some of them have been doing, and it's why the Senate wants my testimony on some of the fine points of stock transactions. They know I won't be afraid to tell the truth. But someone's trying to stop me and make me hand over a chunk of money besides. Jerry, show Hammond the letter they sent you."

It was on the same order as Kelly's. "If your uncle goes to Washington," it said, "we'll get you, too. Neither of you has a chance. For your own sake see that he doesn't testify."

"They didn't ask for money," said Kelly grimly, "because they know he's always broke. Spends every cent he has on his damn racing cars. And if they think Jerry here can stop me they're crazy. He'll have to run the same risk as I do. Are you man enough to take it, Jerry?"

Herd flushed and was silent. Wade said: "A man who can handle racing cars should be pretty hard to scare." Then Wade turned to Kelly. "What are you going to do?"

"Do! I'm going to stop over in my apartment in New York, get these arms fixed up, and straighten out a few things so that if I'm killed it won't make my executors too much trouble. Then I'm going on to Washington and appear before the Senate in the morning."

Wade Hammond started to answer, but stopped as a sudden noise came through the stateroom panel. He saw Grace Archer jump.

"What's that?" cried Walsh excitedly. "Sounds like a shot!"

Wade Hammond had already identified the noise. A window somewhere in the car had been slammed shut. He turned, yanked open the door into the aisle and ran to the car's rear platform. Leaning across the body of Tracy, he thrust his head out into the darkness until a faint crunch of shoes on cinders sounded on the side opposite from the station.

Wade instantly vaulted the brass observation rail, landing beside the tracks. He leaped ahead, and halfway down the length of the car a running figure struck him, knocking his flashlight from his hand. A man gave a smothered, angry cry and arms beat furiously against Wade's body.

Wade grappled, lurched toward the car and struck his head. It was a stiff blow, making lights dance before his eyes. But he kept his grip. The man he held began struggling desperately, silently now, fighting as though his life depended on getting away. He hunched his shoulders downward, tried to butt Wade with his head. His heavy overcoat dulled the force of the blows Wade Hammond struck. Wade twisted, sought to get in an uppercut with his right fist to the other's jaw. He felt the stranger sway a moment. Then something struck the side of Wade's face with a smack like a piece of plank. It wasn't a hand. It was something hard and smooth and heavy. The full force of it was close to his temple, making his ear ring, dazing him.

He reached up, clutched the heavy thing, hanging on with a deathlike grip to make sure the blow wouldn't be repeated. With another smothered cry the man suddenly let go and fled. Wade Hammond was left alone, hanging onto an oblong something which he couldn't see in the darkness. With his flashlight gone, pursuit of the man was futile.

He struck a match, groped around among the cinders, and recovered his light. Then he saw what he had got in the struggle—a bulging briefcase stuffed, apparently, with letters.

He swung the light in a quick arc, but saw no movement. Someone called to him from the car, then, and Wade retraced his steps. Detective Stull was peering anxiously down from the back platform.

"What is it, Hammond? What's going on out there?"

Wade's lean face went blank. He held the briefcase easily, as though it were his own. Lithely he reached up, grasped the car railing and drew himself back on board. He brushed moisture from his coat, straightened his tie. "It was nothing much," he said. "I thought I heard a noise and jumped down to take a look."

"A window somewhere in the car slid down," Stull said. "The doctor's just come. He's inside fixing Mr. Kelly. The Norwalk constable wasn't home, but Swinton's man phoned the Stamford police and they're coming."

Wade grunted. His eyes were ranging quickly along the aisle on the side where he'd had his fight. "Who stays in those compartments, Stull?" he snapped.

"The first two are for guests," Stull answered. "They're empty now. That one beyond, just across from Kelly's door, is Miss Archer's. The next one's a file room, and the next is Mr. Walsh's. There's one more beyond that, empty. It belonged to Walsh's assistant, a fellow they fired in Boston."

"Fired? What was his name?"

"I don't know. Walsh will tell you. Swinton had all those rooms searched before we left Boston. They were empty, alright."

"Didn't he look in the others?"

"Not in Walsh's and the girl's. They've been with Kelly years."

"Thanks, Stull. Tell Kelly I'll be in in a minute. And there's not much good waiting for the Stamford police. They'll only hold us up. It will take a lot of figuring anyway to find out what county those murders happened in."

Wade Hammond opened the first of the empty staterooms and stepped inside. It was fitted up more luxuriously than any Pullman. A thick rug on the floor. Mahogany furniture. Reading lamps and a shelf of books. He glanced at the window and saw that it was locked on the inside. Undisturbed dust on the sill showed that it hadn't been opened.

With a grim frown creasing his forehead, Wade Hammond stepped under an electric bulb and opened the briefcase he had captured. It was filled with letters, papers, a dozen typewritten briefs. All the letters were addressed to one "Mark Kendall." The miscellaneous papers also bore that name and the same address. The briefs told him little, except that some of them dealt with cases in which J.P. Kelly figured.

Wade stepped out of the empty stateroom and examined the one next to it. That, too, was undisturbed, the window locked. He came into the aisle again, looked along it, and tried the door of the compartment belonging to Kelly's secretary, Grace Archer. It was locked.

Quickly Wade Hammond reached for the special bunch of keys he carried in an inside pocket. He had given his others to Swinton's man to drive the car. These he only used occasionally. They were skeletons, and one special key of his own devising, an adjustable gadget which would fit any lock tumblers. In a moment he had the door open and had entered.

It was a neat stateroom, narrower than those for the guests and not quite as luxurious, but still snug and attractive. A few feminine touches were visible to Wade. Knickknacks on the miniature dresser, a pair of high-heeled slippers under the berth. A small vase of flowers.

He moved quickly to the window and gave an almost soundless ejaculation. The catch on the inside, that held the window up when it was raised, had been wedged with paper, making it possible for a person on the outside to push the window down. There were finger marks along the sill. Obviously, this was the window which had made the gun-like crash. With the catch wedged it had dropped more forcefully than someone had anticipated.

Wade left it as it was, straightened his lean body, and suddenly turned his flashlight off. A key had grated against metal. An instant later the door of the stateroom opened and against its lighted oblong he saw the slim figure of Grace Archer.

CHAPTER III
Bullet Greeting

SHE came in and closed the door before pressing the light button. Then she gave a startled, throaty gasp, her eyes riveted on Wade. There was a look on her face which hadn't been visible even in Kelly's compartment; a look of abject terror. One slim hand rose and fluttered against her throat, fingers nervously curling. Wade spoke quietly, watching her every move.

"I'm sorry I had to do this, Miss Archer—enter behind your back. But I had a reason for wanting to search through all the staterooms on this side of the car."

She stood silent, staring at him.

Wade pointed to the window. "That catch has been wedged, Miss Archer. It looks as though someone in here left that way. I'm hoping you can tell me who it was."

Grace Archer shook her head, her eyes still fixed and bright with fear.

Wade brought the briefcase from behind his back and held it out. "Who's Mark Kendall?"

Breath came from between her bloodless lips in a sharp gasp. Her eyes moved and focused on the briefcase with horrified fascination.

"Better come clean," Wade said patiently. "I had a fight with a man outside—after he'd climbed out of your window. There are letters and papers in this showing his name was Kendall. Considering what's happened on this train tonight it's enough to have him indicted for murder. If you know anything about him you'd better spill it."

The girl's hands clenched; she seemed to fight an inward battle.

"I can't," she gasped. "You'd—never believe me."

"You know Kendall, then?"

"I tell you I'm not going to say anything."

Wade shrugged. "All right. I won't try to force you." He passed her, strode to the door.

"What are you going to do?" she asked quickly.

"Turn this over to the police. They're on their way now. Kendall, whoever he is, will be hunted down for a killer. He wasn't supposed to be on this train. I've got evidence that he was. Three men have been murdered and Kendall will have to answer."

He was watching the girl narrowly. He saw her flinch and whiten. She reached out, caught his arm. "Wait," she pleaded. "I'll tell you—everything I know—if you'll promise to believe me, and help Mr. Kendall."

"I can't make promises," said Wade. "If Kendall's guilty he'll have to answer."

"He isn't, I tell you! He'd never kill anyone."

Wade stood close to the door, feet wide apart, and spoke with exasperation. "Just what's this all about? Start at the beginning."

"Mark Kendall worked for Mr. Kelly as Walsh's assistant. Just before we left Boston, Walsh had him fired. They never did get along very well. Walsh was jealous of Mark, I think. He told Mr. Kelly that Mark had become slipshod and inefficient. Mark accepted his dismissal; but he was afraid something might happen to Mr. Kelly. And then he hoped he might get his job back by having Mr. Kelly's nephew, Jerry Herd, intercede for him. They knew each other. Mark asked me to hide him in my stateroom on the trip to New York." Color swept the girl's cheeks. For a moment her eyes wavered from Wade's piercing ones.

"Sounds complicated," said Wade. "But I gather that you're fond of Kendall. Otherwise you wouldn't have taken this risk for him."

The girl nodded. "It didn't seem like a risk," she admitted, "until this terrible thing happened. Then I knew how it would look if Mark were found on the train. I slipped into my stateroom before we got to Norwalk junction and told him he'd better try to leave as soon as the train stopped. If that window hadn't made such a noise—"

"But it did," Wade said dryly. "And now listen, Miss Archer. You may have faith in this man Kendall, but you can't expect me to take his innocence for granted. The police won't. So you'd better answer my questions straight. Were you here in the stateroom with Kendall when the shooting took place?"

For a brief moment the girl's eyes wavered. She caught her breath, said huskily, "I want to lie to you, but—I won't. No, I wasn't here at the moment. I was up in the file room getting out some papers. But"—her look was pleading again—"I *know* Mark Kendall isn't a murderer."

Wade Hammond shrugged. At that moment there was a grinding sound beneath their feet and the car gave a sudden lurch that threw them together. Wade knew what it meant. Kelly had grown impatient and had given the order to proceed to New York, dead men and all. As the wheels began to rumble and gather momentum, Wade spoke grimly. "What I do about Kendall will depend on what turns up, Miss Archer. That's all I can say just now."

J.P. KELLY'S city apartment was a penthouse. Sixteen stories up, it overlooked the river. It was late, but the bright lights of Broadway still made an orange blaze in the distant sky. The apartment was rich in expensive furnishings. The apartment was crowded with police detectives. Wade Hammond's friend, Inspector Thompson, was there, owlish-faced, bald-headed and fuming. He stood in front of J.P. Kelly, waving a finger at the financier. "You bring in a trainful of corpses—and expect me to solve the murders over night. They didn't occur in my territory, Mr. Kelly. I've just had a call from the Stamford police. They say you skinned out before they got there. Why didn't you wait? There's going to be hell to pay."

Kelly, pale but still in a fighting mood, spoke violently.

"My staying there wouldn't help Swinton and the others, inspector. And there's something bigger afoot even than their murders. If the bucket-shop people prevent my testifying before the Senate tomorrow, this country will be flooded with bad securities."

"Yes," objected Thompson, "and if you go to Washington and try to testify you're going to get yourself bumped off."

Kelly nodded shortly. "It's a chance I've got to take."

Wade Hammond stood on the sidelines listening. The thing was out of his hands for the moment. They had come away from the Grand Central station in Kelly's limousine, leaving the New York police to worry over the bodies. Kelly was too big to be held up by red tape. Stull had stayed on the private train to answer questions, while Thompson had come to hear Kelly's own version of the shooting. He was hearing it now.

Grace Archer, hovering near her boss, kept looking worriedly at Wade.

"What are you going to do, Kelly?" persisted Thompson.

The financier turned suddenly and scowled at his nephew. "I'm going to get Jerry here to help me—if he's got the guts." He stared at the young man in disapproval for a moment, said: "Probably you'll be too scared to do it, Jerry, but for once I think I've found a way to use you. You like racing. It's foolishness and some day you'll break your neck, but tonight I'm going to give you a chance to do some racing—and maybe prove to me that you're a man and not just a fast-stepping sport. I'm going to dictate my testimony to Miss Archer here, and you're going to drive down to Washington with it. It's nearly midnight now. I won't rely on any mail to reach Washington by morning. And in case I don't get there alive you'll hand my testimony to the Senate committee. What do you say to that?"

Herd flipped a cigarette butt into the fireplace, said lightly: "Okay, uncle."

For the next half-hour Kelly dictated in rapid-fire sentences and Grace Archer's pencil raced across the paper. Then Kelly paused, nodded, and the girl withdrew. Her typewriter in the next room clattered. In twenty minutes she was back with the finished copy. Kelly said: "Come here, Walsh. You've got power of attorney. Sign it."

A sweat of terror glistened on Walsh's face as he took out his pen and signed for his employer. His hand shook so that his signature was barely legible. Wade Hammond had seldom seen a man so gripped by fear.

JERRY HERD pocketed the signed testimony and left the room, while Walsh withdrew, mopping his face and trembling as though the thing he had signed was somehow his death warrant. Kelly turned to Miss Archer again. "Take these letters," he snapped. "There are some things I've got to straighten out before I start for Washington. This may be the last chance I'll have to do it."

While the girl's busy pencil flew over the paper again, the butler appeared and spoke softly: "Someone on the telephone for you, Miss Archer."

Wade Hammond pretended not to hear. He was sucking lazily at the stem of his black pipe. But as Grace Archer left the room he followed. He saw her slip into the telephone closet, and he moved close to it. Her voice came faintly through the panels. Twice he plainly heard her speak the name "Mark."

He was waiting outside when she came out. She started and flushed angrily.

"Sorry to sneak up on you again," Wade said. "But where's Kendall now—back in the city?"

She shook her head. "I'm not going to tell you where Mark is; but I'll tell you what he said. The real reason he had me hide him on the train was because he suspects Walsh of doublecrossing Mr. Kelly. He thinks Walsh accepted a bribe from the bucket-shop men to find out what Mr. Kelly's testimony before the Senate would be, so they could build up a case against it. You understand? Walsh fired Mark so there'd be no one to interfere with his double dealing."

Wade Hammond nodded thoughtfully. "A good story, Miss Archer. But don't forget, Kendall knows he's in a tight spot. What I want to know is where I can find him." The girl was silent. "I can trace that call," Wade added.

"It won't do any good," she said defiantly. "He called from a dial phone. Why don't you question Walsh? If he would accept a bribe, he might be back of the murders."

Wade smiled grimly. "I'll question Walsh all right. And for your sake, I hope Kendall isn't guilty. If he was, you'd be guilty, too, as an accomplice."

He walked away, entered the front room and looked for the lawyer. Walsh wasn't in sight. He sent the butler to look for him and the servant came back, frowning.

"Mr. Walsh has gone, sir. I understood that he was going to accompany Mr. Kelly to Washington. But he's taken his hat and coat and left without a word."

"Where does he hang out when he isn't here?"

The butler frowned a moment. "Let me think, sir. I forwarded some of his letters once when Mr. Kelly was away. I believe I can find his address."

He disappeared, came back a minute later with a slip of paper, which Wade Hammond pocketed, then turned to the door.

Wade took a taxi to the street number on the slip. It proved to be a high-class rooming house in the fifties. Wade asked the landlady to show him Walsh's room. She led the way up two flights of carpeted stairs and knocked at a door under which light showed. Through the panels a faint sound issued.

"Mr. Walsh," she called, "a gentleman to see you, sir."

The noise inside ceased, but still there was no answer. The landlady turned startled eyes at Wade. "I don't understand, sir," she whispered. "He's always so polite; but perhaps he's getting ready for bed and doesn't want visitors. You'd better go away."

Wade Hammond made a sudden grim decision and brushed her aside. His shoulder went down. His head turned sidewise. He struck the door like a battering ram, using his full weight. The lock ripped from its fastenings and Wade Hammond stepped inside.

Then he froze, staring down in horror, while behind him the landlady gave a terrified shriek. A bright glow filled the lawyer's room, coming from a big bowl light overhead. In the center of the carpet Walsh was lying in a pool of blood. There was a gaping hole close to his temple, and his eyes were glassy, dead.

Wade took three steps into the room, stopped and glanced sidewise, catching a flash movement at his left. Instinct quicker than thought warned him of danger. He let his legs sag under him, dropped to his knees, and got a glimpse of a masked, corpselike face framed in the door of another room. The long barrel of a silenced gun thrust through curtains like the black head of a snake. There was a dull cough, flame fanned out, and a bullet bored across Wade's shoulders, brushing his coat.

CHAPTER IV
Death on Wheels

HE felt the impact of it against his skin, as though death's fingers had caressed him. There wasn't time to turn and fire. The masked killer was lowering the gun's muzzle to pump lead into his body. Wade swept up a light straight-legged chair and flung it at the curtains with all his might. It spoiled the murderer's aim, made the second bullet strike too low. The shot ploughed the carpet close to Wade's thigh. Wade streaked his body forward and followed the chair in a flying tackle like a football star.

The masked man stepped back as Wade's plunging figure struck him. Curtains ripped from their rings. The two of them went down together in a struggling, panting heap.

Blazing eyes gleamed up through the mask at Wade. He could get no sight of the features. He pinioned the killer's body, reached forward to tear away the mask, as a muffled cry came from the man's hidden lips, sounding like a signal. Wade turned in horror as a shadow fell across the floor.

There was another man in the room, seemingly an accomplice of the murderer. With photographic vividness Wade's mind registered a swift impression. A handkerchief covered only the stranger's mouth and nose. Above it hard, black eyes shone like agate. The man's skin was sunburned, brown as leather, except for lighter circles around the eyes themselves. The flesh there looked as though the sun seldom struck it.

The man hurled himself down at Wade with a guttural curse. At the same instant, working like partners, the rubber-faced gunman tore his arms free and clutched Wade's wrist. The hands of the other met around Wade's throat and began to throttle.

Wade fought like a tiger, desperately, grimly, knowing that he was battling death while the thumbs of the strangler pressed into his flesh. The masked man he could have beaten easily, but this other had taken him by surprise. He couldn't breathe. All air had been shut from his throat as though by steel hands. He freed his right wrist and balled his fist for a savage blow, then saw the masked killer lifting his gun. While one strangled him into insensibility, the other was getting ready to shoot. Wade crouched, then pulled backwards, lifting the strangler off his feet. They struck against the man with the gun and all three went down. A table tipped over with a crash. The straight-backed chair that Wade had thrown got in their way and cracked like matchwood. The wall itself shuddered.

Above the sound of his own pounding blood, rising like a trip-hammer beat in his brain, Wade heard the frenzied screaming of the landlady. The killers suddenly noticed it, too, realized their danger. He heard the rubber-masked man give a curse. Abruptly, both men left him and plunged across the room toward the window. Through swimming eyes he saw their hulking forms move like specters. He tried to get to his feet and follow, drawing his own gun from his pocket, but already the two had disappeared. The shot he slammed after them only smashed glass in a tinkling cascade.

Wade swayed groggily to his feet, cursing. He breathed in great gasps, lurched toward the window. It seemed to take him hours to cross the floor. When he reached the sill and peered down he heard a clatter of feet in a courtyard two floors below. Then a gate slammed and there was only silence.

Wade Hammond jerked around and surveyed the room. Papers and articles of clothing were strewn about in wild confusion. A desk was open, its contents spilled. The two men had obviously been searching for something which Wade's entrance had interrupted.

The landlady was still screaming in the hall, while answering voices sounded through the house. Wade called to her to telephone the police. He recovered his strength, began moving catlike and questing around the room. Walsh had had something valuable which the masked murderer wanted to steal. Wade's coming and the landlady's screams had scared them away. Fear of being captured by the police had outweighed greed. Wade went back into the room where he had almost been strangled and abruptly tensed.

An old-fashioned china clock had broken when the table overturned. It lay on its side with its base smashed to pieces. From the hollow interior a packet of green bills had spilled. Wade snatched them up, saw the figures on their corners. These were five century notes—his quick fingers counted twenty. Ten grand in all, and Walsh had used the clock as a hiding place. A guilty conscience had prevented him taking the bills to a bank. Here was the bribe from the bucket-shop men that Kendall had spoken of to Grace Archer. But was Kendall innocent or guilty? A harsh, humorless smile creased Wade's face as he turned. He walked over to Walsh's still body, thrust the ten thousand inside his coat and rose. Walsh had paid for the money with his life. Perhaps it would be passed on to more deserving heirs.

Wade strode out into the hall and down the steps, ignoring the questions hurled at him by a dozen terrified tenants. He located the landlady's phone and made two quick calls. One was to the homicide bureau. The other was to Inspector Thompson at J.P. Kelly's apartment. Five minutes later Wade had left the house.

J.P. KELLY'S special was on the move again. The fighting financier, both arms in splints and bandages, was tense and grim. There was a light of battle in Wade Hammond's eyes. He and Inspector Thompson's men had searched the car, the locomotive and the tender. He had looked along the roof and under the trucks. Every possible hiding place in and out had been investigated. Wade was satisfied that no gunman was hidden on board. But trouble, he felt sure, lay ahead.

His eyes swung to the stained carpet in Kelly's stateroom. The porter had scrubbed it, but a brownish spot that was Swinton's blood still showed. The bodies of Swinton and his men had been removed, but it was still a train of terror, with the menace of unsolved murder pressing around it in the night.

Detective Stull had volunteered to stay. Other of Swinton's men, hired for the job, were still on board. But Wade had greater faith in the two police detectives Thompson had detailed to go with him. Still more, he depended on himself.

He left Kelly's stateroom and stayed near the end of the car for a time, tense and alert. The .45 automatic which had seen strange service in many lands was in its shoulder holster. His coat was unbuttoned. Few gunmen could beat Wade Hammond to the draw. But once this evening he had been placed at a disadvantage. He didn't want the thing to be repeated.

It was after midnight now. Outside, the locomotive's whistle wailed eerily through the dark. The mist had settled into a drizzling rain. It drove past the windows in hissing sheets as the train sped on.

The tension seemed to increase. Twenty minutes passed and Wade walked to the forward end of the car. He gave quick orders to Thompson's men, asking them to stay away from the rear platform and keep close guard at Kelly's door. Wade went to an empty stateroom, then, opened a suitcase he had brought with him and slid his arms into the sleeves of a light waterproof jacket. He buttoned it around his neck, leaving the front open to give easy access to his gun. He left his hat off, walked to the car's forward end, and, in the darkness, unseen by the engineer and fireman up front, he climbed to the back of the tender. From here he got up on the roof of the car.

The train was hitting seventy miles an hour again. Wind swept along the flat roof with hurricane force, threatening to tear Wade off his feet and hurl him to the tracks. He got down on his stomach, gripped the sides of the car roof and snaked forward toward the rear, while rain and wind pelted the back of his neck. It was a daredevil stunt like others Wade Hammond had performed, but he was confident. His special talent lay in doing the unexpected.

Ten minutes later he'd reached a spot over the observation platform. Crouching flat here, he could look over the rear curve of the car roof and see the long, unwinding ribbon of the rails.

The killer hadn't struck till the train had been nearly three hours out of Boston. But circumstances had been different, then. And the flat Jersey country they were now speeding over was in some respects like Connecticut along the shore.

Wade's eyes never left the blackness in the rear. Light from the end of the car made a dim glow in the mist along the track, stretching out now like slender spears. The train was roaring over a long straight stretch.

It was then that Wade Hammond flattened still more, eyes narrowed into the gloom behind. Something that looked like a moving shadow was coming into the range of light, slowly blotting out the rails. It emerged from the mist, took on form and shape. Wade's pulses quickened with triumph. His hunch had been right. The blunt radiator of a racing auto was clearly discernible now. Wade swore softly. The thing must be fitted with handcar wheels; it was sliding along the track at terrific speed. Fast as the train was, the auto was catching up easily. It showed no lights. There was a low windshield with two goggled heads behind it.

The car came up, lessening the intervening space, creeping out of the darkness like some sinister phantom. The two men looked like demons with glaring goggled eyes.

Wade inched a little forward, holding his breath. The car had a sidestep running forward to the front fender. There was a high metal bumper reaching to the radiator cap. One man was driving while the other peered forward, holding a gun with a long barrel in his hand. Wade Hammond saw him leave his seat and slide over the side of the car and along the step. Keeping a hold on the car's engine hood, he moved cautiously forward.

The car came closer still. Its bumper was within a foot of the train's platform. The man with the gun reached up and swung on board. The auto lessened its speed and slowly fell behind.

Wade Hammond dared wait no longer. He slid forward, clutching a metal brace on the car's roof. He swung his body down and inward so as to clear the observation rail.

AT the instant that he dropped there was a pinpoint of flame behind. A bullet went screaming by his shoulder. He turned and crashed a shot back at the ghostly car whose driver had seen him slide from the car roof and was shooting. Wade's automatic cracked twice in quick succession. A faint cry lifted out of the darkness and the driver sagged behind his wheel.

Wade dropped to his knees and turned. His shots behind had given warning of his presence to the masked killer in front. A puff of flame blazed almost in Wade's face. The wind of a bullet from the silenced gun fanned his cheek. For one brief instant he stared up into the corpselike rubber mask of the mysterious killer. The long gun jutted from one gloved hand. He had taken his goggles off. Through the slits in his mask his eyes blazed with savage hate. Braced against the wall of the aisle, he swung his gun to fire again.

Wade was ready this time. He did not seem to aim, but his automatic cracked a second before the muffled report came from the long silenced barrel. The masked killer gave a cry, then lurched and fell. The long-barreled weapon dropped from his hand.

Wade Hammond was at his side in a moment. Thompson's men had heard the shots. They were coming on the run, puzzled as to how Wade had reached the rear of the car when he had gone up front.

Wade tore off the mask, but, even before he did so, knew whom he would find. Under the strange rubber covering were features he had seen before that night—the now familiar features of Jerry Herd. Wade's bullet had knocked him out; but Hammond knew he would pull through—for a murder trial.

Thompson's men arrived, Stull with them, and a second later Grace Archer opened her stateroom door. Wade Hammond looked up into the fear-blanched face of the girl.

"You don't have to worry about Kendall now, Miss Archer. What you say he told you has all checked up. The bucket-shop men did bribe Walsh to doublecross

Mr. Kelly and find out what he was going to say against them; but they weren't the killers. Herd and his crook mechanic did all the shooting and threatening."

He turned to Stull then, said softly: "You see now why Tracy was shot first. Herd boarded the train in Connecticut just as he did here. He knocked Tracy off on the back platform before he entered the car."

"I don't quite get it," said Stull dazedly. "How—how did he swing it?"

"Easy enough. He had two racing cars hidden beside the track, one in Connecticut, one here. Both were equipped with handcar wheels. He had seen his chance to get money from his uncle at the time Kendall told him about Walsh taking a bribe. Herd used the bucket-shop crowd as a shield. But, in case his uncle wouldn't come across, Herd planned to bump him off. Settling an estate takes a good while. Herd was Kelly's heir and would have got some cash; but he preferred the quick way of extortion if he could work it. He thought crippling his uncle would scare him.

"It didn't work, so Herd stopped at Walsh's place to grab the bribe. After the killings Walsh was scared to death. He skipped out and Herd found him at home, planning probably to skip the country, figuring he'd got himself mixed up with a gang of murderers. Herd made a big mistake going after the bribe. Something I saw at Walsh's put me wise. Herd's mechanic showed goggle rings around his eyes. I've seen other racing drivers. Most of 'em have 'em from wearing goggles all the time. When I thought of auto racing I thought of Herd—and the rest was easy to figure after that."

"Six are destined to die!" intoned the voice of the Reaper from loudspeakers in every home. Even Wade Hammond, that astute criminologist, shuddered when death struck and he heard each marrow-chilling announcement of the next doomed one's name. For Wade had to find a weapon to fight murder on the air that came with invisible bullets.

Murder on the Air

CHAPTER I
Voice of the Reaper

FEAR held Radio Station WOB in an icy grip. Faces had whitened. Those in the big expensively furnished lounge stood rigid, tense. All eyes were turned toward the polished cabinet at the end of the room—staring as though the voice that came from it could be seen as well as heard. Wade Hammond, freelance investigator of crime, was listening with the rest.

"I am the Reaper," the strange voice said. "I come to repeat the message I gave this afternoon. I come to bring tidings of death. The hour is near. Six there are who are destined to die. Nothing can save them. I, the Reaper, will slay—with invisible bullets. This is the Reaper signing off."

There was a low chuckle, a click inside the cabinet as if ghostly fingers had moved a hidden switch. Silence followed, broken suddenly by the nervous, high-pitched laughter of a girl radio star, over by the wall. Her hands were twitching. Her red lips looked unnaturally bright below the stark pallor of her face. Her husky, frightened voice belied her words. "It's the bunk!" she cried. "Someone's trying to kid us. It's all the bunk!"

A chorus of assenting voices answered her, running in quick, uncertain murmurs around the room. "Sure, it's a trick!" "Some new advertising stunt." "There's nothing to it!"

A reporter from one of the city papers jabbed a match unsteadily at his cigarette and turned to Wade. "What do you make of it, pal? Who's this chap who calls himself the Reaper? When do you figure the killings will start?"

Wade Hammond's lean sunburned face was impassive. His lips, below the pencil-thin line of his mustache, were grim. He shook his head. The reporter pressed his questions in an impatient whine. "Give me a break, pal, will you? That harness bull won't let me in to talk to the Druccis. You're in at headquarters. What racket's this guy on the air trying to pull? What did he mean by that spiel about invisible bullets? Where does he hang out?"

Still Wade was silent. He turned as a loud voice sounded behind the door at the end of the lounge that the policeman guarded. Without answering the reporter's hurried queries he moved quickly toward it.

The bluecoat glanced at him, touched his cap respectfully and stood aside. As an expert in crime analysis, Wade Hammond had taken part in more than one bizarre homicide case. The whole police force knew him by sight, knew of his reputation.

There were three people in the room that he now entered. A big man with a thin dark face sat tensely behind a desk gripping the edge of it with clawlike fingers. Two police detectives stood in front of him, their hats pushed back.

Wade recognized the detectives. The dark man, he guessed, was Sam Drucci, who handled the publicity for WOB. Drucci twisted in his chair. His dark eyes focused on Wade, glaringly. He turned back to the plainclothes men. "I thought you said that officer outside wasn't going to let anybody in?"

Before either dick could answer, Wade Hammond flipped open his wallet and presented his special investigator's card. "My pass," he said.

Drucci nodded nervously. "All right, all right!" He struck the desk and began talking loudly to the two detectives again. "You heard his broadcast just now! You heard it! We've got to stop this thing! I'm not mentioning any names, but I think I know who's behind it. Trace the wire from here to the concert hall at once. Somebody must have cut in along that. I'll get one of our electricians to go with you."

Veins in Drucci's thin face stood out. Fear battled in his eyes with anger. Sweat glistened on his upper lip. "This thing is going to make us look cheap," he added hoarsely. "People will think it's a racket of some kind. The public will laugh at our expense. We've got to grab the man who calls himself the Reaper before any more damage is done. If you people can't do the job right, I will!"

THERE was sudden harshness in Drucci's voice; the harshness of desperation. His snapping dark eyes were those of a man accustomed to making quick decisions. His tone showed that he lacked faith in the methods of the law. He and his brothers, Wade knew, had operated a successful speakeasy in the days of prohibition.

Station WOB was in the same building that had once housed the notorious Sunrise Club where illicit liquor and a blaring jazz band had turned night into day. Drucci had rubbed shoulders with the underworld. When the bootleg business was ended, he and his brothers had invested their money in a radio station with an interstate charter. His unwillingness to tell whom he suspected showed the influence of his former life. Drucci was afraid to squeal.

Wade Hammond opened his mouth to ask a question, then clamped his lips. A clatter of sound came from somewhere down the corridor, echoing through the office and making them all jump. There was no mistaking what it was. A gun had been fired close by, two shots in quick succession.

Drucci sprang to his feet. His thin face had suddenly grown lax. The look of fear in his eyes had deepened into haunting terror. He turned and ran jerkily toward the door.

But Wade Hammond beat him to it. He reached the knob, twisted it, and heard a shrill scream following closely on the shots. It, too, was down the hallway. It seemed to Wade like the cry of a girl in abject fear. He got the door open, then stepped out and saw her.

She was running straight toward him from the door of another office. Her head was thrown back. Dark hair framed a face contorted into lines of horror. Her eyes were glassy, fixed.

Drucci pushed Wade aside and stood with feet braced wide beneath him, staring. When the girl came close she pointed behind her with a shaking hand.

"Your brother!" she gasped. "He's there—in his office. He's just been shot."

Drucci made strangled sounds in his throat and his thin hand pawed at the girl. "Shot—Ed shot! Who—how?" His voice was hollow, croaking.

The girl shook her head and words tumbled breathlessly from her. "I don't know! I didn't see anyone. I heard shots—and I looked in. He's lying right by his desk—dead, I think."

She clenched her hands and backed away. Drucci shoved past her. Wade and the two detectives followed close behind. They raced along the corridor, entered the other office and stared through the door of a room that opened off it.

Ed Drucci, business manager of station WOB, was stretched on the floor beside his desk. He was a smaller man than Sam, older, with a seamed, hard-bitten face. His body was slumped now and his lined features were grayish white.

Wade Hammond stared a moment, then strode to a window that was raised a crack. He pushed it up farther, looked down on the fire escape below, his right hand resting on the butt of the automatic in an armpit holster beneath his coat. There was no moving thing in sight. He turned back to the man on the floor and stared in wonder.

Sam Drucci was bending over his brother. "Ed! Ed!" he cried. There was the thickness of grief in Drucci's voice. His hands moved over his brother's body searching for the wounds that the gunshots must have made.

Then suddenly his arms grew tense. He raised his head, his features set in frozen horror, and a baffled, anguished look grew in his eyes.

Both detectives had crowded up close and their faces were rigid, too. Drucci didn't state in words what it was that had shocked him. But Wade Hammond and the men beside him understood.

Ed Drucci was dead. The corpse-gray pallor of his face showed that. They had all heard the shots plainly, but there was no mark on the fallen man's face or body. No wound of any kind in sight.

If a gun had killed him, then the Reaper's sinister, fantastic threat had been made good. Ed Drucci had died under the lash of invisible bullets.

CHAPTER II
Invisible Bullets

WADE HAMMOND felt a sensation of crawling tightness along his spine. He grabbed the phone off the dead man's desk, sent in a message to Inspector Thompson, head of the city homicide squad, advising him to hurry. Often before they had worked together in difficult cases. This gave promise of being as tough a mystery as any they'd ever tackled. The murder cycle had only just begun. According to the Reaper's broadcast there were five others destined to die.

Wade turned back to the dead man and heard one of the detectives mumbling to himself. "Invisible bullets. That's what he said he'd use—and he did."

Sam Drucci's face was still ashen, and he thrust a hand in his brother's coat and drew something out. He waved it under the detective's nose. "Look!" he said hoarsely. "Look at this."

The thing he held was a slip of paper with the numeral "1" scrawled on it. He put his hand in his own pocket and drew out another slip. "4" was written on this.

"We all got them!" he gasped. "Ed here, Charlie, Joe and I. They came in the mail this afternoon. Now—now I know what they mean. This man, the Reaper, sent them. We're among the six he's going to kill. Number one was Ed—and the Reaper got him first. Joe comes next, then Charlie, and then—then—"

A young man entered excitedly, interrupting Sam Drucci's speech. He was tall, clean-cut, stylishly dressed. He looked more like a gentleman than thin-faced Sam, but the family resemblance was plain. The newcomer was a Drucci also; Charlie, the younger of the four.

"They just told me!" he gasped. He stood and stared in growing horror at the sprawled figure on the floor. He said huskily: "Then—then it's true!"

Sam Drucci nodded. "Yes, he's dead—shot by the man who calls himself the Reaper. But there aren't any wounds—no bullet holes, Charlie, no blood—do you understand?"

Wade Hammond, watching, saw Charlie Drucci give a violent start. A slow pallor spread across his face. Words came from his lips in a groaning burst. "The Reaper! That's what he said he'd do—kill with invisible bullets!"

Men and women were crowding into the outer office. Horror was reflected on their faces, too. News of the murder had spread. The radio stars in the lounge outside had followed the policeman in, led on by morbid curiosity. They looked frightened—all but one.

A sleeky handsome man in his early thirties, his smooth pale face and sloe-black eyes impassive even in the presence of death, moved forward. He was tapping a cigarette, manicured fingers steady. Wade recognized him from pictures in the radio sections of the press. He was Gordon Vance, Romeo crooner of the air, the man whose sentimental love songs had touched the hearts of thousands.

Vance raised an eyebrow. He stared at the form of Ed Drucci on the floor, stared next at Charlie Drucci, and spoke with malice. "The Reaper, eh? I was afraid of something like this when I heard you and Ed quarreling over Joyce."

Young Drucci whirled, his pale face suffused with red. "What the hell do you mean?"

The malice in the crooner's eyes was veiled. He stared at Drucci innocently. "Nothing, except that everyone around this joint knows you and Ed have been fighting for a week because of Joyce. Now Ed's dead, so I thought maybe—"

Charlie clenched his fist and moved close to Vance, his features furiously convulsed. "You leave Joyce Withersteen out of this. Hear me? Another crack like that and I'll sock you."

"Charlie!"

It was a girl who had spoken. Unobtrusively she had come through the door, and now stood looking from the body on the floor to the two who glared hatred into each other's eyes. Her small, piquant face was anxious. She was unconscious of the curious glances she was drawing from all sides. "Charlie," she repeated, "please don't fight because of me."

Young Drucci dropped his hard fist and turned to the girl. "Stay out of here, Joyce. Haven't you heard? . . . Ed's been murdered."

She nodded. "Yes—they told me! I—it's horrible!" Her eyes switched to Gordon Vance and her tone was scathing. "I heard what you said just now—hinting that Charlie had killed his brother over me. I know why you did it, too. You lying beast!"

Tears came to her eyes suddenly and she turned and fled. Charlie Drucci walked toward Vance again, till his brother Sam's cold voice stopped him.

"Stay away from him, Charlie. He's got to go on the air tonight. Get out of here, Vance, before I throw you out!" Sam Drucci stopped speaking a moment. He was breathing hard. He banged his fist on his desk, said: "I know who's behind this, and—"

Again fear mingled with fury on his face. He opened a desk drawer suddenly and lifted out a gun. He held it up for Wade and the others to see. "I've got a permit to use it; and I may have to. I'm fighting for my life. Do you hear—my life?"

Wade Hammond nodded. But he leaned forward and said quietly: "You'd better tell us whom you suspect."

Sam Drucci shook his head. "Leave that to me." He paused a moment, said in a strained voice: "I'm going to settle it in my own way—I've got to. But you can help me. My brother Joe's at his home right now. He's crippled. He stays in a wheel chair all the time. Get the police and throw them around his place. See that he gets protection. Don't let anyone in. Then trace the line to the concert hall where the Reaper must have cut in to make his broadcast. Some of you work on that. Here!"

He picked up the phone on his desk and gave a quick order. "Send Bittner up!"

They waited, and an emaciated man in a rusty black suit appeared. His face was gray and twitching, his manner scared. But there was intelligence in his high forehead and deep-set burning eyes.

DRUCCI eyed him a moment, and abruptly, as though a sudden thought had struck him, his voice lashed out. "Bittner, how do I know you're not mixed up in this? You're chief engineer here. You know more about how the place is being run than anybody else. If I thought you were in conspiracy with that devil, I'd—I'd break you!"

Sam Drucci waved his gun, and Bittner shrank away.

"Ed's been murdered," Drucci continued, "shot with invisible bullets. What do you know about the Reaper's broadcasts? These men are detectives, you'd better come clean."

"Nothing!" said Bittner hoarsely. "Nothing—I swear to heaven!"

"Where were you a moment ago when that devil was talking?"

"Down in my office, working on the new testing equipment you want installed. But if you think—" Bittner held out his trembling hands, face set in resignation. "Have me arrested if you think I'm guilty! That's all I can say, sir."

Drucci swore. "Give these men information about the line to the concert hall. Get them a map showing how the line lies. Send somebody along it with them."

"Yes, sir!" Black-coated Bittner rolled frightened eyes at the body on the floor. His long fingers twisted.

Fear lay like a pall over everyone in the room. A redheaded radio star who had come in from the lounge pointed a trembling finger and spoke huskily. "This is the room," she cried. "Right on this floor, I remember! It's the spot where Adoree Estrellas was shot. That's where she died—where Mr. Drucci's lying now. Lord, it gives me the creeps. It's just as if—"

A sound like a sigh moved through the crowd. Another girl gave a single frightened moan. A man muttered: "The Reaper!"

"What's she driving at?" growled one of the police detectives.

Sam Drucci looked haunted again, and ran a nervous finger inside his collar, along his thin, dark neck. "Miss Estrellas was a torch singer who used to work for us—when we had a nightclub here. She was shot when some bandits pulled off a stick-up in the place."

"Shot," echoed the red-haired girl. "Shot—and she lay there dead, right where Mr. Drucci is now—before they put those office partitions up. I was doing a number right after her. It might have been me who got it."

"Shut up," said Sam Drucci, his features livid. "Get out of here, all of you. Get out, I say."

A police siren moaned outside. The elevator beyond the lounge doorway clicked in a moment. Inspector Thompson with his group from headquarters entered. With him were an official photographer, a fingerprint man, an assistant district attorney in charge of homicides, and the chief medical examiner. The police had come in full force in answer to Wade Hammond.

The inspector jerked off his hat and slid quick fingers over his bald pink pate. His bright eyes were set in an owlish face. They glittered as he nodded at Wade.

The medical examiner got to work while the photographer pulled his camera open. He bent down quickly, ran tentative fingers over Ed Drucci's body, stared at his face and neck. In a moment he clucked his tongue and looked up grimly. "Nothing doing," he said. "There's not a mark on him."

Inspector Thompson glowered. "How did he die?"

"Can't tell till we get him on a slab. Maybe he was only scared to death. Might be a cerebral hemorrhage or cardiac stoppage; occlusion—maybe."

Thompson spread his hands and turned to Wade. What about those shots? You say you heard 'em, Hammond."

"We all did, chief. They were in or near this room. No mistake about it. But that's all we know."

The inspector crossed to the window and peered out. Wade did likewise, then stepped to the fire escape, flashed his hand light and started down. Thompson followed, agile for all his years.

There was a courtyard below, with fences and an ally beyond. The killer could have climbed into the yard, or come from some window in the broadcasting building itself.

At the bottom of the escape Wade stopped suddenly and picked up something off the concrete of the court. It was a piece of cardboard, small and round that had apparently fluttered down from above. He put it on his palm and held it out for the inspector to see. Thompson nodded.

"Wadding," he said.

"Yes—but not from a cartridge with a bullet, chief. There's no mark of lead. Only powder on the bottom. It came from a blank shell, caliber .38."

"A blank! And a man shot with no bullet wounds. I'm beginning to think this Reaper—" He trailed off, swore harshly under his breath.

Wade found another piece of wadding a few feet farther on. He gave this to Thompson also.

"Have them checked over, chief. They might tell something."

Wade's voice was grim. Here was concrete evidence of the shots that they had heard, yet evidence that deepened the mystery of the man slain above. Ex-gangsters didn't die of fright alone. Wade took a black pipe from his pocket and thumbed tobacco into the bowl. He struck a match and sucked smoke thoughtfully in heavy puffs.

They climbed the fire escape back upstairs. Wade angled from the office where Drucci had been killed, and began exploring the station. He visited the studios, the big control room with its technical experts and hundreds of dials, the generating room in the basement, the broadcasting tower far above. He snooped, asked questions and took brief notes.

THE medical examiner was fighting for permission to perform an autopsy when Hammond returned to the scene of the crime. Sam Drucci, his hat and coat on, was objecting. Charlie was standing by, hands in his pockets. He had his hat and coat on, too. They were evidently ready to shove off somewhere; but Thompson wouldn't let them go until the question of the autopsy was decided. It looked to Wade like the beginning of a long argument.

He shrugged. There was a lead he wanted to follow. Sam Drucci had stated that he thought he knew who was behind the Reaper broadcast, but he was keeping mum about it. This pointed at some underworld rival, and Wade had many records in his files. He had some dope on the bootleg exploits of the Drucci brothers themselves.

He quietly left the station and sped downtown in his roadster. Parking in front of his bachelor apartment, he entered and began looking through his files.

He searched for items on the Druccis. Newspaper clippings saved from prohibition days. He pulled out the story of the holdup in which the singer, Adoree Estrellas, had been slain. There was a picture of her. She was a pretty, dolllike girl in her late teens. The holdup men had been caught by the police. Both had paid in the chair for the death of Adoree.

Wade found an item then about a man named Felk. Felk had been with the Druccis once, before he had struck out for himself, become their rival and opened up a more elaborate joint than theirs.

Wade paced the floor of his apartment, fingering his pipe. He looked at his watch, switched his radio in on Station WOB. A hotel orchestra was playing. Once again the studio was getting its music from an outside line. These were the conditions under which the Reaper had broadcast in the afternoon. Suddenly Wade Hammond stopped his pacing, grunted.

"Stand by! This is the Reaper again. One of the fated six is already dead! I killed him—I, the Reaper. The second will meet death tonight!"

The Reaper's chuckle rang through the room. It seemed to mock Wade as he stared at the radio's front. A light sweat dampened his forehead. The thing was unbelievable, uncanny. The Reaper, like his invisible bullets, seemed to have inhuman powers. The voice of the unseen killer continued, more grating than before.

"Destiny is moving along the course which no man can stop. Yet there is one who will try to interfere—an officious meddler whose name I know. Wade Hammond, drop the case! Leave the police alone. It is their business to fight crime. Their meddling is excusable to me; but yours is not. Interfere, and my invisible bullets will strike you down. This is the Reaper signing off."

Wade Hammond stood grim-faced. With tense fingers he drew out the automatic that had served him in the far places of the world. He snapped a fresh clip of cartridges into it, not blanks, but ones with steel-jacketed lead. He strapped it under his arm in the well-worn shoulder holster. It might not be much good against invisible death, yet its presence gave him confidence.

He put on his hat, strode to the door and yanked it open. Then suddenly he froze.

A girl stood in the hall outside—the same girl he had seen in Station WOB— Joyce Withersteen, singer of old-fashioned songs. She was reaching for his bell button with a trembling finger, and she spoke quickly as she met his eyes.

"I was going to ring. I wanted to talk to you. I—I've come to ask your help." There was embarrassment in her gray eyes, fear in the husky tremble of her voice. "It's about Charlie Drucci," she continued. "I don't want anything to happen to him. I'm terribly frightened."

Wade looked at her sharply, and color crept into her pale cheeks.

"I love him," she said simply. "I was fond of Ed, too, but not in the same way. Charlie isn't like the others. He wasn't old enough to do the things they did. He was the kid brother—out of it all. He's straight and fine, and I don't want him to get killed or jailed because—" Her voice broke. "You'll help me, won't you, Mr. Hammond?"

"Is it the Reaper you're afraid of?" Wade asked.

"No. There's something else that frightens me more. Charlie's straight, but he'll do as his brother, Sam, tells him. Sam thinks he knows who the Reaper is. I heard them talking. They've gone to get the man they think is behind the thing. They're going to make him confess, or—"

"Who is he?"

"Felk's his name. He's a nightclub owner. I can take you to him if you'll go."

Wade smiled with grim amusement. Felk, the man his own clippings showed had been the Drucci's biggest rival. Murder guns would flame again, unless . . . Joyce Withersteen came closer, eyes appealing.

"You will, won't you?" she pleaded. "I've read about your helping people before. You'll see that Charlie doesn't get mixed up in some terrible shooting?"

Wade Hammond smiled and nodded slowly. The Reaper had warned him to lay off, on pain of death. The Reaper had proved that he could kill mysteriously, quickly, in some unknown way. But now a good-looking girl was asking Wade to mix in deeper. It was a choice between the grim Reaper and a pretty girl—and that was no choice to Wade. He took Joyce Withersteen's slim arm and said: "Let's go."

CHAPTER III
The Second Victim

A CAR was standing in front of Felk's nightclub when they arrived. Joyce Withersteen gasped when she saw it and dug pointed nails into Wade Hammond's arm. "It's Charlie's coupe," she said. "They're here now. Hurry—please."

Wade Hammond did. He swept into the building in long-legged strides with the girl running to keep up. An orchestra was playing at the head of a flight of stairs, which Wade took three at a time. He paused a moment at the top. Joyce Withersteen came up beside him, pale and out of breath.

There was a big room at Wade's left, dimly lighted, with small booths and tables showing along the walls. Couples were dancing in the center of the floor. Black-coated waiters moved silently along the carpeted aisles.

A man who didn't look like a waiter suddenly edged from behind a booth and stepped in front of Wade. His eyes were hard and black, his expression suspicious. "Got your reservation, mister?"

Wade ignored the question. "Where's Felk?" he said.

The agate-eyed man came closer, squinting coldly at Wade. "He's not in. Anything I can do?"

For a moment Wade Hammond's gaze swiveled around the room, missing nothing. "Show me where I can find Felk and the Druccis," he snapped.

The man before him spoke without moving his lips. "I said the boss wasn't in and I meant it. I haven't seen your pals. We don't want any trouble. Beat it quick."

Wade lifted his arm, drew up his cuff and glanced at his wristwatch calmly. "I'll give you five seconds," he said, "to tell me where Felk is. Then I'll start working on you. Is that the door of his office over there?"

The black-eyed man didn't answer. His right hand plunged suddenly into the pocket of his coat. Wade Hammond gave Joyce Withersteen a push that sent her stumbling. In the same movement his own hand doubled into a fist and caught the man before him on the point of the chin.

An explosion sounded as knuckles cracked against flesh. Flame streaked from the man's coat, and a bullet seared close to Wade Hammond's side, missing him by inches. The man's head flew up. He did a backward flip-flop like an acrobat and fell against the table.

The dancers gasped and screamed, freezing in their tracks. The orchestra came to a sudden stop. In the brief, tense silence that followed, Wade Hammond crossed the room toward the door he had already spotted as leading to Felk's private office.

Joyce Withersteen tried to follow, but he clutched her shoulder and snapped a quick order in her ear. "Stay here. If I don't come back in ten minutes, call the cops."

The girl nodded in a terrified daze. Wade strode to the door, jerked it open, and stepped into a corridor with another room beyond. He edged toward this. Harsh voices sounded from where light came through a frosted transom.

He listened a moment, then drew the heavy-handled automatic from his coat. He held it ready, softly turned the knob of the second door, threw his whole weight against a panel. The door sprang open. Wade Hammond barged inside.

Three men stood staring with mouths open at his sudden entry. One was Felk, small and oily, cringing back against his desk. The other two were the Druccis, Charlie and Sam. Guns gleamed in their hands. Sam stood with his feet apart, face menacing, a desperate gleam in his eyes. Charlie was pale but determined. There was sweat beaded on Felk's forehead and his skin was greenish. He looked like a man getting ready to die. Close behind him, in an open drawer, another pistol glinted. Felk's hand was poised for a desperate dive for the gun.

"Hold everything!" said Wade. "Nobody move!"

His voice came through his teeth between tight lips. It was like the lash of a whip. Sam Drucci stiffened. "Drop the rod, Drucci—even if you have a permit. I've got you covered."

DRUCCI was the first to get over his shock. Anger thickened his voice. "You're not a policeman, Hammond. You can't tell me what to do. Get out before I hurt you. I'm going to kill this rat."

"Don't be a fool, Drucci. You and your kid brother will land in the hot seat if you murder Felk. Drop your gun."

"Felk, or someone he hired, killed my brother tonight. He's trying to put me out of business. He's got it coming to him, and—"

"You don't know it was Felk," Wade grated. "Where's your proof? There weren't even any bullets." Wade turned to the nightclub's cringing proprietor. "Don't you go for your gun either, Felk. Stay where you are. I'll stop him."

"You won't!" screamed Drucci. "I'm not going to wait like a sap till we're all murdered. Get Felk, Charlie. I'll fix this guy!"

Drucci's gun swung toward Wade Hammond, but Wade didn't fire. There was a light, straight-backed chair close to his leg. He stuck his foot among the rungs, ducked and pivoted his body. Drucci's gun belched flame as the chair sailed through the air and struck him, spoiling his aim.

Wade followed the chair in a flying leap and jolted a hard left fist into Drucci's body. He slapped his gun hand down on Drucci's wrist, knocking the weapon from his fingers. Charlie, cursing, swung his gun toward Felk. Wade kicked the youngster in the shins viciously. In the same movement, he sent a bullet crashing into the drawer where Felk's automatic lay. Felk's hand remained suspended halfway to the gun.

"Leave it alone," snarled Wade. "Beat it while you can."

Felk took the hint. He ran like a frightened rat to the door and whisked through it. Charlie Drucci, his face convulsed with anger, tried to play the part of hardboiled gangster and get the drop on Wade, who opened his palm, slapped him across the face and grabbed his automatic. He pocketed the gun quickly, said: "Behave, both of you. It was a fool stunt to come here. You haven't a thing on Felk."

Sam Drucci was cursing in incoherent fury as Wade talked like a Dutch Uncle. "It's none of my business," he said, "and you won't thank me, but I wanted to save you boys from the chair, especially Charlie. Don't let Sam get you into mischief. Joyce Withersteen's outside waiting. Better go out quick and show her you're not shot. She's a good kid and deserves a break. She seems to like you."

"You'll regret this," said Sam Drucci fiercely.

"Forget it," growled Wade. "Go back to your radio station and let the cops hunt down the Reaper. If Felk's guilty, you can bet they'll get him. If he isn't, there's no use hounding him. I'm going over to your brother Joe's now and see if he's getting enough protection."

He stared hard at Charlie Drucci. With the tension over, the youngster looked relieved. But Wade picked up both automatics and shoved them in his pockets. "I'll keep these for a while. Better scram out of here, both of you, and take Joyce with you. I'll see you later."

He stalked ahead of them, passing the frightened girl with a smile and a whispered word of reassurance. People were bending over the man he had knocked out. Others were crowding out the door to the stairs. Wade shouldered through them and descended to the street just as two cops climbed hurriedly from a radio car. Someone had got excited and sent in a call. Wade buttonholed the officers.

"It was a false alarm," he said. "Just a little private brawl upstairs. It's all over now, everything settled and no one hurt."

The cops knew Wade. They nodded, climbing back into their car. Wade stepped into his roadster and headed for Joe Drucci's place. He felt uneasy. Joe was number two on the Reaper's list. So far the Reaper's threats hadn't been idle.

HEADQUARTERS men were stationed all around the Drucci residence. The house itself was an old-fashioned brownstone affair with an air of grave respectability.

Wade drew up to a curb and spoke to the headquarters man who hailed him.

"Anything happen?"

"No, all quiet, Hammond. We haven't seen a soul."

"Good! I'm going in to look things over and have a chat with Drucci. I want to talk to him about a man named Felk."

Wade climbed the steps and pulled an old-fashioned wire clapper. A bell tinkled somewhere in the depths of the house. A moment later a scared-looking butler opened the door on a chain. Wade showed his card, stated his purpose in calling, and the butler let him in.

Somewhere in the rooms overhead a radio was playing, filling the old house with whispering echoes.

The butler went up to announce Wade, returning a moment later. "Mr. Drucci will see you at once. His room is the second at the right."

Wade climbed the softly carpeted stairs with their polished walnut railing. The sound of the radio grew louder. He came to a high-ceilinged hall, saw a half-open door with a lighted room behind it. He had almost reached it, walking swiftly along the hall, when something stopped him.

With a gasping cry Wade reached out to steady himself. The walls of the hallway seemed to be closing in upon him. Lights danced and gyrated before his eyes, and a great weight appeared suddenly to have been pushed against his head. He could feel it, pounding, pressing, and there came an intolerable torturing ache that lasted for a moment. He fell to his knees, dazed, almost senseless, groping like a blind man along the carpet. As he did so, above the roaring in his own head, he heard a frenzied scream.

CHAPTER IV
Motive for Murder

WADE got up, fighting, battling the giddiness that was like a crushing weight. He lunged forward desperately, staggered across the threshold of the lighted room, banging the door open.

Through swimming eyes he glimpsed the contorted face of a man who had the characteristics of a Drucci. Hands gripping his head, mouth open, eyeballs rolling, the man had half-risen from the wheel chair in which he sat. Another scream came pulsing from his throat. Before Wade could reach him the man fell sidewise, knocking the chair over.

Wade jerked at his gun. He turned dazedly, searching for a hidden assassin. But all the windows of the room were closed. There had been an explosion. It had felled Drucci, knocked Wade almost senseless, but no one was in sight.

Wade whirled toward the man in the chair. Joe Drucci was also dead. Wade's fingers, hastily thrust beneath his coat, told that. But there was no mark of a bullet. Again, through dazed faculties, Wade felt the uncanny tingling along his spine.

The radio he'd heard below was in this room. It had ceased playing directly following the crash. It was close to Drucci's chair. A dialed panel with switches controlling a piece of apparatus unfamiliar to Wade was connected with it. On the table close beside it was a telephone.

Wade went to the radio and examined it quickly, face tense with thought. But he could find nothing wrong with the mechanism inside. He stared around the chamber, suddenly caught his breath. Something gleamed dully on the carpet under a small table near the wall. He lurched across the room and picked it up. It was a small cylinder of copper—an empty cartridge.

Holding the shell in the palm of his hand, Wade studied it. The edges of the open end curled in slightly. If a bullet had been fired out they would have been spread flat. This meant that the shell was a blank. Wade's hand balled into a fist. He cursed harshly. Another blank, another invisible bullet! He sniffed at the end of the shell and could smell no fresh fumes of powder. The metal was cold.

The butler entered, followed by two headquarters men from the street. They, too, had heard the explosion. The butler's jaw dropped slackly at sight of his dead master. His face turned white. The two detectives gaped in horror.

Wade thrust the blank shell under the servant's face. "Ever see this before?"

The butler stared with chattering teeth, gasped: "No, sir!"

Wade dropped the shell in his pocket and turned toward the radio apparatus. "This panel here—what is it?"

He had to repeat his question before the butler answered. Fear had almost made the man speechless. "The Druccis, sir! They're all in the radio business, as you probably know. Mr. Drucci was handicapped by his lameness and couldn't get about. He didn't want to miss things. He liked to get the tests and tryouts straight from the studio by wire. That—that panel operates some sort of converter, sir. It connects the radio with the studio wire when tryouts are to be made."

"And this telephone?"

"A private line direct to station WOB."

Wade Hammond was silent an instant. The butler's eyes remained fixed in horrible fascination on the corpse of his master. The two detectives crowded close, trying to ascertain the cause of death. Wade Hammond spoke again sharply. "Has anyone called Mr. Drucci recently on this phone?"

The butler nodded. "There were several calls this evening."

"Did you hear the last one?"

Again the servant nodded. "I came up to Mr. Drucci's room with a glass of water just—just before you arrived. Mr. Drucci was talking on the telephone then."

"Who was he speaking to? Do you remember?"

"Yes, sir. To Mr. Gordon Vance at the station. I gathered that Mr. Vance wasn't feeling well and wished to be released from his broadcast tonight. Mr. Drucci sounded very angry."

Wade Hammond swore. He turned to the phone and lifted it off its cradle. A girl's voice answered at once from the studio. Wade said: "Give me Charlie or Sam Drucci."

"I'm sorry, they're not in."

"Give me Vance then."

"You're at Mr. Joe Drucci's now, aren't you? Didn't he tell you Mr. Vance felt too ill to sing tonight? He left for his apartment ten minutes ago."

Wade Hammond's voice was steely. "Mr. Drucci didn't tell me anything. He's just been murdered—shot by invisible bullets. Tell that to his brothers as soon as they arrive."

He heard the girl operator's cry of horror as he slammed the receiver up and looked sharply at the two headquarters men. "I'm leaving," he said. "There's nothing I can do here. Give this shell to the inspector when he comes and tell him I picked it up on the carpet, over there under the table. Tell him it's a blank."

He turned on his heel and left the room with the detectives gaping after him. Outside, he climbed into his roadster and roared away. The night seemed suddenly blacker. The uncanny threat of the man who called himself the Reaper hung like a cloud of death. Twice now in the space of a few hours the Reaper had snuffed out human lives. And there were still other men who were destined to die.

WADE found the address of Gordon Vance in the telephone book and sped to the singer's apartment. Vance was the last man who had talked with Joseph Drucci. More than that, Vance had suddenly and mysteriously been taken sick. Wade scowled at this, recalling that at the time of Ed Drucci's murder Vance had seemed perfectly well.

He was informed by a snooty telephone girl at the high-priced apartment where Vance resided, that the singer was receiving no visitors tonight. Wade took out his special police card and held it close to the girl's face. "He'll see me. Never mind an announcement. What number is it? I'll just go up."

She told him, looking scared, and Wade took the elevator to a suite at the very top. No one answered his ringing for more than a minute. Then cautious footsteps sounded faintly behind the door. Vance's voice, muffled, fear-strained, came through the panels. "Who—who is it?"

"Wade Hammond calling. I want to see you."

There was an instant's silence. Then Vance spoke more weakly. "You're the man who came to the studio tonight—the detective."

"Yes."

The door opened slowly. Vance's face showed in the crack. Wade thrust it wider, stepped inside. He stared sharply at the singer. Vance didn't look ill to Wade, though his features were pale. It seemed like a pallor of fear. Something had shaken Vance badly, something very sudden. For he had been self-possessed at the time of Ed Drucci's murder. Now Vance was trembling. "Why," he said, "did you come here? Has anything happened?"

Wade spoke softly, watching the effect of his words on Vance's face. "Joe Drucci was killed by the Reaper fifteen minutes ago."

Vance staggered an instant like a drunken man, clutching the wall for support, then found his way to a chair, and sank weakly in it. His forehead, Wade saw, was glistening with sweat.

"They said at the studio that you were sick, Mr. Vance. Sorry to trouble you; but I thought you ought to know . . ."

Vance nodded slowly. More slowly still, seemingly in a daze, he reached into his pocket and drew out a paper slip. He held this out to Wade. "I wasn't sick. It was this. Now you—you understand?"

Wade did. There was the numeral "5" scrawled on the piece of paper.

"I found it in my pocket. It means I've been marked for death by the Reaper," said Vance. "That's why I wouldn't stay at the studio; wouldn't sing. I phoned Mr. Drucci and told him I was ill."

"Why didn't you tell him the truth?"

A sickly grin overspread Vance's face. He made a deprecating gesture with his manicured hands. "He might have thought I was yellow because I wouldn't stick around. I wanted to leave the studio as quickly as I could."

"It may not help you," said Wade grimly. "Joe Drucci was in his own home and he was murdered. This man, the Reaper, is no common killer."

Vance choked. "I know it. It's got me, too!" His voice grew high-pitched. He almost slobbered. "I'm not yellow, Hammond. I can face anything I can see. But the Reaper—with these invisible bullets!" He clenched his hands and groaned.

SUDDENLY Wade crossed the room in a casual walk, staring at a string of photos of pretty women that graced the wall. Musicians. Nightclub girls. Screen stars. Some were inscribed to Gordon Vance with love or best wishes. Wade's eyes came to rest on one, a doll-faced beauty whose white shoulders gleamed above a low-cut dress. Across the bottom of the picture was a childish scrawl. "Love and kisses from Adoree," it said.

"Miss Estrellas," Wade muttered. "I was looking at a newspaper cut of her tonight. She's the kid who got shot in the Druccis' nightclub four years back."

Gordon Vance gulped and lifted a haggard face. "Yes, I knew her."

"How well, Vance?"

"She—she was one of my flames," said the singer weakly. "You know how it is—a fellow in my profession gets around a lot."

"What was she—Spanish?"

"No, Estrellas wasn't her real name. She wasn't Latin at all. She called herself Adoree just for the glamour. A lot of them do it—entertainers, I mean. Her name was Charlotte Smith. She was a good-looking kid all right. Plenty of pep. I was very sorry when she was shot. I—saved her picture."

"Did she have a family?"

"I guess so, but she ran away from home. The old stuff, you know. Another pretty face on Broadway—and nothing to eat. She was hard up when I got her a job at the Sunrise Club; but she had a voice . . ."

"I see," said Wade. He was silent a moment, then spoke with grimness. "It's funny, Vance. Charlotte Smith was shot close to the spot where Ed Drucci was killed tonight. You heard the redhead say so?"

"Yes, I did. What of it?"

"Motive, that's all. Every killer unless he's cracked has a motive. And these murders have been deliberate. What would you say if I told you someone who liked Charlotte Smith a lot was guilty?"

Gordon Vance gasped, turned deathly white and suddenly cringed. "Look here, Hammond, you—you're not accusing me!"

Wade's face was hard, unsmiling. "I'm not accusing anyone yet, but—" He walked over to Vance's radio and studied it closely, shoving it out from the wall and peering in back.

"I'm no killer!" Vance stated wildly. "And I don't want to get shot. How—how can I keep from being murdered?"

"Maybe you can't," said Wade. "The best thing for you to do is sit tight here."

He left the trembling singer. Down in the apartment lobby he grabbed a phone and made a hasty call. "Give me police headquarters." To the sergeant at the desk he snapped an order. "Wade Hammond speaking. I'm nosing around on the Drucci case. Better set a couple of men to tail Gordon Vance. He's had a threat from the Reaper. He might take it into his head to skip; and—we might need him as a witness."

ONE hour later, Wade Hammond, Inspector Thompson, and the two remaining Druccis were back in Station WOB. Nothing else had happened. The police were baffled by the uncanny murders.

The evening broadcasts were in progress; but fear lay like a miasma over the whole place. Sam Drucci and his brother Charlie were tense and white. Horror at the two killings seemed to have wiped from their minds their late unpleasantness with Wade.

The studio was swarming with detectives, prowling, poking, searching everywhere.

"We'd better call a conference," said Thompson hoarsely. "We've got to do something, get somewhere before there's another killing. Maybe the whole station will have to be closed."

Wade Hammond nodded grimly, agreeing. "I'd like to know who the sixth victim's going to be. There were six on the Reaper's list, chief. Only five have received slips so far."

Inspector Thompson didn't answer. He got hold of a sergeant of detectives, said: "Round up the technical staff. Tell them to come to Sam Drucci's office just as quick as they can."

Sam Drucci came out of his fear-clouded daze. He leveled malevolent eyes at Wade, pointed a stubby finger.

"Police protection, Hammond! A lot of good it did my brother Joe! You and your damned cops! If you hadn't butted in tonight when I was going to kill Felk, Joe'd still be alive. You'll be sorry for this."

"Cut it!" snapped Thompson coldly. "And don't insult the force. There wasn't any killer at your brother's place tonight."

"No!" sneered Drucci. "Just invisible bullets!"

The heads of the technical staff of Station WOB assembled nervously in Drucci's office: Nordhoff, the sound expert; Reisling, who had charge of the broadcast tower, and Bittner, the chief engineer. The inspector addressed them grimly.

"It looks as though someone was trying to put this station on the blink. We may have to close it if we can't do something. I don't believe in spooks; but there's something queer going on. Twice now, we've heard shots, and two men have died. Neither time were any bullets fired. Have any of you men got suggestions to offer?"

There was dead silence. The scared, white faces of the men who controlled Station WOB showed only shocked puzzlement. But out of the silence a sound came, making every man in the room jump. It was a metallic click, then a grating, hollow laugh. A radio cabinet stood against the side of the wall. Out of this a voice suddenly issued.

"I am the Reaper come again. Greetings, gentlemen! The little farce continues, and I wish at this time to announce whom my sixth victim will be. Ed and Joe Drucci have met their deaths as promised. Sam and Charlie Drucci will be the next, then Gordon Vance. My sixth victim will be Henry Bittner."

CHAPTER V
The Unseen Death

THE voice stopped speaking as abruptly as it had begun. A gasp went up from those assembled in the room. All eyes swung to Bittner.

The engineer in his rusty black suit was deathly pale. He stood with fists clenched, lips working. The Reaper's sentence of death, coming so unexpectedly, had struck home like a bolt.

Inspector Thompson swore like a madman for an instant.

"This settles it. There's something wrong with this station, Mr. Drucci. The place is hoodooed. These are radio murders. That killer's using WOB for his infernal threats. I'm not going to allow it. The station will have to be closed."

Sam Drucci, slouched and trembling at his desk, was like a man resigned. He threw up his hands, said hoarsely: "See if I care! Ed's dead. Joe's dead. We're on the spot, all of us, and you can padlock the place for all of me."

Inspector Thompson gave swift orders. Charlie Drucci, more poised in this emergency than his brother, volunteered to help see that they were carried out. All the artists were to be sent home for the night, the employees dismissed, the station shut down. "It's one way to put the screws on the Reaper," said Thompson.

Wade Hammond, black pipe in his mouth, face thoughtful, drew the inspector aside.

"It's not getting the killer, chief. You can't keep the station closed forever. If you don't get the Reaper now, he'll be back."

"Have you anything better to offer?"

Wade's voice was suddenly tense. "I may have. I'll let you know in the next half-hour. I'm going to look around."

Wade didn't mention to Thompson that he himself had received a threat of death. But it wasn't out of his mind. He was still on the case, deeper in it than ever. The unknown killer might unexpectedly strike.

Wade spoke to Henry Bittner, the sixth who was to die. The Reaper had placed a bond between them now—a bond of doom. Wade sank his voice to a pitch that others might not hear.

"I want you to let me have a key to the station, Mr. Bittner. I'm coming back later tonight, after the rest have gone. I don't want either Sam or Charlie Drucci to know it, that's why I'm speaking to you. But I want to take a look at the office where Ed Drucci was murdered. I heard those shots myself. I can't believe there isn't something there."

Bittner nodded, his face drawn and gray. "You can have my key, but you'll be a fool, Mr. Hammond, if you come back to this place alone. There—there's death hidden somewhere in it."

Wade nodded and pocketed Bittner's key. He knew he'd be taking a chance. He did not tell Bittner, either, of the Reaper's threat. The man would think him mad. But he had a plan of his own, which might or might not work.

He looked around the studio again, found nothing, and returned to Inspector Thompson. "I've got a scheme, chief. I'm coming down to your office in about an hour. I'll be seeing you then."

"Where are you headed now?"

"Back to my apartment. There's something I've got to do."

Wade Hammond didn't state what it was. He often used strange methods in his battle with crime. Thompson knew better than to question him now. There was a silent bond of understanding between the two. A facetious newspaper writer had once dubbed them "Twins of Trouble."

Back in his bachelor apartment Wade Hammond opened a trunk. It was one of many he kept in a huge closet filled with some of the more cluttered relics of his past. Old guns. Books. Skates. Riding boots and sporting equipment.

He selected a worn leather helmet that recalled memories of his varsity days. Once on a bright November afternoon he had worn that helmet in a winning dash with a pigskin ball under his arm while thousands cheered. He handled it fondly, slipped it over his head and found that it still fit. It would accompany him in no bright sporting contest now. He planned to use it in a grim, black game of life and death.

There were pads with holes in them over the helmet for his ears. Wade got a tube of rubber cement and carefully plugged these up. He inserted inner squares of cemented rubber, cut from an old tire tube. Finally he drew from a medicine cabinet a box of impregnated wool, used as ear stuffing when the street sounds became annoying and he wanted to concentrate. He stuffed the football helmet and the box of wool in his pocket.

WADE HAMMOND and Inspector Thompson moved back in darkness to Station WOB. Wade had picked up the inspector in his office. Thompson was puzzled, but willing to oblige. He was ready to do anything that might trap the man who called himself the Reaper.

Wade, stopping his car two blocks from the station, said: "I'm going in alone, chief. There's a courtyard out back. You can reach it from a side alley. I want you to wait for me there. This may be a wild goose chase. There's no telling. But we mustn't be seen together."

He got out of the car grimly, spoke a word of warning. "Be on your guard, chief. It would be a hell of a note if the head of the homicide squad got bumped off. The crooks would all die laughing. With me it doesn't matter."

Wade silently approached the building which housed the station, and which had now been cleared. A curse of death hung over it. The body of a murdered man had been taken from it that night. Wade let himself silently in with his key. He passed along a dark corridor where not even a watchman was now posted. He passed the elevator shaft which was silent and still. He moved up a flight of marble stairs to the executive offices above.

At the top landing of the stairs, in deepest shadow where no glow from the street penetrated, Wade put wads of impregnated cotton in his ears and slipped the helmet over his head. His eyes gleamed brightly. He looked like a warrior going into battle. He drew out his automatic and gripped it in a steady hand. He could not hear. He had deafened himself purposely. But his gaze was alert and watchful.

In the hallway above, he slipped to the door of the murder office. He opened it, entered the place where two people had died. Charlotte Smith years ago, her white, youthful body stained with blood. Ed Drucci tonight, stricken by no bullets a man could see.

Wade Hammond's flashlight was in his hand. He played it over the still office with a grisly sense of horror. But there was nothing of interest here that he could see, no bloodstain even. He walked to a spot on the wall directly behind Ed Drucci's desk, and examined it intently. Seen closely, the surface of the process board that formed the wall was slightly rounded.

Wade's breath hissed between his teeth. His fingers groped along the wall. He pressed. The rounded surface of the board behind Ed Drucci's desk was thin, thinner than was natural.

Wade's fingers tore through into an open space beyond. He ripped away the paper, disclosing a radio loudspeaker concealed within the wall. It had been a neat, clever job, with hidden wires. He tried to trace them, saw that they went down, and quickly crossed the room.

He opened the window next and moved out on the fire escape. There was no movement in the courtyard below. Inspector Thompson was waiting in darkness.

In darkness, too, Wade Hammond's fingers explored the outside surface of the window frame. Far down under the left-hand edge he located a threadlike wire. He traced it, pulled it out from beneath the wood till it refused to come any further. He pressed against what appeared to be wood, and his fingers broke through taut oil paper. Inside was a circular disc hardly larger than a watch. But Wade Hammond knew what it was. A microphone! He was getting closer to the cause of the murders every second.

He went into Charlie Drucci's office next, found another microphone outside his window. Sam Drucci's office had been wired in the same way. Then Wade crouched expectantly. From the corner of his eyes he had seen a shadow. A wan glow came from a streetlight far away. Something, a ghostly bluff, had touched the edge of the windowpane for a moment. To Wade it seemed that a man's face had peered in.

Deliberately he clicked on his flash, turned it on Sam Drucci's desk and bent above it. His back was turned to the wall. He kept the flash from throwing light on his own helmeted head. He directed it down only on the papers.

A SECOND passed. Wade's heartbeats rose to a throbbing pitch. Fists seemed hammering on his chest. Then what he expected happened.

There was a thunderous explosion in the room. No flame, no smoke, but a report that struck like a physical blow against Wade's head. Even through the wads of wool and the helmet he felt it. It was a concussion that made him fall dazed for an instant. His flash fell from his hand. He sprawled over the top of Drucci's desk. But only for a moment. His padded ears preventing the full force of the sound from striking. The wool close to his eardrums deadened the vibration.

He sank to his knees, recovered his flashlight, raced for the window. With the butt of his gun he smashed out one of the big panes, and swept his flash along the outside face of the building. The fire escape landing ran the full length from corner to corner. A man was running along it.

Wade called a halt, but the man ignored him. Like a scuttling rat he continued, back turned to Wade. Wade fired then, sending a shot screaming close to the man's head.

At that the man let out a desperate cry. He swerved to the right, stepped over the fire escape and tried to swing down to the floor below. He dropped. His feet missed the next platform. He fell with a piercing, agonized scream into the blackness of the court. Wade heard the dull, sickening thud of a striking body.

He turned, ran back through the office, raced down the dark stairs. He groped along a corridor, found a rear exit, and undid a latch. Out in the court, Inspector Thompson was swearing, running forward. His flashlight made a bobbing circle on the stones. Wade called out quickly: "It's okay, chief!"

Relief sounded in Thompson's voice as he bent over. "You had me scared Hammond. I thought—who's this?"

The man who had fallen from the platform above was lying now in a crumpled heap on the hard court. A faint sound of breathing whispered from his half-open lips. He was still alive, obviously, and the inspector's flash swept down across his face. Thompson spoke in quick amazement. "Henry Bittner!"

Wade Hammond nodded, voice accusing but unexcited. "Yes, the Reaper—the man who fooled us all."

The black-suited engineer of Station WOB opened his eyes. A faint glaze filmed across them, but they still held understanding—life. He opened his lips wider, and whispering words came from them. "I got two of them, two at least who were to blame for Charlotte's death."

The white lips closed. A shudder passed over Bittner's broken body. The sound that rose from his mouth was like an echo from the grave. "You wouldn't take your dad's advice, would you, Charlotte? You knew so much better than the old man! You had to run away, make a name for yourself—and get mixed up with criminals. Then—then they killed you. So your old dad had to come back—to square things up."

A twisted smile of satisfaction crossed the dying man's face. A harsh laugh shook him. "Two lives for one," he muttered. His eyes closed slowly. He was still.

WADE HAMMOND spoke in the silence that followed. "His name wasn't Bittner, chief. He was Smith, the father of the girl who called herself Adoree Estrellas. You heard what he said. She came to the city, ran away from home. Smith blamed Gordon Vance and the Druccis for her staying and getting shot. He used his profession of radio engineer to get a job here, work in secret and plot his daughter's revenge. His mind must have become warped, or he wouldn't have done it."

Inspector Thompson grunted. "Okay—but Smith was in the room with us the last time the Reaper talked!"

"Sure, chief, I know. And didn't it strike you as funny then that the other five victims got paper slips, while Bittner's name was spoken by the Reaper? Right then I began to figure it was Bittner. So I took him into my confidence, told him I was coming back here alone tonight. The Reaper had threatened me. If Smith was the Reaper I wanted to give him his chance. When he talked to us in Drucci's office he must have had a dictaphone or phonograph record fixed up somewhere. It was hitched to a mike, probably in his private room. He set it going just before he came up. Naming himself as a victim looked like a good way to keep clear of all suspicion. He wanted to give himself time to polish off the rest."

Wade stared at the inspector sharply, said: "You heard him fire a blank, chief. You should have been inside. It was like a ton of TNT exploding—even with this on."

Wade touched his helmet, which he had shoved back on. "Just amplification, of course. He had a microphone outside the window, a loudspeaker hidden in the wall behind Drucci's desk. He was a shark at such things. He probably helped build the station, and had plenty of chance to work. And he knew what sound can do to a guy. Burst a paper bag close to a man's ear and his brain pressure goes up four times. Amplify a blank a thousand times and you get an explosion that will give a man a hemorrhage fired close to his ear."

Hammond paused, then concluded: "When I saw Joe Drucci dead in front of his radio that got broadcasts straight from the station, I began to figure this must be murder on the air. I unhitched Vance's radio when I went to see him—just in case. Smith was back in the station when he fired the shot that killed Joe Drucci. He planted the blank cartridge in Drucci's room. And sound waves made invisible bullets."

Appendix: The Wade Hammond Stories

(**Bold-face** titles: included in Volume 1; ***bold italics***: Volume 2)

		Detective-Dragnet
1	1931 September	Depths of Doom
2	1931 November	The Curse of Kut-Amen
3	1931 December	**Murder in the Mist**
4	1932 January	**Murder by Minutes**
5	1932 February	Craven Manor
6	1932 March	***Satan's Shrine***
7	1932 May	**The Murder Monster**
8	1932 July	**Ghost Fingers**
9	1932 September	**Tarantula Bait**
10	1932 December	***The Corpses' Carnival***
		Ten Detective Aces
11	1933 March	**Skyscraper Horror**
12	1933 April	**Doctor Zero**
13	1933 May/June	***Teeth of Terror***
14	1933 July	The Screaming Clue
15	1933 August	Tentacles of Doom
16	1933 September	Gun Trap
17	1933 October	***Fangs of the Cobra***
18	1933 November	**Trance of Terror**
19	1933 December	Shrouds of Horror
20	1934 January	The Face from the Grave
21	1934 February	Steel Corpse
22	1934 March	Murder Magic
23	1934 April	The Gilded Corpse
24	1934 May	Sinister Shrine
25	1934 June	Murder to Music
26	1934 July	Killer's Carnival
27	1934 October	**The Skeleton Scourge**
28	1934 November	Death Double-Crosses
29	1935 May	Dead Man's Threat
30	1935 June	***Murder Bait***
31	1935 July	Diamonds of Doom
32	1935 August	**Corpse Cheaters**
33	1935 September	***Scented Murder***
34	1935 October	***The Murder Maker***
35	1935 November	***The Grinning Ghoul***
36	1935 December	***The Terror Train***
37	1936 February	***Murder on the Air***
38	1936 June	The Kiss of Korma
39	1936 August	Murder Bride

ALSO FROM OFF-TRAIL PUBLICATIONS

The Weird Detective Adventures of Wade Hammond
by Paul Chadwick
10 stories from *Detective-Dragnet*
and *Ten Detective Aces*
180 pages, $18

The City of Baal
by Charles Beadle
introduction by John Locke
7 stories of African adventure
from *Adventure* and *The Frontier*
240 pages, $20

Pulpwood Days
Volume One: Editors You Want To Know
edited by John Locke
Writers' magazine articles by and about pulp
editors; with ample biographical info
180 pages, $16

Doctor Coffin: The Living Dead Man
by Perley Poore Sheehan
introduction by John Wooley
8 novelettes of Hollywood detection
from *Thrilling Detective*
174 pages, $16

Check or MO to:
Off-Trail Publications
2036 Elkhorn Road, Castroville, CA 95012
Paypal: offtrail@redshift.com

Printed in the United States
208231BV00002B/220-384/A